The Secret Women

A NOVEL

Sheila Williams

AMISTAD

An Imprint of HarperCollins*Publishers*

HarperCollins books may be purchased for educational, business, or sales promotional use. For information, please email the Special Markets Department at SPsales@harpercollins.com.

FIRST EDITION

Designed by Terry McGrath

Library of Congress Cataloging-in-Publication Data

Names: Williams, Sheila (Sheila J.), author.
Title: The secret women : a novel / Sheila Williams.
Description: First edition. | New York : Amistad, 2020
Identifiers: LCCN 2019054637 | ISBN 9780063005150 (trade paperback) | ISBN 9780062934246 (ebook)
Subjects: LCSH: Mothers and daughters—Fiction.
Classification: LCC PS3623.I5633 S43 2020 | DDC 813/.6—dc23
LC record available at https://lccn.loc.gov/2019054637

ISBN 978-0-06-293422-2

20 21 22 23 24 LSC 10 9 8 7 6 5 4 3 2

For Dorothy Turner Johnson
1915–2015

In almost all of us, there is the secret woman who does not appear for her friends and acquaintances, perhaps not even for the man she marries.

—from *The Secret Woman*, Victoria Holt (1970)

The
Secret
Women

PART 1

PART I

CHAPTER I

Elise

I am not feelin' Namaste today, Elise Armstrong said to herself as she struggled through her Monday evening yoga class.

It wasn't as if she was stressed out or in a bad mood. On a normal Monday, Elise looked forward to the class. She enjoyed yoga, appreciating the discipline of it and the flexibility the practice brought to her body. Yoga had strengthened her posture and toned her arms and legs. And it worked better than a pill for the back and shoulder pain she'd had lately, probably from sitting too long hunched over her computer. It was a part of Elise's beauty regimen. But tonight? It seemed that all the star signs, chakras, and incense from Sergeant Jasmine, the instructor, had aligned to create a perfect storm of I-just-don't-feel-like-this syndrome. Yet she couldn't explain why.

All the meditation she'd done over the years had flown out the window. Elise had taken off her watch, and Sergeant Jasmine didn't believe in clocks, so she had no idea what time it was or how close it was to the end of the ninety-minute class.

Considering it was the first yoga class she'd attended in almost two months, one would think she'd be more . . . *mindful*. Instead, she was un-mindful. And starving. *I'm thinking tacos, guacamole, and a margarita . . . then a hot bath and a couple of Tylenol, not necessarily in that order.* By the time the class reached its fifteenth downward-facing dog, Elise's thoughts had wandered from Mexican to Thai cuisine. *Yep. That's it. Pad Thai, a couple of fresh spring rolls . . .* She worked it all out as she set up for her headstand. It would be the perfect evening. Her son, Wade, had headed back to Chicago, his weekend visit over. Tonight it would be just her with a bubble bath accompanied by vanilla-sandalwood candles and the new Esperanza Spalding CD, followed by the mystery she'd picked up by that new Scandinavian writer what's-his-name. And . . . oh yes, that thick manila envelope from the lawyer.

"Class, remember, don't let monkey mind distract you from your purpose as you prepare." Jasmine's voice had cut through Elise's reverie like an F5 tornado. And was it just her imagination or was Jasmine making a comment about *her*? Elise stole a peek at the teacher. Jasmine's eyes quickly moved in another direction.

"Puff out your kidneys and tuck in your tailbone!"

Are you kidding me? Puff out your kidneys? How the hell do you do that?

"Spine straight!" The yoga teacher was standing two mats away. She tapped one woman on the back. "Tailbone!" Jasmine's freight-train voice was earsplitting against the muted sitar music playing serenely in the background. "Focus! Concentrate!"

Elise took a slow, deep breath, tucked her tailbone, adjusted her shoulders, and concentrated: on a small white dish of green curry chicken, plated with slices of lime on the side. That worked until the image of a plate of overstuffed tacos dripping with super-spicy salsa replaced it. That was all it took. Her arms began to quiver. Her shoulders buckled. Disaster was then inevitable. Her legs swayed, and down she went.

"Daammnn!"

She caught herself just before a complete bone-breaking collapse on her mat.

The woman on her left chuckled, and her headstand evaporated too. Unfortunately, she bumped her funny bone on the way down.

"Ouch!"

"Shit!"

Headstands across the studio fell like dominos.

Jasmine was not pleased.

"Ujjayi breathing, class." The instructor frowned in Elise's direction. "No negative energy. Let's regroup."

Elise was tempted to stick out her tongue.

"Ohhh . . . let's not and say we did," said the woman on the purple mat.

"I've got some negative energy for you." This loudly whispered comment emanated from the woman two mats down from Elise, now seated and rubbing her knee, a sour expression on her face.

Elise suppressed a giggle.

"Well, shit and double damn!" the woman added.

To Elise's right, a woman Sergeant Jasmine had called Deanna unfolded from her headstand and crumpled into a heap of giggles.

"My feelings exactly," the woman on the purple mat said, her low voice shaded by suppressed amusement.

Soon afterward, Jasmine concluded the session with "Namaste, class." She bowed, her hands clasped together. She was frowning at Elise as she rose.

"Namaste," the class responded in unison.

"Whatever," Elise murmured. She limped over to the cubbyholes to collect her things and put on her shoes.

The woman called Deanna plopped down on the floor beside her and laced up her sneakers. "Thanks for that," she said to Elise, grinning. "That's the most fun I've had in a headstand pose since I came here!"

"Me too," came a voice from behind them. The woman from the purple mat grabbed a gym bag from one of the cubbyholes. "Most of the time, I look forward to class. It helps me reduce my stress." She rummaged around in the bag for a moment, then pulled out a towel and draped it around her neck. "But I have to tell you," she said with a sigh, "I just was not feeling it tonight."

The two women laughed and introduced themselves as they dressed. They were relative newcomers to the class, having joined only a few months before Elise's brief absence.

"Deanna Davis, but call me Dee Dee—everyone else does." Dee Dee's wide smile lit up her face. She was tall and slim with an elegant neck and smooth features that reminded Elise of a fashion model. She moved with the confidence of an athlete, and Elise wondered if she was a runner.

"Carmen Bradshaw," said the woman from the purple mat, extending her hand first to Elise, then to Dee Dee. Carmen's almond-shaped hazel eyes sparkled with mischief. "I just love it that you cursed in class. Sometimes I think our esteemed leader is a bit of a tight ass." Carmen's cheeks brightened as she laughed, soft peach against her light caramel skin sprinkled with freckles. Her light brown hair, a profusion of corkscrew curls, was corralled with an animal-print scrunchy. "She gets just a little bit too serious for a Monday night."

"Amen to that," Elise said, fumbling around in the bottom of her purse to find her keys. Her fingertips brushed against a cool, smooth surface. "Got 'em!" she said and added, "I'm Elise Armstrong." And then she thought with amazement how she had taken this class for over two years and had shared floor space with a revolving group of twelve to twenty people, including these two women, and this was one of the few times she'd actually held a conversation with her classmates beyond the perfunctory "Hi, how are you doing?" Why was that? All that focus on tadasana feet, puffed out kidneys, and downward-facing canines, then out the door to rush off to their respective busy lives and no time out for the real Namaste moments. Life went too fast to throw those things away.

"You haven't been in class in a while," said Dee Dee, shrugging a sweater over her toned shoulders.

"Uh-huh. We've missed you," Carmen observed, hunched over a tote bag the size of Vermont. "You know you're the role model for the class, right? We spend half the class trying to figure out what the hell Sergeant J is saying and the other half copying you. Not successfully, by the way." She sighed.

Elise stared. "What?"

Dee Dee chuckled. "I can run a marathon, but I have all the subtlety of Shrek when it comes to yoga. And then I'm so tall!" Her voice held a slight whine, leftover perhaps from the days when she was a kid and towered over everyone else. "I look like an inebriated female Goliath stumbling after David!"

Flattered, Elise shook her head. It had never occurred to her that anyone was watching. Now she felt self-conscious. "All I can say is, if I can do these poses, anyone can. And that's the truth."

"Well, it's good to see you back and to meet you, officially, at last," Carmen said. "I thought you'd dropped out. Did you pull a muscle or something? Or maybe . . ."

Elise had quickly returned her attention to her bag. *Now, where is that lip gloss?* It wasn't lost; she knew exactly where it was: in the first place she'd looked. Over the past few months she'd become an expert at dodging or, if cornered, answering questions like Carmen's.

"Just . . . taking care of some work issues." The image of the manila envelope popped into her head again. This time she banished it, like she briefly had banished the image of a small bowl of pad Thai with three spring rolls, and she switched the conversational gears. "You know what? I'm starving. I barely ate lunch today, and I have a craving for overstuffed tacos, salsa, and a salty margarita. What do you say?"

"Are you talking about the place on the next block?" Carmen asked. "I've been there. Their fajitas are to die for. Count me in."

"Hold on a minute." Dee Dee's thumbs flew across the surface of her mobile. "Just texting Satan's spawns."

"Satan's . . ."

"My daughters. They're going through puberty. Both of them."

Elise winced, remembering the days when she wondered if she or her sons—now grown—would survive their teens. "You have my sympathy."

With a flourish, Dee Dee tapped the SEND key. "There. Car pool activated. Okay. I thought I heard something about food. Like red meat, tequila, guacamole, none of which are on my North Beach diet."

Carmen grinned. "There is no North Beach diet."

Dee Dee clapped her palms together. "Perfect."

Now it was Elise's turn to smile.

* * *

Margaret Rita's—the restaurant was named after Chef Francisco's grandmother—specialized in an excess of everything bad for you: loud music, oversalted house-made tortilla chips, chunky guacamole, strong margaritas, and noise, lots and lots of noise. The mariachi band CD was playing so loudly that Elise was shouting just so Carmen and Dee Dee could hear—and they were sitting less than two feet away. Between the eye-watering hot salsa, the coarse salt, and the yelling, her throat was getting sore. But she was having fun, a rare treat for her these days. Elise ran her finger along the ridge of her glass and licked off the salt. *Mmmm* . . .

"I said," Carmen shouted, "how long have you taken yoga? You move so effortlessly. I'm jealous."

"Me too!" yelled Dee Dee, leaning over the table in the booth. "I'll be a hundred years old before I figure out pigeon pose."

"It's nice of you to say that. It just takes practice. I know, that's boring," Elise yelled back. "I took yoga for the first time years ago, before the boys were born. Some woman had a TV show on PBS. Then Alexander came along, then Wade, and suddenly"—she snapped her fingers—"I was too busy to take anything except the bus to work. I started again a few years ago to increase my flexibility and build strength—I didn't want to be a brittle old woman. It is challenging, but really, if I can do it, you all can."

The booming mariachi music morphed into a ballad at a lower volume.

Carmen sighed as she scooped up a dollop of shredded chicken with her fingers. "Yeah, it only takes concentration, which is the one thing I don't have. I'm too ADHD. And meditation baffles me. My mind flies off in a million directions."

Dee Dee nodded in agreement as she swallowed, then licked salt from her upper lip. "Me too, plus with the kids, the job, there's no time to be peaceful, mindful, or any of the other 'fuls' that bag of bones nags us about."

"I think Jasmine's full of shit," Carmen murmured.

The other women laughed.

"Don't worry," Elise commented. "Children do grow up, much faster than you think. How many do you have, Dee Dee?"

"Just the two girls, and that's enough. Phoebe and Frances, twelve and fifteen going on twenty-five and thirty!"

"I have nieces about that age," Carmen chimed in. "Lord, they're a handful. They stay with me for long weekends sometimes, in the summer. They run me here and there—buy me this, buy me that. I'm ready to crawl into bed for a week by the time they go home!"

"No kids of your own?" Elise asked.

Carmen shook her head. "Nope. Career woman. No kids, one ex-husband, just a few African violets and an aloe plant. It's hard to kill an aloe plant." She dunked a chip into the salsa and scooped up enough of the chunky treat to fill a small coffee cup. "Good thing you don't have to water them very often."

Elise settled back in her seat in the booth, glad to feel the cushion against her spine. A little soreness was there, and her shoulders felt tired. A hot bath was just what she needed. Dee Dee and Carmen continued their conversation about children, careers, and corporate politics, and for a moment, Elise's mind flitted off to other branches of thought, then wandered back in time.

God, that balancing act! Career, children, husband, home, the mantra that you couldn't do it all or have it all. And yet she had. Somehow. But perhaps the mantra should have been expanded: you can have it all at the same time just as long as you don't expect to remember it! Her past lives were a blur: teaching, her master's, more teaching, consulting, marriage—thirty-plus years—kids, school football games, college trips, divorce, then a book, then travel, and Daddy's illness, and the images slammed into each other and became one multilayered collage of color, texture, sound, and light. A few moments stood out. For many years there just hadn't been enough money and Elise's throat would close with angst whenever she wrote a check. Her father's stroke had been a family challenge and painful. Daddy always had been so vibrant, so much in control of himself. She'd tried to be there for the family, for her mother, but Lord, it was hard. Most of the time she didn't think she had the strength.

"Elise dear, you can get through this. You can get through anything," her mother had told her. *"You're stronger than you know."*

Her mother.

". . . so I said to him, 'Look, it's been nice but the smell of eggs in the morning turns my stomach, and the only thing I want to grab that early is . . .' Elise? Are you all right?"

She hadn't even realized she was crying until Carmen's words cut through the renewed mariachi, the yelling, and the clinking of dishes that had numbed her eardrums. Her brain had stopped functioning when the word "mother" had entered her consciousness. Her vision blurred, and she wiped away the tears with the back of her hand, then reached for a napkin. A large packet of tissues swam into view.

"Here! You can't wipe your eyes with that! It has salsa

on it." It was Dee Dee's voice, firm and businesslike. "Take these!"

Elise sniffed. "Thanks."

Carmen's hazel eyes bored into hers. "What's wrong? What is it?"

She wanted to answer, but nothing coherent came out as the words disintegrated into fragments like the pasta letters in alphabet soup. But one image came in strong and clear, and it bludgeoned her. Her mother, Marie, stretched out on the hospital bed, wearing a necklace of tubes, her eyes closed, and her face waxlike.

"I-I'm sorry. I don't mean to be . . . a downer." The yoga teacher's words broke through her thoughts: *"Ujjayi breathing, class."* She inhaled. "My mother died ten months ago. And I . . . still feel as if it was yesterday. I . . . I didn't mean to blank out like that." She sniffed and then sighed. "Or send everybody into depression. I seem to do that a lot these days."

For a moment, all three of the women were silent and the lively music had the floor to itself.

"I know how you feel," Carmen said, studying the dregs of her Corona as she rotated the beer bottle slowly on the table. "You feel as if someone took your liver out using a sharp rock and no anesthetic."

"Or like you've been sideswiped by a Metro bus, T-boned by a semi, and run over by a freight train." Dee Dee's eyes were moist. "Twice."

Elise stared first at Dee Dee and then at Carmen.

Carmen extended her hand across the table. "Hello, I don't

believe we've met. I'm Carmen Bradshaw. My mother, Joan Bradshaw, died last year as well. And I still wake up in tears thinking about her."

Dee Dee held out her hand too.

"I'm Deanna, Dee Dee Davis, attorney, wife of Lorenzo, mother of Satan's spawns, and daughter of . . ." She closed her eyes for a moment, then opened them. "Daughter of Laura O'Neill, artist, writer, free spirit, who died fifteen years ago." Dee Dee paused again. "I hardly knew her. She was . . . sick a lot when I was growing up. But it still hurts. And it still feels as if it was yesterday." Dee Dee took a tissue from the packet she'd passed over to Elise and blew her nose.

Carmen wiped her eyes with the back of her hand and picked up her Corona bottle. She held it up.

"I hereby call to order the first meeting of the Daughters of Dead Mothers Club. Our first order of business is to devise a punishment for those well-meaning folks who tell you that God never gives you more than you can handle."

"If I had a dollar for every time I heard that . . ." Dee Dee murmured.

"I like the Red Queen approach myself," Elise said, taking a sip of her drink. "Off with their heads."

"Drawing and quartering," Dee Dee countered, a wicked grin lighting up her face. "It sounds so clever."

"But messy," Carmen commented. "What about boiling in oil? That's more hygienic."

Elise nodded. The idea had merit.

"Firing squad," Dee Dee said in an ominous tone.

"So moved," said Carmen.

"I second." Dee Dee smiled. Her eyes were gleaming with moisture.

"But which one?" Elise asked, a smile curling her lips upward.

"All of them," Dee Dee said firmly.

Two glasses and one bottle touched together with a *clink*.

CHAPTER 2

Elise

Friends are formed out of shared experiences by people who, sometimes, have similar interests: who attend the same class at school, who enjoy the same music or art, or who have grown up together and enjoy the contentment of memories across the landscape of their pasts. Elise had friends from all of these categories, but she had not thought she could bond so instantly or deeply with two women, outside of a weekly yoga class she hadn't attended in two months, she barely knew. She hadn't been sure of their names before tonight. But that didn't matter. Because Dee Dee and Carmen were more familiar with her inner feelings than anyone, feelings she hadn't felt safe sharing until now. Their mothers, too, had left them feeling both bereft and empty. Like the orphan Paddington Bear, Carmen had commented as they walked out of Margaret Rita's that night, they'd been left on a train platform with only a worn-out suitcase and a jar of marmalade for company. Lots of people had mothers who'd died. So why hadn't Elise "gotten over it," "gotten on with it," or "moved forward"? And why hadn't Dee Dee and Carmen?

"It's un-American," Carmen had said earlier in the evening while rotating a tortilla chip around in her hand. "That Puritan thing about not showing emotion, the work ethic, about moving forward, and, you know, eminent-domain thinking. Bored? Sad? Conquer somebody!"

"We don't know how to cope with expressions of grief. It makes people uncomfortable," Elise said. "I mean, it's okay to cry—"

"A little," Dee Dee interrupted.

Elise smiled. "Yes. A little. Cry a bit at the wake. Sob if you must at the funeral—"

"And you know black folks can perform at a funeral!" Carmen said, chuckling. "I'm a preacher's kid—I should know."

"But once that's all finished. Put your tissues away, get out of the black clothing, and move on. Outward expressions of grief make people squirm."

Elise had said this, had uttered the words aloud, although she hadn't intended to. She thought about the expressions on her sons' faces when she got teary-eyed. She heard the words of her ex-husband, Bobby, in her head: *"Now, Lisee, you need to get over this. You can't keep this up. It's not good for you."*

What you mean is, it's not good for you, she remembered thinking viciously.

The grief counselor's comments had been illuminating. *"It'll be over when it's over. There's no stopwatch marking the time you need to grieve for a loved one. Get that concept out of your head. There's no formula, protocol, or rule. It'll take as long as it takes."*

But if Elise was honest with herself, there were times when even *she* thought it had gone on too long. The problem was: she didn't know what to do about it.

After pushing the MUTE icon on the car radio, she drove home from the dinner in silence, let herself into her house, ignored the blinking light on the answering machine, and, contrary to habit, left the TV remote exactly where it was: on the arm of the couch. She put away her clothes, turned on the taps of the tub, and sat on the edge of the bed while it filled, her mind a thousand miles away.

It was strange, even sad, to think that she'd gotten more out of this evening sharing her pain and loneliness with her new friends than she had in all the months since Mom had died, but that was the way it was. They had laughed, cried, vented, and shared anecdotes about their mothers: Joan, the minister's wife; Laura, the artist; Marie, the globe-trotter. Elise felt better than she had in weeks.

She lit candles and set them beside the tub, but she didn't turn on the music that had filled her head today: Valerie June, Emeli Sandé, Tony Bennett, the energetic *thump-thump* of her favorite Beyoncé tune, the song that always got her going in Zumba class. No, now was the time for silence; it filled the emptiness just fine. Kashmir, her ageless Siamese, padded into the bathroom on ghost feet and settled himself next to the heater vent. Elise took a deep breath, inhaling the gentle, exotic scent emanating from the candles, and sank into the water until it covered her shoulders. The warmth was delicious and soothing. She closed her eyes.

Three women, different in background and experience yet united in their pain over the loss of their mothers. Carmen was almost fifty, a vice president and product manager, overseeing a division at Procter & Gamble, single, an extrovert who loved salsa dancing, travel, and gourmet cooking. Northern Italian cuisine was her newest passion. She was taking a crash course in Italian in anticipation of a trip to Italy next year.

Dee Dee was married—almost twenty years—and had two daughters who were driving her crazy not only with their teenage drama but also with their piano, cello, gymnastics, and ballet lessons. She was a lawyer specializing in products liability and claimed that her hobbies would be "reading, jazz (especially John Coltrane and Thelonious Monk), and interior decorating" she added, "if I only had the time," singing the words to the tune from *The Wizard of Oz*. She was in her forties.

And then there was Elise, in her early sixties, with two grown sons and one granddaughter, who had retired from one career and was now deeply ensconced in another, with one published book and another one in the works. Her hobbies were—

The phone rang. Elise's train of thought and the warm serenity of the bath shattered like glass. She closed her eyes, exhaled, and groped along the bathmat until she found her phone, forgetting that her hand was covered in white, fluffy bubbles.

"Hi, Bobby."

"Hey, babe, how you doin'?"

"Fine. How are you? How'd the meeting go?"

Her ex-husband's baritone filled the phone receiver. Elise

closed her eyes again. She supposed it was a good thing that she and Bobby got along; it made life easier. She knew the conversation by heart, as if it was a play and she was now "off book."

"Uh-huh, and what did he say?"

She turned the tap on again, adding hot water to the warm. The sensation was delicious. Now the water was up to her neck.

"Right, right, I get it. So what's next?"

Bobby was an IT manager, proficient in all things software, bits, bytes, cookies (the inedible kind), and internet security. He knew spyware, malware, and every other kind of "ware" there was. Elise knew enough to turn on her laptop, move the mouse around, and do her work. The insides of the computer were a mystery that, unlike the books she read, she was content to ignore. Unless there was a problem, and then she simply turned the machine over to him.

"*I think you only keep me around because you need someone to take care of your laptop for you,*" Bobby would tease. Elise didn't bother to persuade him otherwise.

"Sure, baby. Uh-huh, I called Dan. He'll be over tomorrow and take care of that. Right. Sure." She yawned.

". . . won't be able to help you at your mother's . . ."

She'd been listening on automatic, but the key words "your mother's" woke her.

"Sorry? I . . . uh . . . didn't catch that."

"There's an issue with the off-site servers and I'll have to go in on Sunday, so I won't be able to help you at your mother's condo. Can you manage on your own?"

She said, "Yes," and eventually, "Good night." She wiped

the bubbles off the phone, made sure it was dry, and set it down. And then she sat up in the tub, oblivious to the rush of cool air across her body.

"*. . . your mother's . . .*"

She was her mother's executrix, going about the business of after-death and following the probate attorney's instructions. Order the death certificates, file this, copy that, email here, sign there, find the deed for the condo, and inventory the contents.

Oh Lord. Just the thought of the property inventory was enough to turn Elise's hair white—whiter than it already would be if she didn't color it every five weeks. Because Elise's mother did not just have a house full of the usual household goods: dishes, clothing, TVs, furniture, whatnots. Marie Wade had several collections of household goods—their very order and nature was all that had kept her from being classified as a hoarder and earning a place on a reality TV show. Marie had loved beautiful things, she had loved to travel, and she had brought home mementoes from every destination. She had adored jewelry and had learned enough about each style and era to become an expert. She had adored music and had collected not just one but two or three different recordings of her favorite works. And on and on. And so there were, by Elise's initial count, ten sets of china (including the Christmas and the zebra patterns), five distinct collections of jewelry (including southwest Indian, Victorian, and art deco styles; white, pink, pale amber, and black pearls; and silver and 18- or 24-carat gold pieces), and art from Marie's southwest phase and her Asian phase, plus her collection of African masks from various nations, her modern African American pieces, and the land-scapes she'd purchased in her later years when she joined the Sierra Club and became passionate about natural environments that were in danger of pollution or erosion. Her favorite piece had been a mountain view of eastern Kentucky, an area that had piqued her interest when she learned that mining compa-nies were blowing the tops off the rugged hardwood-forested hills. Marie Wade's two-bedroom condominium was not just a home; it was a museum of arts and cultural artifacts.

And it was up to Elise to sort through every piece, itemize it, and record it on the estate household-contents inventory form. And then do something with it.

The thought of the task made her want to submerge herself in the tub like a submarine.

She'd started the process several times, but it was a daunting mission. Each time she'd given up in frustration and anguish. These were her mother's things—Marie's treasures—each item lovingly chosen and used or displayed with pride. It broke Elise's heart because she knew there was no way she could keep everything. In fact, there was no way to keep hardly anything. She didn't have the space. And while their tastes were often similar, Elise's style was more minimalist and modern than her mother's. For Marie, every era had appeal.

An image of the ground-floor coat closet—full of . . . stuff from ceiling to floor—flitted across her mind. The closet wouldn't clear out by itself. Elise sighed.

CHAPTER 3

Carmen

Carmen stopped at Starbucks for a coffee, then headed home to her house in Mason, fielding three business calls (from the offices in Shanghai, London, and Dubai) and a personal one from her father. Bluetooth was her savior—considering the time differences with her clients and the length of Carmen's commute, it had made sense to convert her car into a moving satellite office. Technology was a wonder. She took care of Spring Chu's issue, Eric Needham's question, and the brief meeting to check in with Jehan Muhammad and Rory Jones within the thirty-minute drive so that by the time she reached her neighborhood, the only call remaining was the one to her father.

"Dad, how are you? Am I calling too late?"

No, her father explained, but he couldn't talk long, the ten o'clock news was about to come on, and among the things that Reverend Howard Bradshaw—now retired—was religious about was the evening news.

"Okay, well, I would've called earlier but I was out. What's going on? Are you all right?"

"I'm just fine, baby girl. Don't you worry about me," her father replied. "I didn't want anything particular other than to remind you about the dinner coming up next Wednesday night. You haven't forgotten, have you?"

I tried to.

"No, of course not," she said. "Seven o'clock. The Prime. I might be a few minutes late, but I'll be there. Just order me a glass of wine."

At first she heard nothing, but she could feel her father's disapproval.

"You know that I don't drink, Carmen," he said sternly. "And neither does Elaine."

Of course, she said snidely to herself. "Right, I remember," she said aloud to her father.

Mrs. Reverend Doctor Elaine Oakes. How was it that a minister's widow (and said minister's Ph.D. in divinity was questionable), got away with calling herself Mrs. Reverend Doctor? Or was it Mrs. Doctor Reverend? *What is that about?* Carmen wondered. She also marveled at the speed with which her father had returned to a normal life after her mom died. "Getting on with it" was what he told her as he juggled the persistent and tenacious attentions of single church ladies across the Cincinnati metro region. Every widow and divorcée over or near the age of seventy—and a couple who were much younger or older than that—had set their sights on the newly widowed Reverend Bradshaw.

"That is what you should be doing," he'd advised her sternly with the same tone he used when reading or preaching from

the book of the great softie, the prophet Jeremiah, *"getting on
with your life. Your mother wouldn't have wanted you to continue with this unseemly grieving."*

"Yes, Dad," she'd answered through her teeth.

Yeah, whatever. Somehow Carmen didn't think her mother
would have been pleased to see her husband of fifty-plus years
stepping out with every available widow, divorcée, and otherwise single female within a twenty-mile radius of town either.
But Carmen hadn't said that aloud. She felt bitterness and
jealousy. Her own mother would have said that it was *very*
unbecoming. And her dad was right: Joan Bradshaw would
not have wanted Howard to sit at home, alone, eating dinner
for one in front of the TV and having only Wednesday prayer
meetings and Sunday services as his social outlets.

But still . . . *Elaine Oakes?* Identical St. John suits in every
color of the rainbow, including a baby-poop yellow that did
not flatter; acrylic nails sharpened to talon-length (appropriate, Carmen thought); suspiciously colored hair (reddish gold
with blond highlights); and a penchant for Opium, a cologne of
exotic fragrance and nuclear-level strength. Contrasting Elaine
with Carmen's mother was like comparing the Arctic with
the Amazon Basin. Of all the women he could have chosen to
spend time with, why on earth did it have to be Mrs. Reverend
Doctor Oakes?

"Sorry, Dad, I didn't catch that," Carmen said quickly, realizing she'd zoned out on their conversation. "A semi just went
by," she lied as she pulled into her driveway and pressed the
button to open the garage.

"Don't forget that you should pick up the rest of these boxes and things that belonged to your mother. They're in the basement."

Carmen's chest tightened with sadness and fury. She wanted to scream at her father. *You've put her things in the basement out of sight . . . in her own home? Already?*

"Sure, Dad, I'll take care of it. I gotta go, okay?"

It took all of the strength Carmen had to keep from punching her finger through the steering wheel when she tapped the button to disconnect the call. Her eyes flooded with tears.

Oh, Momma, he's forgotten you already. And for Mrs. Reverend Doctor Elaine Oakes, for Christ's sake! Jesus . . .

Carmen, darling, her mother would've said. *Now, what'd I tell you about that cursing? Cut that out now.*

Carmen gripped the wheel, wiped the tears away, and focused on maneuvering the car into the garage. Three of the boxes containing her mother's things that her father had packed up were stacked on the workbench, her mother's initials written boldly in large-print letters with a bright blue Sharpie: "JAB," for Joan Adams Bradshaw. They'd been there for weeks—months, even. At least once a week or so Carmen would come out to the garage, usually on a Saturday or Sunday, pick up a box, take it inside, and plan to open it and unpack and sort its contents. The weekend would go by. Carmen would pick up the box again—unopened—and take it back to the garage. She didn't have the heart to do it. She could not think of her mother as a box or two of . . . *things.* Nor was she ready to handle her mother's personal belongings, which Carmen knew would carry the scent of L'Interdit, a classic French perfume her mother had always worn.

The garage door closed with a soft *thump*, and Carmen unlocked the door that led to the kitchen. She looked at the three boxes again, thinking of the remaining ones stacked neatly in the basement at her family home. Then she turned out the light and went into the house.

CHAPTER 4

Dee Dee

Every room in the house was glowing with light when Dee Dee pulled into the driveway. She groaned. It had not been her goal in life to be Duke Energy's favorite customer. Obviously Lorenzo and the girls were home. She opened the door and smiled, then took a deep, cleansing breath. The *thump-thump* of Frances's music (why didn't she use the $150 headphones they'd given her for Christmas? Had she misplaced them already?); Pauly the cat cowering under the table, hissing at the Labrador puppy, Dallas, who was too young and inexperienced to know that he was about to be scratched; Phoebe hunched over her laptop, her glittery blue polished fingertips skating along the keys, earbuds buried in her ears, eyes glued to the computer screen; and in the middle of it all . . .

A yelp from Dallas distracted her. Out of the corner of her eye she saw Pauly slinking off toward the hall and mudroom, where the litter box was. Dee Dee knelt down and petted the golden Lab pup, whose expression was a mix of pain and incomprehension. She could imagine what he was thinking: *I was just playing! Can't he take a joke?*

"Dallas, baby, you cannot play with that cat. That's not how he rolls." The puppy's nose didn't appear to be damaged, so she scratched him beneath the chin, then quickly checked the hall floor for puddles as she whistled for the animal to follow her to the back door. "Out you go, monster."

The remnants of pizza and salad looked like leftovers from an archaeological dig on the granite island counter, and the kitchen TV was on even though no one was watching it. Dee Dee rolled her eyes, clicked off the TV, and poured herself a glass of water, then let the dog back in and turned toward the great room. This time Phoebe saw her and waved.

"Hi, Mom."

"Is that homework?" Dee Dee asked as she returned to lean over and kiss the top of her daughter's head.

"Yes," Phoebe answered. "Algebra. Almost done."

Times sure had changed. Phoebe hadn't heard one word she'd said—the earbuds were still in her ears. But she could read lips. Incredible!

The music was getting louder, as if trying to win a decibel competition with ESPN blaring from the great room, where her husband, Lorenzo, was ensconced. Dee Dee stopped at the foot of the stairs and sent a text message to Frances.

"Turn music down."

She counted to ten. The volume decreased one hundred percent. So Frances did know where the new headphones were.

Now it was Lorenzo's turn. *SportsCenter*, his favorite program, was on, and even Dee Dee was impressed by the sharp definition and color of the 75-inch flat-screen mounted over the mantel. It was new and Lorenzo's pride and joy. She was not as impressed with the audio since the three commentators insisted on talking at once. Of course it didn't matter what they said since Lorenzo was asleep. Dee Dee smiled. He was buried in the cushions, so closely hugged by them that he was practically wearing the couch. She picked up the remote and turned off the set.

Lorenzo sat up. "I was watching that." He scratched his head and yawned.

"It was watching you and got bored, so I turned it off."

Lorenzo shrugged and stretched. His shoeless size 15 feet landed on the floor with a *thud*. "How's work?"

"Fine. Work was good, class was good, and I met a couple of interesting women. We had dinner together. Anything new with the girls?"

Lorenzo shook his head slowly and yawned again. "Nope." He glanced around. "Humph. France found the headphones. Thank God."

"She did after I texted her. When I came in it was the battle of *SportsCenter* and Rihanna. Phoebe's in the dining room doing her homework."

"Oh yeah, meant to tell you. She's joining a math/science club at school; I got an email from Mr. Holiday. They'll meet once a week, and there's some kind of competition in the spring. Phoebe's excited."

Now it was Dee Dee's turn to scratch her head. "I don't know where she gets this math ability from. It sure isn't me."

Lorenzo chuckled. "It ain't me either," he said, standing up. "Do you want anything? I'm going to the kitchen."

"No. France okay?"

"Yep." He padded out of the room on his large sock-covered feet. "But I'm going to have a conversation with Mr. Devon Carmichael very soon. A come-to-Jesus meeting."

"What?" Dee Dee chuckled as she took a seat on the couch. "Lo, you need to leave that boy alone."

"I will," he called back at her. "When he leaves my daughter alone."

Poor Devon, Dee Dee thought. He was a sweet kid and Frances's newest infatuation. Dee Dee hoped his phone plan— and hers—could accommodate the constant calls and texts. She also hoped—for Frances's sake—that Lorenzo didn't frighten the boy off. It wasn't unhealthy for her to have a little boy–girl attraction going on at fifteen. No dating yet—she and Lorenzo were united on that issue. But there wasn't any harm in Frances having the heady experience of a boy liking her. Convincing Lorenzo of that was going to be a challenge, however.

"Lo, she can date when she's sixteen," Dee Dee had said during one of their many conversations about the girls.

Lorenzo roared at that notion—like the MGM lion. "Hell no! Twenty-two. After she graduates from college."

Dee Dee chuckled again. "Yeah? Good luck with that, okay?"

"I'm serious!"

"Get real. You won't be there when she's in college."

"Why not? She's only going to UC. She can commute."

And that was when the conversation had turned into a gladiatorial match.

"Oh, hell no!" It was Dee Dee's turn to bellow. "There can only be one queen bee in a hive at a time. Those girls are going away to college."

"What if they don't want to go away?"

Dee Dee shook her head. "They're going to have to go somewhere," she said firmly. "I can barely keep from strangling them now. Can you imagine what this house will be like when Frances is eighteen and Phoebe is fifteen? Please—that's too many hormones. She's going away to college. And that's that. And you will not be in control."

She sighed now, thinking about it. She wouldn't be in control either. *Lord, have mercy . . .*

"Oh yeah, I forgot," her husband shouted from the kitchen. "Debora called."

Dee Dee froze, her ears pricking up. "What'd she want? Is she okay? What's going on?"

"Calm down. She's fine," he said, coming back into the room, a glass of water in his hand. "She just called to remind you of your aunt Lou's birthday next week. Said she called your cell but the mailbox was full."

The ice in Dee Dee's veins began to melt a bit. "D-did she sound all right?"

Lorenzo picked up the remote and clicked the TV back on. This time the volume was set on low. "Uh-huh. She sounded fine."

Dee Dee exhaled slowly. "As if . . ."

Her husband patted her knee as he sat down. "Yep. As if she's taking her meds. Dee Dee, relax. Deb's okay."

And she was and had been, actually, for over two decades. She'd been working as a senior accountant at the same company for years. So why did Dee Dee still freeze up whenever her sister's name was mentioned? Was she afraid that Deb would have that . . . tone in her voice, the one that preceded a manic phase? She couldn't help it—she panicked whenever her sister or her brother-in-law called, her shoulders tightening up, the fear choking her voice: *"Amory? Everything okay?"*

Amory was like a huge teddy bear, gregarious and trusting. He never seemed to notice the anxiety in Dee Dee's voice, or if he did, he generously pretended to ignore it. "Hey, Sis-in-law!" he would say. "Girl, how you doin'? Those girls still driving you crazy? We are A-OK out here. Listen, is Lo home? I'm returning his call."

"I'm fine, Amory. The girls are great, and I'm ready to pack them up and send them to boarding school! Wait a second, here's Lorenzo."

Dee Dee would then hand over the phone to her husband, embarrassed by her overreaction, and grateful to Amory for cutting her some slack and not calling her out for being ridiculous.

No such luck with Debora, who was always on to her from word one.

"Hi, Sis!" Dee Dee had opened with during their most recent conversation.

"'Hi, Sis, my ass,'" Debora had fired back, her voice tinged with humor and sarcasm. "Before you say anything else, here's the status report: yes, I'm taking my meds, including a new one with a thingamabob name that I can't pronounce without my tongue turning inside out, I'm going to support group biweekly, Mass weekly at Saint Stephen's, kickboxing, tai chi, and a monthly massage given by Gerald, the patron saint of magic fingers. What'd you say, Amory?" Debora's voice faded as she spoke to her husband. Then there was a chorus of laughter. "That fool I married says I'm having an affair with my masseuse. Really, Amory?"

Then it was Dee Dee's turn to laugh, as much with relief as with humor.

"Gerald's gay, isn't he?"

"Uh-huh. So now that I've told you what you really want to know, what *do* you want?"

Their conversations would eventually morph into normal banter between sisters, the sharing of family activities, coordination of holiday or birthday celebrations, and a reminder to email this link or that address. For almost twenty years, Dee Dee's interactions with her sister had followed this pattern. Debora's last episode was in the early 1990s, resulting in a family intervention and hospitalization. But since that time, she had been well—aware of her condition and doubly aware of the tools and practices she needed to maintain equilibrium. So why was Dee Dee still so anxious? Just the sound of her sister's voice over the telephone—a voice so much like their mother's that it was eerie—would send Dee Dee into a state of terror.

Debora teased her about it once. "Do you take anything for it?" she asked.

No, but I should, Dee Dee had said to herself.

She tried to convince herself that her continued anxiety was because Deb's voice reminded her so much of their mother. But Dee Dee's vigilance had the potential to strain her relationship with her only sibling. She knew Debora was weary of having to account for herself at the beginning of every conversation.

Dee Dee turned to Lorenzo on the couch and asked, using a neutral tone, "So does Deb want me to call her or what?"

"Nope," Lorenzo answered, his eyes on the TV screen, his thumb working the buttons. "She'll send you an email. She and Amory are having a twenty-year anniversary celebration in a couple of months—spa stuff, a golf outing, and then a dinner dance."

"When is this?"

"May . . . June? The ninth and tenth . . . or tenth and eleventh . . . or twelfth . . ." Lorenzo's eyes and concentration were fixed on the T. Rex-sized TV screen.

"Wow," Dee Dee said and meant it. "Okay. Well, I'll let you know when I see the email. Then we can plan the road trip to Chicago."

"Uh-huh," her husband replied, his mind now in sports-chat oblivion.

Dee Dee patted him on the shoulder, rose, and walked back toward the kitchen, grabbing her tote and purse. Frances's music was audible again, and Phoebe's thumbs were flying across her phone.

"Phoebe! No texting! Homework," she said, shaking her head from side to side because her daughter still had the ear-buds in. Phoebe shrugged her shoulders, sighed, then pressed a button and set the phone down. Dee Dee smiled and headed upstairs.

She yawned as she walked down the hall toward her elder daughter's room. Work, yoga, dinner, margaritas . . . It used to be, back in the day, she could go twenty hours on four hours of sleep. But that was twenty years, Lorenzo, two babies, and thousands of ten-hour workdays ago. Now she needed seven hours of sleep, and sometimes even that wasn't enough.

Dee Dee knocked on Frances's door, then opened it a crack and peeked in. Frances stood in the corner with her back to the door, the ceiling lights illuminating a large sheet of sketch pa-per mounted on an easel. Frances didn't turn around—she was plugged into her phone—and she stood nearly motionless as she applied a detail to the painting with a near-miniature paint-brush, leaning in close to add a nuance of color or detail. It was an impressionistic painting, reminding Dee Dee of Monet and the colors of Giverny. Frances was so absorbed that she didn't sense she was being observed. Dee Dee smiled and gently closed the door.

Frances was artistic, excelling at the cello and with a paint-brush. And her temperament was volatile, optimistic, and brave. *So much like my mother.* Dee Dee pushed that thought away.

She'd enjoyed the evening with Elise and Carmen. It had been a long time since she'd had an evening out with friends, old or new. The laughter and conversation had lightened her mood and had provided a much-needed retreat from the stress of her hectic day. But still . . . Dee Dee continued to feel as if something was following her. She didn't look over her shoulder because she knew what it was: *fear*, a loyal but unwanted companion for most of her life.

Dee Dee didn't remember how old she was when she first realized that her mommy behaved differently from the other mommies. Was she five? Six? It was a gradual awareness, and, at first, she had no words for "it." She was too young and still guided by instinct, having no idea what "it" was, only that it was as strong as she was and suffocating in its completeness. It was as if the blankets on her bed were being pulled up before she went to sleep, slowly covering her feet and calves, then her hips and her torso and, finally, her shoulders. By the time the blankets were tucked in, Dee Dee's realization shape-shifted into what she later would identify as cold fear.

"Your mommy crazy!" a boy in her second-grade class said to her one day.

Dee Dee pushed him down on the playground and he scraped his knee. She spent that afternoon standing in the corner of Mrs. Cochran's room. But deep down, even though she didn't have words for it yet, she knew the boy had been telling the truth.

On the way to the grocery store one summer afternoon, Laura O'Neill drove 70 miles per hour in a 40 mile-per-hour zone, zigzagging through traffic while screeching with laughter during a conversation she was having with herself. She told her daughters, crouched and terrified in the back seat, that she was chatting with her friend and was going to get some milk and hamburger meat. It was hours before Deanna and Debora stopped trembling.

The terror Dee Dee experienced on that day, and on many others like it, was the shadow that followed her through most of her life. It was like she lived on a fault line at the rim of an active volcano during a thunderstorm. She never knew when the ground would shift and throw her off her feet, or when the mountain would explode and bury her in heat and misery, or when the sky would open up and send zigzags of lightning down on her head. It would be the most complete destruction there was. She'd seen something destroy her mother, an outgoing and creative woman. She'd seen it try to destroy her sister. Every day, even though she had no symptoms, Dee Dee woke in the morning terrified that it would try to destroy her too. And now, without any evidence or reason, she was worried about Frances.

And then there was the matter of four roughed-up water-stained boxes sitting on the old Ping-Pong table in the back of the basement, the ones she'd never opened. The ones with her mother's name on them.

CHAPTER 5

Carmen

It *was* Carmen's idea. Elise thought it was brilliant, and Dee Dee too was enthusiastic, but Carmen refused to accept the credit.

"I just listened, that's all," she said, explaining how she pulled together the common threads of their stories about their mothers and tied them with a bow. "It's what I do. Listen to stories, true and untrue, pull out useful information, and formulate a solution."

"Hmmm, like Olivia Pope," Dee Dee said, referring to the character in a TV show. But it was more basic than that. It was so easy that Carmen couldn't explain why she hadn't thought of it sooner—the idea had been right in front of her nose. Instead, it had come to her like a lightning bolt—when she was in the shower washing her hair. Or, rather, rinsing the shampoo out of her eyes, blinking to ease the irritation from the suds, her mind wandering off to a new line of hair products she'd seen on QVC, then on to a meeting she had to attend in New York in the coming week. The weather had been iffy—pop-up thunderstorms and tornadoes, especially in the South. What if her plane was coming from Atlanta? Would her flight be cancelled? Carmen loved one of the new display windows at Saks: a minimalist scene with a trio of faceless mannequins wearing red designer clothing and standing next to a tower of boxes stacked haphazardly. It reminded her of the Tower of Pisa. Wasn't there an email in her in-box from the tour group about her upcoming foodie tour of Tuscany? Or was it Umbria? And she wondered if . . .

Boxes. They all had boxes to sort through. Boxes containing things—none of them knew for certain what things, but things that had belonged to their mothers. Elise was still facing the clear-out of her mother's condominium: furniture, dishes and other household goods, books, things, things, things—the whole idea of the project had overwhelmed her into misery. And inactivity. ("When in doubt," Elise quipped, "do nothing!") Dee Dee teased that her mother—dead many years now—was a bountiful person when it came to her art and her life but a minimalist as far as possessions were concerned. Besides a few crates of her works stored in a small gallery owned by one of her mother's friends, she had only four small boxes of her mother's belongings sitting on the Ping-Pong table in the back of her basement. Carmen, on the other hand, had boxes on the workbench in her garage and several more in the basement at her childhood home—the same boxes her father, now enjoying the company of Elaine Oakes, was nudging her to remove.

She, Elise, and Dee Dee each had a task they found sad, difficult, and overwhelming. But three pairs of hands were better than one pair. And three women could not only clear a condo, a basement, and the back of a garage but also celebrate said clearing out with good wine and great food accessorized by energizing music.

The plan came together within days of their first dinner at Margaret Rita's. This time they had gathered at Siam Flower for the pad Thai and fresh spring rolls that had been on Elise's mind.

"Look, here's the way I see it," Carmen said, holding a cup of hot jasmine tea between her palms. It was mild outside, but the restaurant's AC was blowing, and she was cold. "Rome wasn't built in a day, and we have nothing like that grand a project to tackle . . ."

"You haven't seen my mother's condo," Elise said in a low voice.

"Neither were the pyramids or those amazing Gothic cathedrals."

Elise nodded, dipping a fresh spring roll into the sauce and taking a small bite. She chewed for a moment and said, "And the signature dome in Florence . . ." She snapped her fingers, trying to grab the name from her memory. "Brunelleschi's—"

"Cathedral of Santa Maria del Fiore," Dee Dee interrupted.

"Nice pronunciation," Carmen said.

"I spent six months in Italy as an exchange student. Loved Florence, absolutely loved it!"

"Okay, so Brunelleschi's dome wasn't built in a day. Or the pyramids or anything worth our time. So how is it we think that grief should go away in a day? Or that anyone could possibly clear out a house in a short period of time?"

Elise shook her head slowly. "No, dear. Grief is self-absorption on a grand scale, or so I was told by one of my colleagues. One of those 'Get over it' types who drinks himself into a stupor on the weekends."

"Uh-huh," Dee Dee said, nodding her head. "And will have cirrhosis in a few years. I love Carmen's idea. I'm a pack rat, though you wouldn't know it. I like to keep . . . things. You know how it is. Maybe I'll use a thing next month. Maybe the girls would like it."

"Maybe it'll sprout wings and fly away?" Elise added, grinning.

"Uh-huh."

"Only thing is, I have so few boxes of Mommy's," Dee Dee interjected. "It'd hardly be worth your time."

"Except that your mother's been dead how many years and you still have these boxes?" Elise asked pointedly.

Dee Dee pulled a face. "Okay, so I'm the poster child for procrastination."

Elise finished off her spring roll, then licked a splash of peanut sauce from her finger. "You have too few. I have too many. I'm at the other end of the spectrum." She paused. "Speaking of that, I have a whole condo to dismantle, ladies. It's not exactly fair for me to monopolize your time on such a huge project."

"Yes, but I'm nosy," Carmen said, smiling. She gathered up noodles with her chopsticks and held them dangling in the air. "I want to see what you've got in that condo. You said your mother collected art, jewelry, whatnots. There isn't an earring or bracelet that's safe from me. I'll buy the pieces I like."

Carmen slurped the noodles into her mouth, Dee Dee snorted. "I thought the idea was to decrease the amount of stuff we have!"

"No. The idea is to decrease the amount of stuff we have from our mothers! So that's my solution. What do you think?" Carmen asked. She studied the two women closely. Elise was nodding. Dee Dee's expression was thoughtful. "And since Elise has the most stuff, we'll attack her project in phases and work on the others in between."

Elise inhaled deeply. "Okay. But I still think it's generous of you all to even consider what I've got going on in that condo. Maybe I should do some pre-clear-out pruning so the job won't be as overwhelming?"

"Sounds like a plan," Dee Dee said. "Although I don't mind helping with that. I'm curious too."

"Okay," Carmen concluded. "If that's what you want to do. And to sweeten the pot, I propose that we start at my place. I have three boxes in my garage and a few more at my dad's. I'll get those, and we can have a clearing-out party . . . Check your phones, girls. I'll even cook!"

"I'll bring wine," Dee Dee said.

"I'll bring something sweet," Elise added.

"It's too bad there isn't such a thing as a three-pronged wishbone," Carmen said. "That would bring us luck."

"We'll improvise." Dee Dee laughed, extending her fist to the center of the table. Elise and Carmen did the same.

"Our own wishbone," Carmen said.

"Namaste," Dee Dee and Elise said in unison.

PART 2

CHAPTER 6

Carmen

Of all the obstacles Carmen expected to encounter with her plan to sort through and (finally!) dispose of her mother's belongings, her father was not on the list. Shortly before the dreaded dinner with Elaine Oakes, Carmen called to tell her father that she was stopping by to pick up the boxes stored in the basement. She was startled by his response.

"It's not a good time," Howard Bradshaw told his daughter. "It's kinda late."

"Dad, it's only 8:30. This won't take long. Just fifteen minutes or—"

"No. Another time would be better."

Carmen tilted her head to the side. *What is this about?*

A naughty and disturbing thought popped into her head. Was he entertaining Elaine? Was he entertaining some other lady? Just the notion (and the visual that went with it) made Carmen feel queasy. Unreasonable? Yes, she knew that. Her father was a widower now, a single man. But the thought of him with a woman—not her mother—still annoyed her.

"Well, I'm just about to make the turn from Galbraith Road. Dad, I'm sorry about this, I would've called earlier, but I didn't know that I'd finish up work so soon. Is it okay or not?"

She heard him clear his throat loudly.

"Yes, all right," he answered in a sharp tone and hung up the phone.

Humph. He's getting grouchy in his old age.

Her father had sounded like a troll guarding a bridge in a Scandinavian folktale. When she pulled into the driveway, he'd opened the garage and was standing just inside, a stern expression on his face, the one her mother referred to as his "plagues and pestilence" grimace. He looked seriously pissed off. What Carmen couldn't figure out was why.

She got out of the car, pushed the button to open her trunk, and kissed her father on the cheek.

"Why do you want to bother with those boxes and things at this late date?" her father growled. "They've been in the basement for months, and now you want to pick them up in the middle of the night!"

"Middle of the night, Dad? It's a quarter to nine!" Carmen brushed past him and went into the kitchen toward the basement door. "I don't get it. You've been after me for weeks to come and get these things. In fact, not too long ago, when you called me about the dinner with . . ." *Ugh.* She could barely get the woman's name out. "Mrs. Oakes . . . you mentioned clearing the boxes out of the basement. So what's changed? Do they have cooties or something?"

Carmen's attempt at levity didn't work. Howard Bradshaw's

expression looked like a thundercloud about to burst. "No. I think you . . . that your timing is bad, that's all."

She smiled slightly and peeked around the corner into the family room, where the TV was on. "I'm sorry about that. I'll make it quick. Do you have . . . are you entertaining?" she teased. "Why didn't you say so? I don't mean to interrupt."

Her father was not amused. "That isn't funny, Carmen."

Geez, no sense of humor tonight. "Okay, well, whatever it is that's bugging you, I'm sorry. Look, I'll just grab the boxes downstairs and be out of your hair."

"Here, let me help," her father said, sprinting past her and down the basement steps with a burst of energy she wouldn't have thought him capable of.

"Okay . . ." Carmen said, following him down the stairs. Now she was confused. First he didn't want her to get the boxes, now he was helping her. *What the heck?*

There were only four boxes, fewer than Carmen remembered. She thought her mother had had more personal belongings than this, but then she recalled that she, her dad, and her brothers had sorted through Mom's clothes and personal items shortly after the funeral, donating most to a not-for-profit organization that provided clothing for women job seekers. The boxes were stacked on top of an old banquet table the church had had no use for, all neatly sealed, the more dilapidated ones secured with ancient masking tape and fortified with string, labeled in her mother's handwriting: "Jo Adams," her maiden name.

Carmen caressed the top of one of the old boxes and smiled. "Mom must've packed these," she mused aloud. She ran her finger across the name Jo, the once-bold navy ink diminished to the faded blue of old, well-washed denim. "I didn't know Mom used the name Jo. I don't think I ever heard anyone call her that."

Howard nudged the box away and picked up one of the newer ones.

"Nobody here ever called her that. I don't like nicknames. To me—" His voice caught. "Your mother . . . she was always Joan or Mrs. B." He stacked another box on top. "Here, I'll take these and put them in your trunk. Leave those for another time."

"That's okay. I can handle 'em. They aren't heavy," Carmen said, gathering the two worn boxes into her arms. "You go ahead." When she looked up, she was surprised that her father had barely moved and was still standing in the middle of the room, staring at her.

"Dad? Are you all right?"

Howard Bradshaw licked his lips. "Yes. Ah . . . you sure that you don't want to leave those? I could drop them off later in the week. You don't want to do too much at one time. Going through your mother's things could be . . . a bit overwhelming."

Why this tug-of-war?

"It's fine. Besides, I'll have help." Carmen briefly explained about the plan she, Elise, and Dee Dee had concocted. She thought her father would be relieved that she wouldn't be alone, that she was finally doing something with these boxes. Instead, he looked upset.

"What?" he exclaimed. "Who are these women? How well

do you know them?" He was frowning when he turned around to go up the stairs. "I don't think it's right to have . . . strangers picking through your mother's things."

Jesus Christ.

"Dad, it'll be fine. Elise is a consultant and an author. Deanna is a lawyer with P&G. I assure you that they are trustworthy, reputable women. Stop worrying."

None of this made any sense. It was all Carmen could do to keep from showing how astonished she was. Her father had been bugging her for weeks, *months*, about her mother's things. And now that she was actually here, picking them up, he acted as if there was no rush. As if . . .

Carmen glanced down at the old box she was carrying: "Jo Adams."

As if you don't want me to take these. She shook the box gently. There was no sound or rattling, and nothing shifted. The box felt solid but wasn't overly heavy. Paper? Photo albums? No, they would knock together and make noise. She would feel the contents shifting. Clothing, linens?

Howard helped her load the boxes into her trunk and closed it. Then he kissed his daughter good night and stood in the open garage watching until she pulled out and drove away, sounding her horn once. In the rearview mirror, she saw the garage door come down, and her father disappeared from her sight.

On the drive home, Carmen finally analyzed her father's initial hostility, his abrupt change in attitude, and his choice of words. The sea change had occurred when she'd picked up the old boxes, the ones labeled "Jo Adams" in her mother's handwriting. She knew her mother's maiden name had been Adams, but she didn't remember ever hearing anyone call her mother Jo, not even Joan's close friends. And what was it Dad had said?

"Nobody here ever called her that."

That's a strange thing to say, Carmen thought. So *where* had Mom been when people had called her Jo? As far as Carmen knew, her mother had never traveled anywhere without her dad: church conventions, church- or college-sponsored tours, and the cruises they had started taking once her dad became pastor emeritus and didn't have the responsibility of two Sunday sermons plus Wednesday prayer meetings and other obligations during the week. And something else was spinning around in her mind like the icon on her cell phone searching for a Wi-Fi connection. When she had looked up, holding the two older boxes in her arms, her father had been staring at her with a strange expression on his face. Carmen had never seen her dad look like that. He'd looked as if he was about to cry. No, that wasn't it. Something else. A facial expression totally out of character for her father. Was he ill? She couldn't understand it. And then the expression was gone, in the blink of an eye. She replayed that moment in her mind the entire drive home. But it was still an enigma.

Later that evening, it came to her. Carmen sat up in bed, her bare arms covered with goose bumps in the cool darkness. Fear. Her father was afraid of something, something that was in one of the old boxes.

CHAPTER 7

Carmen

Carmen had no time to obsess over her mother's boxes, because the first order of business was a "china sorting party" at the condo that had belonged to Elise's late mother. After that, the trio would move on to Carmen's to assess the situation there, then call it a day.

Marie Wade's two-bedroom condo was in Evendale, and despite Elise's warnings to the contrary, it wasn't cluttered, just full. Of everything. The bedrooms had been cleared out, and the smell of fresh paint and carpet cleaner filled the air. Elise opened the windows to air out the place so it was a bit chilly, but there was laughter, hot tea and coffee, sandwiches and cookies, so no one minded much. They set up their work area in the dining room and gave themselves a time limit: no more than three hours. The goal was to organize the dishes in Marie's 1920s-era china cabinet into sets, then wrap and box them for storage or sale. Elise had found a dealer interested in handling the consignment.

She stood in the middle of the living room floor looking like a goddess rising out of a sea of crumpled newspaper as she surveyed the waves of cups, saucers, dessert plates, and meat platters.

"Okay, girls, here's what we'll do. We'll empty out the cabinet and use the table as a staging area, placing each item with its set. Any odd pieces you unearth, leave them inside the china cabinet." Elise walked over and opened one of the cabinet doors, then sighed. It was packed with cups and saucers. "There should be eight sets of china, water goblets, wine and champagne glasses, pink Depression glass, white Depression glass, and a chocolate set."

"Roger that," Dee Dee said with a salute.

Carmen held up a teacup with a handle so thin and delicate that she was almost afraid to breathe on it. Agility and coordination as they related to fine china or babies were not her strong suits. *Oh Lord, please don't let me break anything.* Gingerly, she turned the cup upside down and read its country of origin along with the manufacturer's name. Elise had already started a grouping of French Havilland, so Carmen extracted the tiny matching saucer from the cabinet and placed the two pieces on the table.

Two hours later, the women stood around the dining room table, which now looked like the successful beginnings of a fine china boutique.

"One, two, three, four, five . . ." Dee Dee was counting the different groupings. She made a face. "I thought you said your mother had eight sets of china."

"Nine, ten, eleven . . . twelve!" Carmen giggled. "Twelve

sets of china!" she crowed, imitating the voice of the Count from *Sesame Street*.

Elise looked both embarrassed and dismayed. "I am so sorry," she said. "I don't know what else to say. I remember Mom going through her 'china phase.' I just didn't know it had gotten so out of hand. If y'all want to forget about this . . ."

Carmen hugged her but couldn't stop giggling. "No, we're in this together. You can't get rid of us. It's just that none of us has ever seen twelve sets of china owned by one person! I don't think I knew there were so many different types of china."

Elise inhaled loudly. "Well, if anyone could find them, it would be my mother."

There was a set of Blue Ridge china made in Erwin, Tennessee, in a factory no longer in business, and it was considered "collectible," or so Elise told them. There was also the French Havilland china in a feminine floral pattern and made in the late 1890s, plus Christmas china, zebra- and leopard-pattern china, a bright white china with square dinner plates, a Fiestaware set from the 1960s . . .

Elise sat down with a deep sigh. "I give up," she said, sinking into the cushions of the single couch in her mother's living room.

"Don't give up," Dee Dee told her. "But only you can decide which sets you want to keep."

"Keep?" Elise exclaimed. "None of them! I have my own china, including a set that Mom gave me." Elise narrowed her eyes as she glanced over at the crowded dining room table. "Which means that Mom had thirteen sets of china, not twelve."

"Mercy!" Carmen said, grinning. "I am in awe. My mother had two sets of dishes, one for special occasions and Sundays, and one for every day. As for me, I have microwaveable dishes from Target!" She glanced over at the clock. "Okay, ladies, it's three thirty. We have half an hour left in our schedule." She picked up a dessert plate with a zebra pattern. "I move that we spend the time boxing up this set of china and head over to my place for the second shift. Any seconds?"

* * *

Carmen opened the blinds in her great room to let in the afternoon sun. She'd brought in the three boxes from the garage and the four she'd taken from her dad's a few nights ago, setting them all on a table or on newspaper she'd spread out on the carpeted floor. It was nearing five o'clock, so she set out cheese, cold meats, fruit, bread rounds, and some snack mix, and opened a chilled bottle of Riesling.

Elise sat down on the floor—lotus position, damn her—and stretched her arms toward the ceiling.

"Carmen, this is lovely. Just what I needed. The thought of those twelve—"

"Thirteen," said Dee Dee, already comfortably seated on the couch.

Elise stuck her tongue out. "*Thirteen* sets of china was giving me the willies. I can't imagine how my mother managed to squirrel away so much . . . stuff!"

Carmen smiled. "As far as my own mother's things, like you, I have a few preliminary instructions."

"Carmen, how hard can it be?" Dee Dee asked sarcastically. "We cut the tape, open said box, and take out the contents one by one. Sort into three piles: save or analyze, donate, throw the hell out. Does that sum it up?"

"Thanks for that summation, Counselor," Carmen said, taking a sip of her wine. "One word of warning. My mom led an organized but dull life. She was a minister's wife, okay? She was a lovely mother, generous with her time and energy, a . . ." Carmen felt her words catch in her throat as the image of her mother's smiling face floated into her mind. One constant about her mother: she was always pleasant and usually smiling. "Mom was a precious darling," she added wistfully. "But there won't be much here worth saving. And everything of sentimental value that I wanted, I've already claimed." She paused. "What I'm trying to say is don't be afraid to put things in the trash sack. You won't hurt my feelings. A few items of clothing that she tucked away, purses—she liked her purses—a scarf or two, perhaps, some scrapbooks. Mommy was a homebody, and she didn't socialize much outside church—bridge with her little group of friends and movies once in a while with Dad. If he approved of the film, of course." Carmen added, "She was your traditional *Mad Men*–era 1950s housewife."

Carmen put on a Branford Marsalis CD, grabbed a handful of snack mix, and opened a box marked "Joan, Misc.," the notation in her brother Howie's nearly illegible handwriting. A couple of blouses; a Bible bound in white leather, now worn and peeling, inscribed to her by a *"Mrs. Workman, with gratitude"*; some Danielle Steel and Jackie Collins novels; old LPs, the vinyl discs encased in shabby and torn covers, the art faded by time, moisture, and handling; a well-worn paperback copy of *Their Eyes Were Watching God*—Carmen set this aside—framed photographs of Carmen and her younger brothers, Ralph and Howie, high school and college graduations, Howie's wedding, her mom and dad on a cruise. *Would Dad like to have these?* Carmen wondered. She wiped a tear away.

A photo of . . . Carmen lost herself in memories as she thumbed through a small album of her own baby pictures and photos of her mother, aunts, and uncles from the '40s, '50s, and early '60s, judging by the clothes, and Uncle Jack in his Army Air Corps uniform from World War II.

"I thought you said your mother never went anywhere!" Dee Dee's voice carried across the room. She held up her hands, one clutching a stack of postcards and photos, the other a passport. Carmen set her wineglass down, rose, and took the passport from Dee Dee, opening it.

"France, Canada, the UK, the Netherlands . . ." She scanned her memory for the itineraries of her parents' later cruise vacations, but none of them matched the countries stamped on the pages of the now-expired document. "This passport is . . . Wow, this is from the late '50s, early '60s." *Hmmm, the stamps are faded. Kind of hard to read.* She frowned. As far as Carmen knew, Mom had never mentioned anything about going to these places. In fact, she hadn't talked much at all about her life before she married Carmen's dad.

"Well, she was definitely there, and in New York, Baltimore . . . no, that's a postcard to her from someone named RS,"

Dee Dee said, her attention riveted to the stack of black-and-white photos she was flipping through. "Oh, wait . . . here's a photo of your mom! At least I think this is her. You tell me. She looks like you—same dimples. Here she is at the Eiffel Tower . . . Versailles! Hmmm. London. Big Ben in the background. She was quite a globe-trotter. And—" Dee Dee stopped.

Carmen stepped closer and nudged her. "What? What is it? Let me see that."

"Oh yes, that's got to be your mom," Elise commented, now peering over Dee Dee's other shoulder at the tiny photo, her reading glasses perched on the end of her nose. "You do look like her—dimples, smile. Is that your father? I used to hear about Reverend Bradshaw and the church a lot, but I haven't actually met him . . ." Elise's voice faded away.

"No, that isn't my dad. So that can't be Mom," Carmen observed, frowning. The woman in the photo was beaming; she looked joyful and appeared to be laughing just when the shutter had clicked. She held herself with a jaunty attitude, and her clothes were stylish. Carmen didn't recognize the man at her side in the picture. Her breath caught for a second, then Carmen smiled. *Of course.*

"No. That isn't Mom. That's probably Aunt Tricia. Well, she wasn't really my aunt. She and my mom were first cousins, but she looked just like Mom, and they were close in age, just seven months apart." But even as Carmen spoke, as she studied the photo more closely, she knew her words weren't true. "No. Wait. That *is* my mother. But . . ."

Who's the guy?

She leaned in to the photo, taking it from Dee Dee's fingers. Her eyes narrowed as she studied the young man standing next to her mother, his arm draped protectively around her shoulders. He wore a military uniform; it looked as if it was from the Army, she thought. Carmen looked up at Dee Dee and Elise. She turned the photo over. The handwriting was unfamiliar.

"Jo and RS, April 1963"

Jo.

For a moment, no one spoke. Carmen knew that the gazes of Elise and Dee Dee were riveted to her face. She felt them staring at her. She continued to study the woman in the photo—now a stranger—looking from her to the soldier and back again. There was no doubt. This was Mom. But who was the man? The photo had been taken before she was born. She glanced at the photographs Dee Dee still clutched in her hand. And then she grabbed her cell phone.

She was startled when a hand that felt like a bracelet of steel encircled her wrist.

"Who are you calling?" Elise's voice was sharp.

"My dad. I'm going to ask him—"

"No, you aren't," Elise interrupted.

Carmen jerked her arm away and glared at Elise. "What are you talking about? This is not your business."

Elise nodded. "You're right, it isn't." She gestured toward the photo. "And have you considered that *this* might not be your father's business? That these treasures of your mother's are hers alone, from the days before she married him? From the days

when she was known . . . to someone, anyway, as Jo Adams
and not Mrs. Reverend Howard Bradshaw?"

Carmen felt tears forming in her eyes. "But . . . h-he would
know . . ."

"He might not know," Dee Dee said, a matter-of-fact tone
in her voice, a contrast to the stern one in Elise's. "Just because you marry someone doesn't mean they know everything
about you. Maybe you should finish going through all of these
boxes before you make that call. You should read through
these letters."

"What letters?"

Dee Dee took two steps toward the coffee table and with-
drew a packet from a box: a neat stack of letters bundled
together and tied with a red ribbon. She handed them to Carmen, whose hand was shaking. The top letter was addressed to
"Miss Joan Adams" in care of a post office box in Harlem. The
return address was "Lt. R. S. Topolosky, Ft. Knox, Kentucky."

Carmen's hand was trembling. "W-what does this mean?"

Elise shrugged her shoulders. "It doesn't have to mean anything other than your mom had a life before she married your
dad. Judging from the address, it looks as if she lived in New
York City for a while. And that—"

"And that she traveled to . . . Europe!" Carmen said loudly,
her voice quivering. "What the hell! My mom never went anywhere!"

Dee Dee giggled. "As far you as you knew."

"It looks like there was a lot more to her than you realized,"
Elise added in a mild tone.

The ribbon holding the letters together was shredded and worn, a bit stretched and barely holding together the assortment of papers and letters. One envelope had worked itself loose and suddenly floated down to the floor.

Elise knelt to pick it up. "Here you go. This one is trying to get away."

Carmen took the envelope and sat down on the couch. Gently, she slipped it back under the ribbon and set the bundle on the table. Her mind was still spinning from the notion that her mother, whom she'd thought of as the consummate "church lady," had not quite been who she seemed to be. Elise and Dee Dee retreated to give her some privacy and continue their sorting while, absently, Carmen's gaze wandered back and forth across the room, then returned to the coffee table and the writing on the front of the envelope on top of the stack. It was in the same handwriting. The words danced in front of her eyes. The return address was the same as the last one she'd seen: from a Lt. Topolosky. The mailing address on the envelope was the same too. Only the addressee's name was different. Carmen gasped.

Elise and Dee Dee whirled around.

"What is it?"

"Is something wrong?"

"Where is it, where is it . . ."

"Where is what?" Elise asked.

"The magnifying glass. Ah! Here it is. Okay," Carmen murmured to herself as she rummaged around the table sending the papers flying as if they'd been attacked by the Tasmanian Devil.

She finally found the tiny snapshot Dee Dee had first excavated, then held the magnifying glass in her hand like Sher-
lock Holmes, moving it close to the image. The photo had been
taken on a sunny day, but neither her mother nor the soldier
were wearing sunglasses, so both were squinting. The soldier's
left hand rested gently on top of Joan's shoulder. Joan's left arm
was bent at the elbow, her hand resting on the soldier's. A flash
of light there had been caught by the camera, the reflection of
sunlight from a ring. A ring with a gemstone. Carmen's breath
caught in her throat. A wedding ring.

Mrs. Joan Topolosky.

CHAPTER 8

Carmen

Elise and Dee Dee were giddy with curiosity about the contents of the letters as well as the photos and mementoes they'd found in the old boxes. Carmen knew that. But they didn't stick around.

"You need some breathing room," Elise said, hugging her gently.

Dee Dee followed suit. "Yes, you do. Some private time to read and absorb your mom's words. I gotta scoot. Satan's spawn number one is probably waiting for me." She sighed dramatically in imitation of her eldest daughter. "Prom season is upon us. Shopping for 'the dress.'"

After they left, Carmen poured another glass of wine, clicked off the music, and sat down on the floor in front of the coffee table. The letters, a stack of papers, and the photo albums were spread out across the top. The two shabby little boxes had contained a lot more than she'd realized when she picked them up from her dad. The memory of his odd behavior and even more odd expression caused her to wonder now if he'd known what they contained. She thought he did.

The setting sun cast a warm glow across the room, one last bow before sinking below the horizon. The light was amber in color and illuminated small specks of glitter that had attached themselves to the red ribbon tied around the letters. Carmen touched it, and a few of the sparkles came off on her fingertip. She didn't know where to begin.

No, that's not true. I know where to begin. I just don't know if I should.

Carmen focused the organizational side of her brain. She started with the documents, resisting the urge to read each one; she smoothed out the old papers and placed each one flat, creating a neat stack. Carmen then picked up the letters, slid off the ribbon, and organized them chronologically by postmark. Many of them were from her grandparents, Nona and Pops, a few were from distant relatives in Georgia, and several had a New York return address. These were from her mother's favorite cousin, Dorothy. The first of these letters was addressed to "Miss Joan Adams" from "Mrs. Dorothy Fortune." Carmen smiled. She remembered Cousin Dorothy—one of her mother's many first cousins—as a ninety-plus-year-old dynamo, before she passed away. The postmark year was 1949.

She moved on to the booklets and pamphlets and other miscellaneous pieces of paper. Next, she looked at the photographs, most of which were in small albums. Unknowingly, perhaps, her mother had helped her: each album was labeled in her mother's or grandmother's handwriting. The earliest date was in 1938, and Joan would have been eight years old.

Carmen chuckled at the image of her mother with plaited hair and scraped knobby knees, skinny and grinning, a cat-that-caught-the-canary expression on her face. Her smile exposed lots of teeth that seemed too large and too many for her small face. Next to her stood a little boy of similar height and age, his neatly ironed and tucked-in plaid shirt a marked contrast to Joan's rumpled skirt. He squinted, as if the sun was in his eyes, and his face had an ambivalent mask, as if he was concerned about something. Carmen smiled. Judging from Joan's defiant expression, Carmen rather thought her mother might have been up to some mischief, an assumption based on some of the stories she'd heard from her grandparents and uncles years ago.

"Oh yes, that Joanie was something else! Always up to some devilry!" Uncle Marshall, her mother's older brother, had often said in the evenings after a huge holiday dinner, which Joan's family was famous for.

"Hush up, Marsh," her mother would say in passing, usually wearing a mysterious smile as she moved quickly from kitchen to dining room and back again.

Uncle Marshall would roll his eyes and wink at Carmen, who was enthralled and incredulous. It was difficult to imagine her mother as anything but an angel and Reverend Bradshaw's saintly wife.

Carmen read the neatly printed caption below the faded snapshot.

"Joanie and Cricket, summer 1943"

CHAPTER 9

Joan

Cincinnati, 1946

C rrriiiccckkket! Ima pop you in your head!"

"Uh-uh . . ."

"Uh-*huh*!"

"Ow!"

Cricket's yell hit decibels unmatched by a Wagnerian soprano.

"What is going on out there?" Winona Adams stepped onto the back porch. She did not look happy.

Cricket stole a quick look at Joanie, who glared back at him, her hand balled into a fist.

"Nothing!" he said, wiping away his tears with the back of a grimy paw.

Joanie was crouched off to the side of him, her face hidden behind the branches of the sticker bush. She could see the bottom half of her mother: white-and-black-checked apron, faded blue housedress, and black shoes. Her mother didn't move. That was a good sign. Then she took a step into the yard. *Uh-oh.*

"Do I have to come over there?" Winona called. Now her hands were on her hips. Joanie's stomach muscles clenched.

"Noooooo," both children called out.

"Humph," Mrs. Adams commented. "Y'all behave, all right?"

"Yeeessss, ma'am," Joanie and Cricket answered in unison. The screen door squeaked when it closed.

"And Joan Ann, don't get filthy out there, now. Dorothy Mae's coming, you hear me?"

"Yes, Momma!" This time only Joanie had answered.

Both she and Cricket looked down at her dress, smudged with grass stains and the imprints of sweaty fingers, and at her bony knees: one was caked with mud; the other had a prominent scrape on it.

Mrs. Adams's voice carried again. Startled, the children froze, and Joanie, who'd started to say something to Cricket, closed her mouth.

"Hubert, will you please oil up that door? I just cain't listen to . . ." The sound of her voice faded as she moved toward the center of the house. Joanie smiled. Her mother was from a place she called "middle Georgia," and when she was annoyed about something, the vowels in her words stretched out and a "fixin' to" or "cain't" would slip into her sentences. Joanie thought that was funny, the way Momma talked, but she would never let her mother know that.

"You in trouble now. Pro'bly get a whuppin'," Cricket whispered loud enough to spook the bunny rabbit they'd been stalking.

"Shut up!" Joanie snapped at Cricket. She swatted at him

too, but this time she missed. "Now look what you done!" A flash of white cottontail caught her attention, but one blink later it was gone.

Cricket grinned. Joanie was always hitting him or trying to. He'd never admit it, but he liked it when Joanie did that. He loved Joanie, and she loved him back. She was his best friend. So he swatted back at Joanie, then ran. And ran and ran, so fast that his legs hurt. Joanie ran after him.

Cricket didn't run out of space—the yard was huge. The street Joanie lived on was one street over from where Cricket lived, both streets within the boundaries of the city but only just. At the end of the block, there was a cornfield and then railroad tracks. On the other side of the tracks, or so Joanie's father said when he didn't know Joanie was listening, lived a man named McCulloch who owned something called a still. Joanie's brothers were warned repeatedly to stay away from it because it was known to blow up occasionally, which Joanie thought was so funny. How could a thing that was supposed to be "still" blow up?

When Hubert Adams got a job on the railroad, he and Joanie's mother, Winona, moved up to Cincinnati from Georgia by way of Kentucky, and as soon as they could, they grabbed up a little "spot" of land, as Hubert called it, as much space as they could afford. They were city folk now, but the country they grew up in was not left behind. Nona, as she was sometimes called, brought as much of the red clay of Georgia with her as she could; Hubert's contribution from Kentucky was a handful of tobacco seeds and a couple of sturdy plants that would grow into his favorite string beans. The same was true of Cricket's parents, transplants from Alabama. The city was growing too fast and expanding too wide for any one person to own real acreage anymore—even old McCulloch's boundaries were being whittled away by development and the Baltimore & Ohio Railroad tracks. But the yards back along their neighborhood were still generous, and there was space for the children to roam, for a family to keep chickens (no roosters—too noisy) and a garden that would yield enough tomatoes, melons, string beans, cucumbers, kale, and mustard greens to feed the family or to give away or to sell if necessary. Hubert's small patch of tobacco thrived (even though he didn't smoke much anymore), as did the Kentucky Wonders, more than Joanie liked because it was her job to pick them, and no matter how hard she tried, she always got a spider bite for her trouble. And when she did, she'd run to her parents, who liked to walk the boundaries of their small domain in the early evening, treading carefully in the rows amidst the thick scent of honeysuckle and the humidity, imagining themselves home again.

Joanie and Cricket were two lonely children who had played in a crib together when their mothers visited, who walked to school together each morning, and who shared the Sunday school lesson paper at church because they were in the same class. Joanie was the youngest child of the Adams household, a hodgepodge of children from Mr. Adams's two marriages, all boys and all older than Joanie. After the first Mrs. Adams died, the second Mrs. Adams—Joanie's mother—took over, raising her husband's sons and then adding two of her own plus one daughter. From her brothers, Joanie had learned to be tough, but she was not their friend. They avoided her like the plague. John—or Jack, as he was called—was two years older than Joanie, but he pretended not to see her when they were at school. And as far as Hubert Jr., Jack, Marshall, and Allen were concerned, she barely existed.

Cricket, on the other hand, was an only child, a much-wanted baby born to mature parents who had given up on the idea of having children. Overjoyed, they set about making his life as carefree and abundant as possible. Nona Adams teased Eleanor that the baby's poop barely got into the diaper good before Eleanor wiped it away. Cricket's mother also put off letting him walk outside because she didn't want him to get the soles of his shiny white baby shoes soiled. Called Cricket by the neighborhood children—because, they said, he looked like Jiminy Cricket in the *Pinocchio* movie—the boy was so pampered that he might have become a spoiled brat had it not been for his friendship with Joanie Adams. She was his conscience and his courage.

Where Cricket was hesitant, Joanie was bold. If Cricket was afraid, Joanie pulled him along, surprisingly strong considering how skinny she was, and made him do whatever it was that frightened him. And so he sprained an elbow when she pushed his swing really high; he climbed trees even though he was terrified of heights; and he skinned his knee when Joanie gave his bicycle a shove to help him go faster. She was with him to face down a pack of bullies who called him a sissy. Cricket had been so scared of the boys that he turned and ran. But when Leander

Shaw pushed Joanie down onto the sidewalk, Cricket ran back and gave Leander a solid fist to the jaw, much to everyone's surprise. But not Joanie's. She knew that Cricket would die for her if she asked him to. They would be friends forever. He'd even promised to protect her from dragons, although they hadn't found one yet.

But even Cricket couldn't protect Joanie from her mother. Nona was not going to be happy when she saw how dirty Joanie was.

Joanie used a handful of leaves to wipe the mud from her knee. It still looked a little dark around her kneecap, but that was okay. A quick spit bath took care of the scratch on her shin. It wasn't even bleeding now. Well, not much. But the grass stains on her dress were a worry.

"You're never gonna get *that* out," Cricket said, leaning down to get a better look, his hands on his knees. His voice had been full of satisfaction.

"Oh, shut up!"

He shook his head, an expression of doubt on his small face. "No, look." He pointed at the stain with his mud-tipped finger. "The more you wipe it, the bigger it gets." Cricket frowned and squinted. His mother was taking him to pick up his new glasses next week. He dreaded it. "And now it's turning gray."

Joanie held up the front of her skirt for a closer look. No. It didn't look good. And it wasn't really gray, more of a brownish-greenish color and . . . it did seem to be spreading. There were blue cornflowers on the fabric. She bit her lip. Would Mother notice?

"Who's Dorothy Mae, anyway?" Cricket asked. "Why is she somebody special you got to keep clean for?"

"She's my cousin. From Cleveland. Her mother, Aunt Ava, she's my momma's big sister. Dorothy's all grown up now. She went to college in Atlanta."

Cricket shrugged. "It's called Atlanta?"

"Nooooo, dummy, it's *in* Atlanta," Joanie corrected him. She couldn't remember exactly what the college was called.

"Is that good?" Cricket asked.

Joanie wiped the front of her dress with the back of her hand, dismayed to see that the once brownish-greenish stain was now just plain brown.

"Uh-huh. All my momma's aunts and sisters went to this college in Atlanta. Dorothy, she's smart. And pretty. She knows things." Joanie wasn't even trying not to brag. She was crazy about Dorothy Mae. Dorothy Mae was everything Joanie wanted to be when she grew up. She was not only smart. She wore beautiful clothes, and she went places and did things. Dorothy Mae had visited San Francisco, she'd been to Mexico to study art, she'd been to a city called Accra—that was a place in Africa—and she'd been to Montreal, a cold place up north where people spoke French. Dorothy could speak French too.

Cricket was impressed. "What's French?"

"It's a . . . language," Joanie said, pronouncing the word carefully. "They use words different from the ones we use, but they mean the same thing. Like . . ." She touched her top lip with the tip of her tongue. "Like 'chapeau.'"

"What's that mean?"

"'Hat,'" Joanie said, looking again at her skirt. Half of the front was now damp and gray embellished with a semicircular stain of deep brownish-gray with streaks of vivid green. The tableau might have made an interesting finger-painting. As a dress, it was a disaster.

Cricket followed her gaze and laughed.

Mr. Adams's oilcan was desperately needed.

The back screen door screeched as it opened. "What's going on out there?" Nona Adams yelled.

The children looked at each other.

"Nothing!"

CHAPTER 10

Joan

Mother was not pleased when Joanie came in, because her dress was a mess, her knees were skinned and grubby, and her hair had worked its way out of the braids and now stood out like a crown of corkscrews encircling her head.

"Joan Ann Adams."

Oh Lordy. It was never a good thing when Mother used her full name.

Nona's expression was grim. She pointed toward the back staircase.

"March upstairs, take off all of those . . . grimy clothes, and put 'em in the basket. Wash your face, hands, neck . . ." Nona grabbed her daughter's ear and looked. "And behind your ears." Her gaze lowered to Joanie's knees. She sighed. "And your knees. Take off those socks, and polish up your shoes . . . Joanie! What were you and Cricket doing to get so filthy?"

Joanie didn't answer at first because she wasn't sure what to say.

Nona smiled and nudged her toward the stairs. "Never mind.

Just hurry up, girl. Aunt Ava, Dorothy Mae, and them will be here shortly."

Joanie scampered up the stairs.

"And bring me down that comb and brush. Your hair's come a-loose."

Washing up and getting her hair combed and braided was a small price to pay for getting a front-row seat at the dining room table when company like Aunt Ava and Dorothy came to visit. Mother's dinner would be a gut buster—all of Joanie's favorite foods: fried chicken and perch, green beans, coleslaw, mashed potatoes, and pies—peach and banana crème. Her mouth watered just thinking about it. But the real treat had nothing to do with food. If Joanie behaved herself, was quiet and didn't ask too many "'pertinent questions" (her grandmother scolded her for asking those), then Mother would let her stay up late and listen to the grown-ups' conversations after dinner. That was almost better than Christmas.

* * *

"Joanie! Honey, are you sick? You hardly ate your dinner!" Nona was clearing the plates. She set the stack of plates down and placed the back of her hand gently against her daughter's forehead. "You feel all right?"

"Yes, Momma." Joanie absently picked up the chicken leg before her mother could pick up her plate. She took a bite and chewed but didn't taste a thing. Not because her mother's cooking wasn't phenomenal but because she was mesmerized by her older cousin: the way she looked and her manners as she ate. Dorothy noticed her little cousin's stare and smiled. Joanie grinned and thought, *I want to be* just *like her when I grow up.*

All eyes were on Dorothy's face, including Joanie's. But unlike the adults, Joanie was concentrating on the way Dorothy looked and spoke, and not as much on what she said. She had a beautiful oval-shaped face framed by stylish dark brown waves—a "coiffure," she called it. Her dark pecan-colored skin was flawless and glowed, and she wore lipstick! A red color that made her look like a movie star. It was a warm day so Dorothy's sleeveless cotton dress was light and cool looking, and she wore a pair of white sandals. Her toenails were painted red too. Joanie thought that was the most amazing thing she'd ever seen. So amazing that she barely heard what Dorothy had said until her cousin winked at her.

"Joan! I don't think you heard a word I said!"

Joanie blushed. "No, I heard you. Honest!" the girl sputtered out, embarrassed. Nona was giving her "the eye"—a look Nona often used on her daughter in church when Joanie wasn't paying attention. "Sorry," she murmured.

"But is it all right?" Joanie's father, Hubert, asked. "You all get along, do you?"

Dorothy nodded, still smiling, a pair of dimples—the "Henry dimples," as they were called—appearing in her cheeks.

"Of course! We're all students. We're serious about this work and want to do well. Besides, discussion is part of the course evaluation." Dorothy looked across the table at her mother. Aunt Ava was frowning. "We're graded on the way we discuss and debate the topics in class as well as on our papers."

Aunt Ava didn't look convinced. "Uh-uh," she said, her reaction duplicated by one of the cousins and Hubert. She locked eyes with her daughter. "You watch what you say 'round them."

"Mother, this is New York City."

Ava pulled her elbows off the table and sat upright. She glanced at her sister and continued to shake her head as if to say, *See what I'm talkin' 'bout, Nona? She doesn't understand me!*

"You think because it's New York City, because it isn't Georgia, that it's all right? That all these white kids like you and respect you? That they don't have the same thoughts in their heads that their cousins do down south? The ones that wear sheets and put 'Whites only' signs on their shops and restaurants? You foolin' yourself, girl. I say be careful. I mean it. You find out the hard way."

Dorothy lowered her head slightly and bit her lip. Joanie was sympathetic, but not because she knew any white kids—the schools in Cincinnati were mostly segregated. She was in Dorothy's corner because she loved her and looked up to her. And because she was drooling over the red lipstick Dorothy was wearing.

Joanie started to listen more intently because she didn't know anything about white folks either. She hoped her mother, Aunt Ava, and the others would enlighten her. White people were a puzzle she could not figure out. They seemed harmless and ordinary. She saw them on the sidewalks and in stores downtown, in automobiles and on the streetcars. They didn't look much different from anybody else except their skin was white. They wore the same clothes and seemed to eat the same food—

Joanie had seen a little boy eating an ice-cream cone; she liked ice cream too. Then there was Brady, the man who picked her daddy up for work sometimes. Brady seemed friendly; he smiled and waved at her and her mother from the front of the truck. He called Daddy "Hubert," and Daddy called him "Brady," not "Mr. Brady," so Joanie thought that was fine. His bright red hair and freckles made him look funny, but lots of people Joanie knew had red hair, and even her mother had freckles on her nose, so maybe he wasn't so different after all. But that was where the puzzle was. Because despite the ordinary appearance of these people, something about them was dangerous, according to her parents and Aunt Ava, something to be wary of, to avoid at all costs. And Joanie was curious to find out what that was. So she took a deep breath and asked.

Her mother said, "This is grown-up time, Joan," and sent her into the kitchen to eat her dessert. If Mother called her "Joan" or "Joan Ann," instead of "Joanie," it was best not to ask more questions. Defeated, she set her bowl and spoon on the kitchen table and gazed longingly at the open dining room door through which laughter floated. It seemed miles away. Joanie couldn't hear anything now but low murmurs. For a few moments, she contented herself with her ice cream and dreamed of the day when she wouldn't be sent to the kitchen, when she was grown up and sophisticated like Dorothy Mae— that was her new favorite word, "sophisticated"—living in a faraway place, traveling to even farther away places, and wearing red lipstick.

The murmuring got louder, and Joanie thought she could

make out Aunt Ava's voice. She looked at the door to the dining room. Her mother had almost closed it, but not quite. The latch hadn't caught and instead the door had creaked open halfway, which was both good and bad. It was bad in that it still blocked the sound. But it was good because it also blocked Nona's view into the kitchen and left just enough room for Joanie to slip into the triangle of space behind the door. From there she could hear just fine.

* * *

Joanie loved listening to her parents, aunts, and uncles talk about "the old days," the family stories so different from the ones she heard in school but better somehow. In these stories, the heroes were people her family actually knew and the situations were true—as far as it was possible to know—and nearly always exciting. Sometimes she'd fall asleep on her father's or Aunt Ava's lap, the murmur of harmonious voices a pleasant substitute for a lullaby. The best stories of all, though, were the ones told after she'd been excused from the table. Sometimes Joan would eavesdrop from the back hall; other times she would pretend to go upstairs but instead crouch on the staircase midway up. The stories were many and various, and yet they were woven together like a knitted scarf with yarns of many colors.

These were the stories Joanie liked best. They were colorful and dramatic, filled with suspense, fire, forbidden love, and gunfights. The best ones involved her mother's grandmother, "Big Ava" Collier, daughter of an enslaved woman, Mary, and the man who owned the land that she worked, whose name was spoken with reverence, whose exploits were recounted with awe. The saga of Ava's life had taken on mythic status, expanding with each telling: Big Ava had followed Sherman's army through Georgia until she was forced to stop to deliver a baby. Big Ava, along with her husband, Harrison Henry, had fought off night riders (she had been interrupted again by childbirth, the fourth of her ten children), and for many of Ava's one hundred years (even reports of her age approached Old Testament length) she and her family had fought her half-brothers and their descendants both in court and at gunpoint to hold on to the two hundred acres bequeathed to her in her father's will, a deathbed bequest that the Scotsman had made to his only daughter following a belated baptism into the body of Christ.

The land remained in Ava and Harrison's hands—several of Joanie's aunts and uncles still lived there, and Big Ava and Harrison were buried there. The stories, and others like them, overflowed with embellishment, accentuated by laughter. But there were points to be made.

"You just cain't trust 'em," Cousin Eugene repeated, shaking his head. He'd come in through the side door, listening to the story through the open, screened window. He'd put his cigarette out, but the smoke swirled around him like the cone of a tornado. "No, sir, you just can't. Don't matter how nice they are . . ."

"Gene, don't say that!" Dorothy interrupted. "Ames Preston over at the lumberyard would do anything for you! Thinks you walk on water!"

"Yeah, he do," Eugene agreed. "And he'd be satisfied if I walked on water too, just as long as I didn't walk 'long the sidewalk when he passed!"

Laughter erupted, and Dorothy swatted at him as if he were a fly.

"They just people," Hubert murmured. He glanced at his wife. She knew he was thinking about Brady.

"We know that, they know that. But it don't mean nothing," Ava chimed in, rubbing her daughter's back. "Momma and Papa fought those Colliers for years. They were like ants— just kept coming back. Didn't matter what the will or the judge said, didn't matter how much it cost 'em." She inhaled and turned her gaze toward her daughter. "Until things change . . ."

"Momma, they *have* changed!" Dorothy exclaimed in frustration. "In the city—"

Ava shook her head slowly. "City or country, it don't matter. Until things change . . . you can be friends with 'em, live near 'em, work with 'em. Even marry 'em." Ava gave a snort to indicate that this was not going to happen. "But when it comes down to it, they still white, honey. And you got to be careful 'cause they can use that against you."

Joanie thought about the boy with freckles she'd seen downtown, the one who'd been eating an ice-cream cone, and she wondered.

CHAPTER II

Joan

New York City, 1958–1966

I still don't know how you did it," Dorothy said as she and Joan unpacked the suitcase. "Uncle Hubert was dead set against you coming here. He said it all the time."

Joan grinned and smoothed the stack of neatly folded slips with her hand before putting them into the bureau drawer that Dorothy had thoughtfully lined with tissue paper. Then she held up her hands and wiggled her fingers as if she were a conjurer casting a spell. "Magic!" she said, then giggled, remembering her father's expression when he realized that he'd agreed to what he had said he would never agree to: letting his "baby girl" move to New York.

Dorothy swatted at her with a brassiere. "Fiend!"

"Give me that!" Joan grabbed the bra and twirled it around her head while she did a little dance. Dorothy clapped her hands. Back in Cincinnati, Hubert Adams was still wondering how he'd been maneuvered into such a spot. If it was magic, it was a spell that Hubert had cast on himself, a self-fulfilling prophecy.

* * *

"Only the best for my baby girl," Hubert Adams had said proudly whenever bringing home yet another expensive dress or doll from Shillito's department store.

"Only the best for my little lady," he had boasted when Joanie's honors scholarship to UC was announced. "The best schools, the best professors."

"Daddy, the best professor in socio-anthropology in the country is at CCNY. I may have to transfer out my junior year," Joanie told her father in the course of a benign conversation one evening after supper as she helped her mother clear the table.

Hubert snapped the evening paper with a sharp, coordinated movement, glancing at his daughter over the top of his glasses. "What'd you say? What's the matter with the . . . what's his name? Dr. Wells over there at the University of Cincinnati?"

Joanie shook her head slightly. "That's what I'm telling you. He took a position at the City College of New York."

"Humph," Hubert said with a tone of disapproval. "That doesn't seem right. How are you supposed to get the best instruction if these fellows move all over the place?"

"It isn't the end of the world. I can always go and study with Dr. Wells in New York. Dorothy Mae's there. I can . . ."

As she talked, she knew her father was in his own world, a mélange of politics, baseball, and racing statistics. "Nona!

That filly of Bernard's, Tomorrow's Dream, looks like it has all of the right things going on . . . It's going to rain Friday, and that two-year-old does well in the mud."

". . . transferred without losing any credits. I can start in September." Joanie was still talking. Standing behind her father, her mother grinned. "I can manage the fees if I stay with Dorothy and Washburn. And Dorothy thinks she can get me a job at the electric company. She has a friend who works there. Dr. Rasmussen's writing me a letter of recommendation."

"Start in September," Hubert repeated. He glanced up at his daughter and nodded. "All right, baby girl, that sounds fine to me. You go ahead and start in September. Only the best for you."

Joanie grinned at her mother. Hubert hadn't heard a word she'd said.

CHAPTER 12

Joan

A transformation began, and Joan became her own fairy godmother. She gave up the "Joanie." Joan Adams was bound for New York and, like a chess piece, one move closer to emulating her role model, Cousin Dorothy. Next, she changed her appearance. She had Eileen cut her hair, and she bought two tubes of red lipstick (Elizabeth Arden) to celebrate her new life. Joan was traveling farther than she ever had in her life. (Summers spent as a child with Grandmother Henry in Georgia didn't count.) This was the jumping off point for adventures new and strange.

In her most recent letter, Dorothy had given her detailed instructions, typed not handwritten. Joan read them over and over, handling the parchment-like stationery until its texture wore down to the slickness of silk. She memorized the words, chanting them like a mantra: "Grand Central . . . 42nd . . . two blocks . . . subway . . . Lexington Avenue northbound . . . Brook Avenue . . . between 135th and . . ."

Dorothy had enclosed a snapshot of the building along with

a neighbor's telephone number. "In case you get scared," she'd scrawled on the back.

Why does everyone think I'll be scared? Joan wondered. This comment—expressed by her mother, father, aunts, uncles, cousins, and friends—irritated her. She wasn't six. And she wasn't scared, wasn't even nervous. And besides, New York was not the end of her journey; it was only the first stop.

After she arrived, she found Dorothy and Washburn lived on the third floor of a four-story prewar building in a three-room apartment with a tiny bathroom and a "stoop" off the back. Joan had never lived in an apartment before; it was the first time she'd lived elbow to elbow with other people. It was like the apartment building was itself a small city.

Mr. Bell upstairs was the skinniest man she'd ever seen, but you'd never know that from the sound of his footsteps clomping around his apartment as if his home had been invaded by a herd of elephants. Amazing, considering how solid and snugly built the Cornell Building was. The Andersons next door seemed to argue a lot, their raised voices often crystal clear despite the thick walls. They argued and sang—an odd combination, Joan thought. Washburn laughed and told her that Connie and Tim were, among other things, actors and musicians—they'd studied at Juilliard and were in the chorus at the Met. "Probably rehearsing," he commented.

The Smiths, both teachers, lived across the hall in 310-B. Mrs. Holland and her sister, Mrs. Nuñez, were at the end of the hall; the sisters baked constantly, infusing the weird yellow-green-painted hall with warm, yeasty aromas of baked bread infused with cinnamon and vanilla. Ellen and Bill what's-their-name (Joan could never remember it, and once she did, to her embarrassment, she didn't pronounce it properly) were medical residents, and Joan saw them infrequently since they worked all the time and mostly at night, while during the day they slept (or tried to, considering the noise emanating from the Andersons or other tenants). Mr. Wakefield, a friend of Washburn's father, lived downstairs and worked at a restaurant in the next block, sharing barbecue, ham, fried chicken, and other delights with them on his days off.

And then there was apartment 310-D and its mysterious occupant, a tall, slim, cadaverous-looking woman in her late twenties or early thirties who only said, "Good evening," and whom Dorothy called Nosferatu because of her nocturnal ways and penchant for wearing all black. Rumors flew about Miss Phillips, and the more ridiculous they were ("She really is a vampire!"), the more they were believed. She kept to herself, and word was she paid her rent on time.

Some nights Joan got buckets of sleep. Other nights she got a lot less. But thanks to the murmurs from the other apartments and the street noise that kept her awake, she picked up a few useful Spanish phrases for her trouble. On still other nights, she shared a shot of whiskey with the tenant in 310-D, Miss Gizzy Phillips (formal name, Griselda) who, Joan was not surprised to learn, was not a vampire at all but a private duty nurse working the night shift.

She was mesmerized by the City College of New York, just the look of the place. There was something otherworldly about it, especially when it came into view near the end of her bus ride, the top of Shepard Hall rising slowly above the other buildings. Of course she could have taken the subway to school. It would have been faster, especially coming from work— Dorothy had indeed gotten her on at the ConEdison office. And it would have been warmer in winter and drier when it rained. But the bus ride allowed Joan the brief pleasure of letting the neo-Gothic buildings take over her imagination. One blink and she would be transported to another continent, another time. She imagined Notre Dame, its massive bells ringing, calling the faithful to Mass. She imagined gargoyles playing tag at the tops of the spires, creating mischief and waving to her. She decided then and there to apply for a passport so she could see the inspiration of her daydreams for herself in Paris. What could be more Gothic than Notre Dame?

"But you just got here!" Dorothy said when she found out.

Joan quickly learned the city's ways. People didn't say "Good morning" or "How are you?" like they did in Cincinnati. Some of her fellow students and instructors thought her accent was "flat" at best, probably "Southern" (not good) and obviously "country" (which was even worse). Joan had grown up thinking of her cousins in Georgia as "country"—and they were, living on a farm of more than one hundred acres, growing crops and raising chickens, hogs, and cattle. Now *that* was country, and self-sustaining if you wanted to make a point about it. It was a way of life. She was dismayed to discover that some of her fellow students considered it a moniker for stupid and inbred, and were boneheaded enough to say so.

"There are studies to indicate a higher percentage of developmental problems in . . . those children—"

"Studies whose results were thrown out," Joan barked back in sociology class one day, "and the authors of the Fielding study, in particular, were thoroughly discredited. Fielding himself admitted that he made up the numbers. He was exposed as a fraud. Even his PhD was fiction!

"The culture is based on agriculture, no doubt. It's rural, but that doesn't preclude it from being modern," Joan also explained, trying to keep her temper in check. She spoke slowly so the nitwit who'd commented could understand her "accent." "The knowledge required to raise beef cattle or grow a strong hybrid of corn is astounding, requiring in some cases a rudimentary background in botany, chemistry, and meteorology. Rural does not equal backward. It equates to growing and harvesting the food"—Joan glared at the man—"that you eat, raising healthy animals so that you can cook a steak or eat fried chicken."

"I was only saying that," the bonehead continued. Just the sound of his voice made her want to smack him. "Pardon me, with your Southern sensibilities."

"My . . . what?" She paused to catch her breath and unclench her fist. She glared at the young man in the black eyeglasses who'd made the comments. "I'm from Ohio, and if your pea brain can recall fifth grade geography, Ohio is not now and has never been a Southern state. As for any sensibilities I might have, Southern or otherwise, they are none of your business."

She was too angry to do anything but gather up her books

and handbag and leave the classroom before her temper got the best of her and she slammed her two-pound sociology book into his head. At the bottom of the stairs, Joan paused to catch her breath, then turned toward the exit doors and almost walked straight into a man she recognized as one of her classmates. Not the bonehead, however.

"Oh! Excuse me! I'm—"

"Sorry! I—" He stepped back quickly as if removing himself from striking range, then he said, "That guy's an idiot. I'm sorry you had to go through that."

"There's no need to apologize. It's not your fault, Mr. . . ." *What the heck was his name?*

"Topolosky. Richard. Just call me Rich." He smiled. "You told him off in brilliant form. Actually, you sorta peeled his skin off." He seemed delighted.

Joan felt her cheeks reddening as she scrutinized him for the first time, taking in his uniform. Army. Lieutenant.

"Yes . . . well . . . I get . . . carried away sometimes."

"He deserved it." Richard extended his hand. "Your name is Joan?"

"Yes, yes, it is. Joan Adams," she said.

He cleared his throat. "Well, Joan, I'd like to take you out."

"Really, it isn't necessary." Joan turned to leave.

"I insist," Richard said.

Okay, she said to herself. "Okay."

It was then that Joan realized Richard Topolosky was still holding her hand.

CHAPTER 13

Joan

Their first date was a disaster. They ate at Omar's, one of Richard's favorite places not far from campus. It was Joan's first experience with hummus, and she loved it. But it didn't love her. The chickpeas gave her the trots, and she vowed never to eat hummus again.

Embarrassed but not defeated (first impressions aren't always destiny), Richard asked her out again. This time the evening wasn't a disaster, just a mild catastrophe.

They went to Teresa's, an Italian place in Little Italy where Teresa cooked, her husband Vito was maître d', and their sons Theo and Domenico served and tended bar. Joan ordered spaghetti alla carbonara. Richard ordered veal scaloppine but barely touched it. He spent the evening scrutinizing Joan with a nervous expression on his face, asking her after each forkful if she was okay.

After the sixth query, Joan had had enough. She slammed her water glass down on the table and dropped her fork onto her plate.

"That's it!" she barked at him. "Stop asking me if I'm okay!"

Water had splashed out of the glass and drenched the starched tablecloth. The fork had skidded off her plate and landed on Richard's. Some of the scaloppine had found a home on the front of his shirt.

"Oh my God! I am so sorry!" She snatched up her napkin and moved to dab up the spill. But the large cloth had other ideas. One edge of it soaked up a tablespoon of rich sauce while another caught on the rims of Joan's water and wine glasses and tipped them over.

Later, as they stood on the sidewalk outside Teresa's— Richard's shirt a damp, rude-looking mélange of brown; Joan's new (purchased for the occasion) and now-damp madras skirt stained dark ruby with Chianti, her white blouse dotted with olive oil droplets—the situation shifted from tragedy to comedy.

Joan looked down at her new purchase. The skirt was probably ruined, the blouse too, since oil stains were next to impossible to get out, and Joan noticed on the toe of her right shoe a small droplet of sauce—whether from the carbonara or the veal, she couldn't tell. She looked up at Rich, whose expression combined horror with embarrassment. Technically, this had been their second date, yet this was the first time Joan took a really good look at him without his uniform on—he wore it only when he worked at the recruiting office. He was tall (at five feet three inches, everybody was tall compared to Joan) and slim, but he had a sturdiness to his body, and somehow Joan knew that his now-ruined white shirt covered muscular arms and shoulders. His face was long, his nose narrow, and his eyes a light brown behind the black eyeglasses. He was, in fact, very handsome despite the mask of self-consciousness he now wore. Richard also wore a small droplet of sauce on his right cheek. Joan couldn't help herself; she reached up to wipe it away, then started laughing. Soon Richard was laughing too, and their giggles morphed into belly laughs.

"I-I better go home," Joan stammered, her words punctuated by giggles. She ran her palm across the wet front of her skirt. "This is sticky. It won't be long before I attract every bug around for miles. And you . . ." She reached up again and touched Richard's veal-hued shirtfront. "Your shirt is a mess."

Richard grinned, his lean face relieved of its self-consciousness. "Are you hungry?"

Joan stared. "Hungry?"

"Hungry," Richard repeated. "We barely ate. Remember?"

Joan smiled. "You're right." She was starving.

"Dimitri's Coney is in the next block. Do you like hot dogs, JoJo?"

She'd been called Joan, Joan Ann, Joanie, and Baby Girl, but never JoJo. She liked it.

"I love hot dogs," she said.

"Good," Richard murmured, taking her hand. "Because I don't think we can go back to Teresa's."

But Richard was wrong. They held their own private wedding reception at Teresa's—sitting at the same table they'd nearly destroyed months before—eating the same meal, toasting the occasion with Chianti.

It hadn't been love at first sight but pretty close. They were nearly inseparable from that day forward. Joan and Richard got married at City Hall, a janitor and the judge's secretary their witnesses. They chose the surreptitious path to matrimony because they wanted the moment to be theirs and no one else's. When she learned of her younger son's choice of bride, Bella Topolosky sat shiva. Nona and Hubert sent their congratulations in a sparsely worded letter. "I don't know what to say," Nona wrote to her daughter. Hubert said nothing.

"What does he do, anyway?" Dorothy asked Joan as they sat together in the East Harlem apartment's kitchen one evening not long after the wedding.

"Do? Who?" Joan's thoughts were miles away.

"Richard. You know, your husband." Amusement brushed across Dorothy's words. She'd been reading her aunt's letter. "What does he do for a living? Uncle Hubert will want to know that he's able to support you in the manner to which he thinks you should become accustomed."

"Army intel," Joan echoed Rich's answer to the question. A flurry of images—none of them pleasant—passed through her mind. "What does that mean?"

Rich smiled slightly.

"Among other things, it means I can't talk about it. For now, I'm on assignment. Civilian. Nothing dangerous. Language school."

Joan was silent for a moment. The war was over. But new conflicts were growing and a few old ones had reasserted themselves. Rich was fluent in German and Russian. "Language school" sounded reasonable. But the unsettled sensation in her stomach was still there.

"So . . ."

"Just tell them I work for the government," Rich had told Joan. "That my specialty is red tape and towers of paperwork."

"You're a spy," Joan had said to him.

A wry smile had come to Richard's lips. "Me? A spy? Think about that. Do I really look like a spy?"

On the slim side, dark brown hair, light brown eyes, and Buddy Holly glasses. Okay, not a spy of movies.

"Army analyst, soon to be poor civilian college instructor. How's that for a profession?" Joan took the cigarette from Dorothy's fingers as she repeated her husband's words. She blew one raggedy smoke ring and then another, smaller but more perfectly formed. This time she didn't cough.

Dorothy shrugged. "I guess it'll have to do," she said.

CHAPTER 14

Joan

From the beginning, it was just the two of them. Aside from Dorothy and Washburn, who loved jazz almost as much as Rich did, family support was in short supply. In the case of Richard's parents, it was nonexistent. Bella and Ira Topolosky were at odds over their son's unorthodox marriage: as far as Bella was concerned, Richard was dead; Ira, as uncomfortable with his wife's reaction as he was with his son's choice of wife, did not seem to know what to do. Richard and his wife ("Dad, her name is Joan.") were welcome in their home, but "welcome" was not the feeling Joan got the first and only time she visited. Bella refused to make an appearance. David, Richard's brother, who lived in Brooklyn, met them for dinner and apologized for his parents' obtuseness, but it didn't change things. Richard could not go "home" again, but he didn't seem too upset about. "Mother and I . . . we've never really seen eye to eye anyway."

Winona and Hubert were similarly at odds with the situation. Hubert was bewildered. Is this what came of living in New York? Winona expressed concern, worrying for Joan's safety. Joan and Richard's first visit to Cincinnati as a couple provoked furtive and sometimes hostile stares on the train and on the streets of the Queen City. But the Adams family celebrated their daughter's homecoming in the usual way, with tables groaning with food and rooms packed with relatives, friends, and nosy neighbors dropping in to say hello to little Joanie Adams and her white husband.

"Your . . . Richard . . . your husband," Winona fumbled over the words. "You didn't tell me that he smokes." She looked toward the window where Richard and a few of the men stood, shivering in the November cold, smoking on the back stoop because Winona didn't allow tobacco in the house. She frowned with disapproval.

Joan sighed with relief. Her mother disapproved of Richard's smoking more than she did of Richard. "Momma . . ."

Winona held up her hand and turned back to the dining room table, where she had been setting up with desserts, plates, and forks. "Don't mind me, Joan Ann," she said. "I'll get used to this. To him, I mean," she added, stealing another quick look out the window at Richard.

"Are you talking about the cigarettes or the fact that he's white?"

Winona looked up. Her lips curled upward in a slight smile. "Both. Joanie, I just want you to be safe. This . . . are you safe in New York? With him, I mean. Things are different there, right? Well, they'd have to be."

Joan smiled at her mother and quickly looked away before her thoughts betrayed her. "We're fine, Mom."

Winona set the cake gently on the stand, licking a smear of coconut icing from her finger. Joan dipped her finger across another stray smear of icing and brought it to her lips.

"Joan Ann!" Her mother swatted at her, a huge grin on her face. "It's good?"

Joan nodded. "It's wonderful!"

The women laughed and went into the kitchen to gather up the other desserts, Winona's question forgotten except by Joan.

That was the thing about New York City, Joan mused, glad that her mother hadn't pressed the issue. Life was different, brilliantly different. The city had . . . well, more of everything: people, noise, smells, buses, cars. More clubs and art to see. More music to listen to and places to go. It *was* different from Cincinnati. And yet . . . the judge's secretary's surly attitude when they'd married; glares from people on the streets; slow service at a restaurant until Rich, furious, threw down his napkin and stormed out, dragging Joan with him; the apartment super who'd hemmed and hawed about renting them a place, finally blurting out that the owners wouldn't like it. New York City appeared to be more open and different. But in many ways it was the same.

Joan and Richard were the same too, the same as any newly married couple. Joan graduated and took a teaching job. Rich continued his "government" work. They had a tiny apartment, argued over whose turn it was to take out the trash, over Richard's socks, which had a way of ending up on the bedroom floor, and Joan's nylons, which took an eternity to dry on the shower rod in the postage-stamp-sized bathroom.

"How many of these . . ." Richard plucked the nylons off the rod, snagging one of them with his finger. "Damn! Do these things multiply at night or what?" He handed them over to Joan, who snatched them from him, then held up the one that now had a prominent hole in it.

"Rich!"

Rich's cheeks colored. "Sorry," he murmured. "I'll buy you another pair."

"Yes, you will," she said. She waved the stocking in the air, the sheer fabric swirling like a magic ribbon until the toe of the stocking, still damp, landed on Richard's nose.

"Hey! JoJo, quit!" He sneezed, then grabbed the stocking, and then he grabbed Joan.

She giggled and waved her hand back and forth in front of his eyes. "You will buy me a pair of Hanes stockings from Lord & Taylor. I repeat: you will buy me a pair of Hanes stockings, size 7½, from Lord & Taylor."

"What are you doing?" Rich chuckled, nuzzling her neck.

"I'm hypnotizing you," Joan said, closing her eyes. "I'm hypnotizing you into buying me a new pair of stockings."

"You don't need to do that," Richard murmured. "I'm already under your spell."

* * *

Joan sat on the couch in the front room, her eyes closed, her back resting on a pillow, her feet submerged in a tub of warm water and Epsom salts. The window was open, and the noise of Greenwich Avenue floated up and into the apartment along with the mild un-March-like evening air. On the outside, she was the picture of Buddha-like serenity. Inside, she was Snidely Whiplash, plotting the imminent demise of all twenty-five students in room 10, her fourth grade class in East Harlem. It had been a dreadful day. Every child in her class seemed intent on working her nerves, to the point that she'd ended up shouting at them and attracting the attention of the principal, Mrs. Bamford. Joan wondered whether she and Cricket had been that bad when they were nine years old. If so, she'd apologize to Mrs. Ferguson, her fourth grade teacher, the next time she visited Cincinnati. Worse yet, it was only March. She had to endure these demons until the first week of June. Joan sighed. The bunion on her right toe was throbbing again.

Six years teaching. And it was always the same. By this point in the school year, her head hurt, her back ached, and her jaw was tight. Would she ever learn?

She heard the sound of the key in the lock and the door opening. "Jo? Are you here? How was your day? I've got some news!"

Joan didn't open her eyes, but she smiled. "In here!"

"Here you are," Rich announced. He leaned over and kissed her on the forehead. "You look done in." Noticing the tub of water for the first time, he added, "And your feet hurt. What happened?"

Joan shook her head. "It's a story longer than *War and Peace*."

"Are you hungry? If your feet hurt, I can run down to—"

"I'm starving. But I'll go with you. I've been sitting here

long enough, reliving every moment of my ordeal in room 10. Sounds like the name of a B movie. What's this?"

A packet had landed in her lap. She picked it up and turned it over. *Pan Am.* "Airplane tickets?"

Richard grinned. "What would you say to a belated honeymoon in Europe to celebrate our anniversary?"

They'd talked about Paris for months—Rich had been there for work once, but his trip had been during the school year and she'd been unable to go with him.

"I'd say yes, but . . ."

"But? But what?"

"Well . . ." Joan lifted her feet out of the tub, swiped them with a towel, and stood to walk into the bedroom. A few moments later, she returned and slid an envelope into Richard's hand.

"Tickets," she said, grinning. "To the Met for *Carmen*, Victoria de los Angeles in the lead role. For our anniversary!" She'd been saving for months to get the money for perfect seats, orchestra, row 17, seats 1 and 2.

"When?"

Joan told him. Richard's initial look of apprehension faded.

"Perfect. Two nights before we leave. We'll start celebrating our anniversary on Thursday at the Met and end it at the Eiffel Tower."

* * *

A few days in London, then a quick stop in Amsterdam, and on to glorious Paris, where they stayed in a small hotel on the

Left Bank, ate croissants and drank strong French coffee for breakfast; bread, cheese, and meats for lunch; and amazing concoctions for dinner at places in the 5th Arrondissement where Richard knew the proprietors. They meandered through the city, taking in every tourist stop with as much unabashed enthusiasm as they could, not worrying about how "American" they looked: le Louvre, l'Arc de Triomphe, Versailles, la Sacré-Coeur. Joan's French was appalling, but she enjoyed trying it out. Richard served as tour guide and translator even though he could read and understand the language better than he actually spoke it. When they visited the Eiffel Tower, he politely asked a passing gendarme to take a photo of them for "posterity."

Leah was born the next year, named for her paternal great-grandmother as well as for her father's favorite opera.

CHAPTER 15

Joan

The teachers at Joan's school threw her a baby shower, as did Dorothy. That afternoon Joan and Rich's tiny apartment was packed with giggling women, a few fussy babies, and pink and yellow wrapping paper variously covered with little bunnies and fuzzy ducklings. "Baby Top," as she was christened by her godmother, Dorothy, had every gadget and doodad available for babies, including an ornate crib sent by Rich's father, Ira.

"Okay, Brother," David said as he and Rich awkwardly maneuvered the gargantuan carton through the narrow door of the apartment, down the tiny hall, and into the front room. "Get your toolbox out. We have work to do." The brothers set the carton on the floor with a *thump* that was guaranteed to elicit a visit from Mr. Ramos in the apartment below.

Joan was pacing the floor, patting Leah on the back to get her to burp.

"Are you sure it's only a crib in there? And not a body? Or two?"

"I'm sure," David gasped out. "I caught a peek of this thing in the window display at Schwartz. It's a doozie."

"It'd have to be," Rich said, returning from the kitchen with a toolbox. "The question is, where will we put it? Our bed takes up most of the bedroom."

Joan scanned the small living room. In the years of their marriage so far, they'd used more of their "extra" money to travel, to attend concerts, the theatre, and the opera, than they had on furniture. A planter in front of the window, one small apartment-size sofa, one Queen Anne–style chair (also on the smallish side), a coffee table (used), and a bookshelf.

"What if we put it in here?" she suggested. "I think it would fit. Maybe." It really was a huge box. "Maybe not . . ." she murmured.

Rich slit the packing tape with his box cutter.

"But what if she cries? You won't be able to hear her," David commented.

Joan laughed. "This baby girl has lungs strong enough to sing Carmen! Or Brunhilde!" As if aware that she was being discussed, Baby Top opened her eyes and stared at her mother. "Leontyne, look out."

Rich planted a kiss on his daughter's cheek.

"How many nicknames does one little girl need? If you don't call her by her given name, she won't know what name to answer to." He nuzzled the baby's cheek and murmured, "Will you, My Little Dumpling?"

Joan smirked. David chuckled.

"Oh, you're one to talk. Let's see. Dimples. Sugar Cookie. Dumpling and, my favorite, Baby Stinky Bottom."

David laughed. Rich's cheeks flushed.

"But only on special occasions," he said.

"And Carmen," Joan added.

Baby-Top-Dumpling-Sugar Cookie-Stinky Bottom let out an ear-splitting cry.

Rich grinned.

"Yes, no doubt about it! She can sing Carmen!"

The crib was gigantic and ornate—French country fused with Victorian. It came in so many pieces that it took the brothers over four hours to put it together. When they were finished, they collapsed on the living room floor—what was left of it now that the crib held court—toasting themselves with beer and Chinese takeout.

"It's different, that's for sure," Rich said, casting a doubtful look at the new crib in which Leah was sleeping.

"And huge!" David added, tiptoeing over to check on his niece. "She only takes up one-tenth of the thing."

"Don't worry. She'll grow into it."

"What on earth possessed Dad to buy it?" Rich asked, although Joan could tell from the tone of his voice that he was pleased.

"It doesn't matter. It's a gift," Joan said. "I'll call him tomorrow to say thank you."

David cleared his throat.

Rich said, "No. *I'll* call him and say thank you. If you call and Mom answers the phone . . ."

She'll hang up.

Rich had explained it to her, but she still didn't understand. As far as Bella was concerned, Richard was dead and Joan was a non-person. Except that Rich wasn't dead, he was alive. It made her crazy to think about it. But, as Rich and then David explained, their mother had performed the mourning rituals, so in her mind it was official.

Even so, Joan wasn't giving up. "Okay. So I won't call. I'll write. I'll send a note to—"

"Dad," David interrupted.

Joan smiled. "Y-e-ssss, to your dad at—"

"His office," her husband piped in. "I'll get you the address."

Joan sighed. "Okay. I'll write the thank-you note to your dad and mail it to his office. I don't want him to think I wasn't brought up right. Momma would be horrified if she thought that I—we—received a gift and didn't send a proper thank-you note."

"Emily Post," David said, his thin face, so like Rich's, splitting into a wide grin. "You married Emily Post."

CHAPTER 16

Carmen

Carmen waved her arms around in a frenzy of searching, scattering notepaper, news clippings, and snapshots into a shower of confetti.

"No! No, no, no!"

She had read the last letter.

She'd been in a cool groove, such a smooth Zen zone of letter reading, Diet Coke drinking balanced with quick potty breaks, that it hit her in the head like a hundred-pound weight. She was out of letters, photos, and scrapbooks. The realization threw her into a panic. Carmen had been sure, had been positively certain, that this mystery—*her* mystery—would be solved once she finished the last letter. That's the way it happened in books. That's the way it happened in movies. That one final letter, the one that *told all*. But it wasn't happening here. Joan's last letter to her mother, quickly scribbled, appeared to be a thank-you note, gratitude for a baby gift paired with a benign comment on the weather ("It was humid"), and that was all. That was it. It was like the ending to *The Sopranos*—ordinary, dull, and a setup to nowhere and anywhere.

Carmen stretched and took a deep breath, then took her place on the floor again in front of the coffee table. She excavated a legal pad from beneath a stack of postcards and read over the lists she'd created, two columns: "Things I know," "Things I don't know." What she knew was that her mother had moved to New York to finish college, fell in love, and married Richard Topolosky, worked as a teacher, went to clubs and concerts, traveled, loved the opera . . .

Which is why she named me . . . Carmen mused, fingering a small stack of faded ticket stubs. Joan must have saved them from every opera she'd seen. *Aida, The Marriage of Figaro, La Boheme,* and others.

Her eyes scanned the "Things I don't know" list. It was a short list with long implications. *Why did the marriage break up? Abuse? Infidelity? What happened to Richard? Is he still alive?*

She hadn't found a death certificate. She hadn't found a divorce decree either. Carmen jotted a few more words on her tablet: "marriage license," "divorce decree," "birth certificates," "death certificates," "the laws of New York governing divorce, adoption."

She looked up and realized that she hadn't drawn the blinds. She reached to turn off the lamp and sat for a few moments in the dark, looking out over the rolling hills southeast toward the twinkling lights of Cincinnati in the distance, letting her mind wander.

She knew a lot and she knew nothing. And what she knew for sure was that she had not known her mother. She clicked the lamp back on and picked up the letters, placing them back into their envelopes in chronological order. There was one in Grandma Nona's handwriting, elegant and strong with well-placed Victorian-style swirls and flourishes. The envelope was missing and Nona had not dated the letter. The last one, the last letter actually received by her mother after her move back to Cincinnati was from Cousin Dorothy. This time the letter was missing and only the envelope remained, Dorothy's address circled most likely as a reminder for Joan to record it in her address book.

The postmark was smudged, as was the return address. Dorothy's handwriting, like Dorothy, was bold and letter perfect. She remembered Cousin Dorothy well, a feisty, irreverent woman with a penchant for whiskey sours and jazz. She was so cool, so hip—she had entertained the likes of James Baldwin, Billie Holiday, and Ralph Ellison—that it was hard to remember she had been a WAC in World War II and then returned to graduate school, becoming an English professor and college librarian.

The paper was fragile, practically coming apart. Carmen wondered if she should wear white gloves when handling it, as curators did with ancient papyrus. The postmark caught her eye again, and she picked up the magnifying glass that had been so useful when she was studying the old photos or trying to read the elaborate handwriting in some of the letters. Dorothy had posted the letter in New York City at Union Station on August 30, 1967. *1967.* Carmen stared at the postmark again.

The fireproof strongbox was a fixed presence in the back of the closet in the second bedroom even though it was nearly invisible, covered by tote bags and long coats. It was gray, un-obtrusive, and as heavy as a concrete block. Carmen had put it in the corner for safety reasons: she had banged her toe on it more times than was good for her. She sprinted down the hall to the back bedroom and dragged it out of its hiding place into the middle of the floor. She paused a few seconds to remember the combination, then turned the dials and opened it.

A few jewelry boxes, the pearls she never wore but cher-ished, her marriage license, her divorce decree, Social Security card . . .

Where is it, where is it . . .

The birth certificate emerged from the gray, felt-lined depths of the strongbox.

I hereby certify that this certificate is an exact copy of the original certificate, which is registered and preserved in the Ohio Department of Health, Bureau of Vital Statistics. Witness my signature and the seal of the Department.

Place of birth: Cincinnati, Ohio

Hospital: Deaconess

Mother: Joan Ann Bradshaw, Negro, 32 years old

Occupation: Housewife

Father: Howard Rogers Bradshaw, 31 years old

Occupation: Minister

Baby: Carmen Ava Bradshaw, girl, Negro

Date of Birth: July 30, 1966, 7:20 a.m.

Carmen had used this document for everything from her marriage license to her passport application. For most of her adult life she'd grabbed up this innocuous-looking greenish-blue sliver of paper without giving it a cursory glance or a second thought. But now it was time to take a close look. The certificate stated that she was born on July 30, 1966. Based on every letter and slip of paper Carmen had read for the past few hours, it was crystal clear that on July 30, 1966, Joan Ann Bradshaw wasn't living in Cincinnati, Ohio. In fact, Joan Bradshaw didn't exist yet. She was Joan Topolosky, living in New York City. And her husband's name was Richard.

Carmen sat back on her heels. Her heart was thumping and she was feeling dizzy. She glanced at the digital clock on the desk: 1:38 a.m. Fat chance she'd get to sleep tonight. She'd had three open items on her list; now she had two. She still didn't know what had happened to her mother's marriage or to Richard. But now she was pretty sure she knew what had happened to Leah. All she had to do was look in the mirror.

CHAPTER 17

Carmen

J esus," Dee Dee murmured, her eyes wide with surprise. The iced tea she'd been drinking was held aloft in her hand as if she was about to make a toast.

Elise whistled, but then silence reigned, each woman lost in thought.

"Tell me about it." Carmen's palms hugged the wide coffee mug as she blew across the hot liquid. She glanced to her left. "Dee Dee, watch it. You're gonna spill that."

"Oh! Right," Dee Dee said, slowly setting the glass down. "But . . . you're sure? That you're Leah?"

"About ninety-nine percent. I've sent off for a copy of the original birth certificate."

Elise frowned. "Original. Aren't they all original?"

Carmen slowly shook her head. "You would think so. That's what I thought. But in adoptions—and this is what I think happened: Dad and Mom got married, and he adopted me. At that time, in Ohio, the courts approved an adoption, then had the state issue a new birth certificate with the names of the adoptive parents as the natural parents. It was perceived to be a protective measure."

"Instead, it was a big fat lie," Elise commented.

Carmen chuckled. "Basically . . . yes. The laws have changed now. They don't do that anymore."

"How long before you know for sure?" Dee Dee asked.

Carmen rolled her eyes, remembering the roundabout conversation she'd had with the man at Vital Statistics.

"Three to six weeks."

Both Dee Dee and Elise said, "Whaaaat?"

Carmen nodded. "Yeah. I'm not happy about that either. The suspense is killing me. But . . ." She shrugged her shoulders. "It is what it is."

"You could ask your dad," Elise suggested.

Carmen grinned. "You said that I shouldn't do that. In case Mom hadn't told him."

Now it was Elise's turn to shrug. "I know. But now it seems as if, well, your dad knows. He must if he adopted you."

"You still could've been twins," Dee Dee chimed in. She was trying to interest the others in a more Gothic theory based on her love for the stories of Alexandre Dumas.

"Twins raised separately? Dee Dee, that was a movie. *The Parent Trap.*"

Dee Dee stuck out her tongue. "It happens."

"Okay. I admit it. I thought about that too," Carmen said. "But there's nothing that points to that scenario. All of the letters back and forth talk about one baby. And the certificate says it's a single birth—"

"Which could still be a lie," Elise piped in.

"True," Carmen said. "But whenever baby Leah is mentioned in letters, it's just her, one child. Ira bought one crib. And Cousin Dorothy's letter refers to a 'Baby Top,' not 'Baby Tops.'"

"So . . . what's next?"

Carmen outlined her plans with crisp precision: the request for her original birth certificate, an application to get a copy of her parents' marriage licenses, and a search for a divorce decree and for a death certificate in case Richard died young. She still had no idea what had happened to him.

"And then you'll sit down with the reverend?" Dee Dee asked.

Carmen sighed.

"It might not be so bad," said Elise, trying to insert optimism into the situation. "He's a pragmatic man from what you've said. He had to know that someday this was going to come out."

"I don't think it will hurt as much as you think," Dee Dee said. "Not as much as going to the dentist."

Carmen giggled.

"Or getting a Brazilian bikini wax," added Elise, her expression folding into a wince. "There are few things as painful as that."

Carmen rolled her eyes. "You're right. And I'm about to participate in one of them."

The other women looked at her.

Carmen sighed again.

"Dinner with Dad and that dreadful woman Elaine, a.k.a. Mrs. Reverend Doctor Theodore Oakes. Now, *that's* painful."

* * *

Elaine had asked Carmen not to call her Mrs. Oakes. It sounded so formal, and they weren't strangers, were they? Carmen had forgotten that Elaine and her parents grew up in the same neighborhood. Elaine mentioned an upcoming church-group-sponsored rail tour Howard and she were taking across the Canadian Rockies. It was the first Carmen had heard of this, and it took a lot of self-control to keep from making a snide comment. When Elaine reached over and touched Howard on the arm, Carmen flinched and reached for her wineglass, provoking a look of disapproval from her father. She counted to ten, then tried to focus on smiling at the appropriate times during the dinner conversation while thinking deeply about something else, *anything* else. But there was really only one thing on her mind: the story of her mother and of the secret child—whether the child was actually Carmen or someone else. It was, as the saying went, a riddle wrapped in a mystery inside an enigma. And then there was the last question: What had happened to Richard?

Carmen turned this question over and over in her brain. She was hoping for an epiphany, a bolt of inspirational lightning that would miraculously (*Ta da!*) reveal the answer since Google wasn't cooperating. It did not occur to her—and wouldn't for a thousand years if she could live that long—that one source of illumination would be Elaine.

Again she remembered an adage that one of her great-aunts used to say: "Baby, you ain't lost; you just ain't got there yet."

Carmen hardly had been listening to her father and Elaine chitchatting. Their easygoing banter made her a little queasy. But then, like a bolt of lightning, something the woman said broke through Carmen's daydream.

"And so I think I just should decorate the grave, Howard. I mean, why not? He was a lovely old man. Honestly, though, I'm so glad that my grandson turned me on to Find-a-Grave.com. I never would have remembered where Pop Pop was buried. It was so long ago . . ."

"What? Where's he buried?" Carmen looked first at her father, then at Elaine.

"Um . . ." For once, the Mrs. Reverend Doctor seemed at a loss for words. But she quickly recovered. "As . . . I was telling your father, I'm driving down to Lexington next weekend with my sister. That's where Mother was from; my grandparents are buried there in the old cemetery next to the Rock of Ages Church. I'd have forgotten where that cemetery was but for this website that my grandson Riley found for me. It's called Find-a-Grave. And it's marvelous!"

"Marvelous" wasn't a word Carmen would have chosen, but a website like that would open up several possibilities. It would be a haven for ghouls. Even the name—Find-a-Grave—sounded like something out of a bad horror movie. And as thorough as she'd been with every other database, Carmen had pointedly avoided searching for death certificates. Looking for her biological father in a cemetery hadn't been on her radar screen until now. She just wasn't ready to accept the fact that he might be dead.

Acceptance or not, she had to face it. So when Carmen got home, she booted up her laptop, located the site, and pushed ENTER, hoping that nothing would appear.

CHAPTER 18

Elise

Elise noticed that her phone was buzzing: it was Carmen. She moved to answer it, then changed her mind. It was one of her pet peeves: people constantly on their phones during meetings, lunch, or dinners out. She was in a meeting with her lawyer. She'd call her friend back later. And anyway, she, Carmen, and Dee Dee were getting together for another clear-out session at Marie's condo in a few days. She looked up and smiled at the man who was talking to her. Maybe he would be reassured that she'd been listening.

Robert F. Adler, Esq., of Adler, Gonzales, and Peters, was an imposing figure in his navy pin-striped suit (bespoke?—it had to be in order to fit so nicely over his gut), red tie (he was a U of L Cardinal fan), and neon-white starched (heavy, please) shirt with monogrammed French cuffs: "R big F A," thank you very much. He'd folded his hands on the clean desktop. What looked like an antique inkwell and a flashy Montblanc fountain pen shared space with a rich dark brown leather portfolio, also monogrammed with the impressive "R big F A." No phone. No laptop or keyboard of any kind. No dust, not one spec. Only Robert . . . Actually, she called him Bob—they'd grown up on the same street. Bob's hands were . . .

Ah! No ring this meeting. Oh, oh, the divorce must have gone through. Divorce number . . .

Everything went together. He looked like a high-end investment firm ad: the hands, the fountain pen with inkwell, and the portfolio. Bob's lips were moving, but Elise didn't hear a word. All she could do was focus on the letters—Bob's initials, embossed in gold—and think that they stood for "Robert's big fucking ass." She yawned and thought about a large mug of coffee. She was delirious from lack of sleep, and it was making her belligerent. At least in her own mind.

Blah, blah, blah.

Elise nodded and smiled at the attorney, wondering when exactly *did* his ass get so big? Really, she would have to call her doctor and get some pills or something to help her sleep. Elise yawned again. This sleep-deprived state was dangerous, almost like being drunk. It made driving an adventure. Not to mention she didn't process a word anyone said.

Blah, blah.

"Elise? Are you all right?"

This time Elise did comprehend the words—her name, at least.

"Yes, yes, sorry." She sat up and cleared her throat. "I, uh, didn't sleep well last night then had an early meeting." She scrawled across the clean page of her open notebook: "WTF!" What she said was "Bob, I didn't catch what you said."

The attorney gave her a dubious look, then returned his attention to his well-manicured digits. Elise couldn't stop staring at the ring finger on his left hand, naked with the recent exit of his wife. Wife number two? Or number three? Really, why was she obsessing over this?

"No problem. I'm not sleeping as well as I used to either." Bob smiled slightly, the incredulity now replaced by an expression of regret. "Let me back up a bit. What I was saying was that the probate account has been filed, we're waiting on Judge Park's bailiff to set a hearing date, and I'll need your signature on a few items." With this comment, Adler produced a few pieces of white paper seemingly from nowhere, like a magician, and slid them across the ice-rink-like desk toward Elise. The SIGN HERE Post-it notes fluttered like tiny orange flags.

Elise slipped on her glasses and picked up the offered Montblanc pen.

"But what's really exciting . . ."

Probate, exciting? Elise flexed her fingers before attempting a signature on the document. Lately her handwriting looked like a sad imitation of ancient Assyrian cuneiform.

"Larry has an offer on the condo. And it's a cash offer."

Elise was dotting her *i*, and the nub of the pen pierced the paper. "Cash!" Now she was awake.

Bob grinned. "Yep. Amazing, isn't it?" He shook his head, producing yet another stack of documents from out of thin air. "Not many folks can do that. Larry says the guy is a finance geek, just moved here from Chicago to be close to his son, loves the real estate flipping game. But he likes your mother's place and

THE SECRET WOMEN   121

thinks he'll use it as his primary home. He has homes on Marco Island and in New Mexico someplace. Taos?" Bob frowned as he consulted a small leather-bound notebook that had just dropped into his hand from an alternate and invisible universe. He peered at the scribbling on the page, then gave up. "Anyway, long story short. Cash offer, your asking price, no quibbles there. Pending a good inspection, obviously, but that's to be expected. He's not asking for any cosmetic upgrades because he'll have his own people do those the way he wants. And he'll be ready to close within thirty days or sooner. So what do you think?"

"Wow! It's great. Thanks. So . . . what's left for me to do?" Elise really could not believe her luck.

Bob shrugged his generously sized shoulders. "Nothing. We're good, I think. Larry will email me the closing date info and we're all set." Frowning again, Bob produced a pair of reading glasses and peered down at his notebook. "Possession at closing." He closed the notebook with a flourish and a smile, pleased with having facilitated a good result for his client. "You won't have this to lose sleep over anymore!"

Elise was wide-awake now. Images of four closets packed with . . . stuff . . . the basement cleared except for neatly stacked moving boxes (as yet unsorted) in the west corner, the dining room china cabinet, its shelves still groaning with pink Depression glass and Royal Doulton figurines despite the three-hour clear-out session with help from Dee Dee and Carmen, and two large country French bureaus in what was Marie Wade's bedroom, full—still—of jewelry: costume, southwestern, Victorian, Bakelite, diamond, gold, jade, and coral, and a collection of purses in the closet that could serve as the foundation inventory for a small store. Elise's heart was pounding in her chest. She thought she was going to pass out.

What am I going to do?

Bob Adler, who'd now cleared his desk, sending every item back to its invisible storage place with, it seemed, a snap of his fingers, was oblivious to his client's distress. This time his attention was on his cell phone, which had just barked out a ringtone that sounded like Donna Summers singing the refrain from "Love to Love You, Baby."

Elise stifled a smile. *Ah . . . wife-to-be. Number four, I think. Who would've thought Bobby Adler would grow up to be such a player?*

"So . . . the closing will be . . ." Stupid question. And asking it again wasn't going to change the answer.

Bob looked up from his text message with the face of a twelve-year-old who'd just been caught surfing porn sites on the family computer. He cleared his throat.

"About thirty days, maybe sooner. Is that a problem?"

Elise felt the air going out of her lungs.

Bob's phone went off again.

Donna Summer was having a vocal orgasm. Wife-in-waiting was getting impatient.

Oooooo, I'd love to love you, baaaby.

Bob's cheeks colored. "Sorry about that." The attorney's chubby thumbs fumbled with the ON/OFF button. Trying to regain his composure, he asked, "The condo's pretty much cleared out, isn't it?"

The image of Marie's hall closet flooded Elise's mind. She kept the door firmly closed to avoid death by avalanche. The stack of boxes in the back bedroom. The trunk in the basement. And the storage locker. She'd forgotten about that.

"Yes. Pretty much," she lied.

Elise hyperventilated as she walked to her next meeting, but that was the only panic attack she had time for that day. There was too much to do: lunch to grab and gobble down, a "pre-meeting" to prepare for the 2:00 meeting and then a "wrap-up" session to discuss what went on in the 2:00 meeting and then a 3:00 board meeting and dinner. She'd have two and a half minutes exactly—between pre- and post-meetings—to pee and swipe lip gloss across her lips. The image of her mother's well-provisioned condo disintegrated to make room for more immediate disasters. Like Scarlett O'Hara, one of Elise's least favorite fictional characters, she would have to worry about the impending sale of Marie's condo tomorrow. She had no time today. But she did reach for the phone to call Carmen.

CHAPTER 19

Carmen

Carmen couldn't sleep. The facts that she'd unearthed—if they were facts—had knocked out her equilibrium. Her mind raced and raced and wouldn't settle, especially at night when she tried to sleep. Nothing worked: not hot tea, not soothing music, not boring books, not a warm bath—nothing. She'd even tried a sleeping pill, an option she would normally avoid. That didn't work either. After four nights with little sleep, Carmen was irritable and loopy. She was so miserable and exhausted that she staggered a bit when she walked, feeling as if she'd had too many cocktails instead of none.

On her way home from work that evening, a Cincinnati motorcycle cop had pulled her over. Elise had teased her mercilessly on the phone earlier after Carmen told her what had happened. Her laughter nearly obscured her words.

"Really? You were stopped for driving too slow? What's the speed limit on that stretch of I-71?"

"Sixty-five."

Elise crowed.

Carmen had to admit that it was hilarious remembering the momentary look of surprise on the policeman's face when she rolled down the window.

"I think he was expecting to see either a very old lady, as in ninety plus, or else a lush with an empty Grey Goose bottle on the front seat," Carmen recalled. "Poor thing."

The cop's cheeks had been red from sunburn. "Ma'am . . . Are you all right?"

Carmen had yawned and nodded. "Yes, I'm fine. Just a little . . . tired. Why did you pull me over?" she asked as she handed over her license in response to his request. She was sure she hadn't been speeding. Pretty sure. Okay. Sort of sure. She sighed. "Was I speeding?"

"Well, no." He leaned close to the car, a slight frown forming across his forehead. "You were going forty in a sixty-five-mile-per-hour zone. That's dangerous! You're going to get run over if you keep that up! Have you been drinking?" He clicked on his flashlight.

Carmen was annoyed but said nothing and only shook her head. "No. No drinking. And no sleeping either." Her yawn was wide enough to pass as authentic.

The policeman paused, then asked her a few more questions before handing over her license. "Okay. Ma'am . . . um, Miss Bradshaw. You're going home now?"

"Uh-huh," Carmen answered, stifling another yawn with the back of her hand.

The young man studied her for a moment.

Good grief, get it over with.

"Is there someone you could call? I don't think you should be driving . . ."

"I'm fine," Carmen assured him, shaking her head a little. She picked up the bottled water sitting in the console. "I'll splash a little water on my face, it'll be good. Besides, I don't have too far to go."

"All right . . . Look, I suggest that you exit at Pfeiffer, all right? You shouldn't be on the freeway. Go straight home and go to bed. Okay?"

Carmen had nodded. "Uh-huh. Sure."

Elise's laughter filled the phone receiver.

"Good Lord, Carmen. You can't drive on 71 north doing forty! It's a miracle you didn't have a wreck! Everybody in Cincinnati knows that when the speed limit is sixty-five, that means seventy-five! Go to bed on time tonight, will ya? Whatever it is that's keeping you up, it can wait until you've had some sleep."

What was "it"? "It" was everything. Carmen's mantra was "Knowledge is power," but now she thought that was bullshit. In less than one week she'd learned a whole encyclopedia of facts that she could have done without. And they were toxic. She felt off-balance, as if one leg were shorter than the other. Her mind was spinning around and around. That night she'd had an awful dream—a nightmare, really. That was what was now keeping her awake. Carmen saw herself in bed, then getting up and going into the bathroom. But when she looked in the bathroom mirror, the woman who stared back was a stranger. Not one feature on her face was familiar. The image was terrifying. And what was worse, she was awake.

Carmen prepared tea, then reached for the honey and added a teaspoon to sweeten it. For a few seconds she was angry. This was Elise's fault, this business of clearing out and sorting through and then finding out things that should have been left unfound. But as she stirred the honey and inhaled the warm scent of the tea that rose from her mug, she gently let the anger go. The blame game was the sleeplessness talking, looking to point a finger. This wasn't Elise's fault or anyone's fault. "Fault" didn't have a part in it.

Carmen had thought she knew who her mother was and she'd been wrong. Now she didn't know exactly who *she* was: her identity had been turned upside down like she was in a head-stand pose, only she wasn't in control of it and no puffing out of kidneys or tucking of tailbones would help. And she couldn't go back. She couldn't forget what she'd learned. The prologue and first chapter of her life had been irrevocably rewritten. Her name, her date of birth—both might be different from what she thought she knew. The research on adoptions had told her that was possible. And then there was her father . . .

Carmen sipped her tea and stared off into the distance at the twinkling lights of the freeway and the city buildings, seeing them but not seeing them.

Beside her computer, a website address was highlighted in neon yellow. She sat down and typed it into Google, the sister site of the one Elaine had mentioned at dinner. The cursor seemed to wink at her, but she didn't see the humor. "Find-an-Obit.com."

She tapped ENTER. The wish flew off to its destination and

could not be recalled. She had resisted taking this leap just as she was resisting talking with her father. She stared at the screen and bit her lip. It was 3:10 in the morning. The adoption records request could take weeks—*would* take weeks, according to the surly clerk she'd spoken with at the Bureau of Vital Statistics. This request could take a few moments.

And it did.

Topolosky, Richard Samuel.
Age 30, died suddenly of a brain aneurysm at his home in Greenwich Village. Richard was an Army veteran . . . an instructor at . . . beloved son of Bella and Ira Topolosky, brother of David L. Topolosky. He is survived by his parents and brother, loving aunts, uncles, and cousins, and many friends. Services will be held Wednesday at Temple Israel, with burial at . . .

The tears in Carmen's eyes blurred the text. She blinked them away to read the date: November 1966.

There was no "survived by loving wife," no daughter mentioned. Loving aunts and uncles were referenced, cousins acknowledged, even friends. But the woman Richard had married? Nothing. And the child . . . Carmen felt sick. The announcement was written as if "we didn't exist," she said aloud.

There would be no sleep for her tonight.

CHAPTER 20

Dee Dee

There would be no sleep for Dee Dee. Yes, she was in bed, the lights were off, the room was cool (just as the sleep doctors recommended), and all of the electronics were either off or covered, including the 32-inch flat-screen that Lorenzo had thoughtfully installed on the wall opposite their bed. The sheets were soft, and the lavender aromatherapy spray was working: if Dee Dee had wanted to, she could have imagined herself skipping across a meadow of purple accented with a soothing soft green before drifting off to a restful sleep. Instead, she was staring at the ceiling, hands wrapped around her upper arms.

Frances had ignored her Friday night curfew, "borrowed" Dee Dee's favorite pair of nude heels, and gotten a D on her Spanish test. She'd told her parents that she was going to an Algebra II study group at Bea's house. Instead, she and her friends Bea and Mei had changed clothes at Mei's and attended a house party in Mei's neighborhood: a blowout *Animal House*–style mega-gathering that had attracted kids from five high schools and police from two jurisdictions. For years to come, at least until Frances's twentieth high school reunion, the event would be remembered with hazy fondness as "the party." Lorenzo and Dee Dee had been totally unaware of any of this until called by the Mason Police Department to come and pick up their daughter. And all of this was *after* Dee Dee had received the text message from Frances's teacher.

Earlier that day, her phone had danced across the conference room table, and Dee Dee had chased it, provoking laughter from her colleagues in their meeting. It had been a welcome diversion from the facts and figures decorating the PowerPoint image, page 14 of the budget discussion.

"Excuse me," Dee Dee murmured, finally capturing the roaming phone and turning it over. She recognized the number of the high school. "Sorry." She felt her cheeks reddening. "Just . . . one . . . minute."

A text message from Mr. Pettiford, Frances's homeroom teacher and counselor, asking if he could have "a word." Despite her concern, Dee Dee smiled. Pettiford was from Arkansas but had spent a year at Oxford, absorbing all things British. The kids said that he spoke like an unpursued fugitive from Downton Abbey. Dee Dee's conversation with Mr. Pettiford lasted about fifteen minutes, and yes, he did sound as if he were auditioning for a British costume drama, but that was the only element of the meeting close to amusing.

When Lorenzo responded to her "CALL NOW" message, he'd said, chuckling, "Is it Armageddon yet?"

Dee Dee's answer was wrapped up in a low growl.

"Oh," he said, his deep voice stripped of amusement. "It's like that."

Dee Dee refused to talk to her daughter in the car on the ride home from the pick-up point at the curb in front of her neighbors Lily and Ray's house, but she and Frances made up for the electrically charged silence with an argument so volatile that it could have had its own Richter scale rating. Phoebe retreated to her bedroom. Pauly the cat and Dallas the puppy retreated to the safety of their safe houses, the center space on the rug beneath the dining room table.

"Sit down, Frances," Lorenzo said, pulling a stool out from the kitchen island.

Frances flipped her hair over her shoulder but not quick enough to hide the smirk on her face as she plopped onto the seat. She slid her glasses to the top of her head.

Dee Dee felt her temperature rising. "You think this is funny?"

Her daughter shrugged. "No. Not funny exactly. Just . . . I don't see what the big deal is. I am allowed to have fun once in a while, aren't I?"

Dee Dee imagined her hands around her daughter's throat.

"No, you are not," she said as calmly as she could. "After the conversation I had with Mr. Pettiford this morning—in the middle of my department budget meeting, by the way—about your attitude issues, your 'B minus, poor effort' in Algebra II, your Spanish grade, your class cutting and disrespect of teachers? No. You are not allowed to have fun. You are on punishment."

Frances gasped. "Mom! For how long?"

"Forever," Lorenzo said. He glanced over at Dee Dee, who nodded.

"That's not fair," Frances commented.

"Fair?" Dee Dee exclaimed. She caught Lorenzo's sideways glance out of the corner of her eye. "Was it fair for you to take my shoes without asking? Was it fair for you to lie? To say that you were at Mei's house when you were somewhere else? Was that fair? To us? To Lily and Ray, was that fair to them? And what about the grades, and the behavior, Frances? What about that? Is that fair?"

Frances exhaled a sound of disgust. "Really, Mom," she said, her words dripping with contempt. "It's not like we were doing anything. We were just listening to music."

"Just listening to . . ." Now Lorenzo's temper boiling over. His baritone reverberated against the stone fireplace. "That music you were just listening to was turned up so loud that half the neighbors in that block called the police!"

This time Frances said nothing.

Dee Dee paced the floor. Okay. Teenagers. She and Deb had done things too. A wild ride in a Mustang down Towne Street, too thrilling for words and too terrifying when the police pulled the car over and discovered that nine people were in it. She pushed the memory to the back of her mind. That was then, this was now. It was Frances she had to deal with.

Dee Dee's voice was like ice. "I'm done with this too. Frances, this can't go on. This won't go on. You're an intelligent girl; you have great experiences ahead of you. But you won't get there if you keep on this way. You have an appointment with Dr. Appleton next week. Monday, four o'clock. Be. There."

Frances whirled around like the cartoon Tasmanian devil.

"Appleton! The school shrink, Mom?" She snorted and whirled her head back. "Mom, I'm not crazy, and I'm not going to see Appleton."

"France . . ." Lorenzo's growl was getting louder.

Dee Dee pounded on the counter. "Yes. Yes, you are. Maybe talking with Dr. Appleton will help . . . what is the word Mr. Pettiford used? Maybe that will help get you sorted out."

"I don't need sorting out!" Frances bellowed. "I'm not crazy like your mother. I don't need a shrink, I don't need a pill. I'm just fine." Frances hopped off the tall stool, nearly toppling it over in the process. "God, Mom! I don't know why you ever named me after her! She was crazy! Even you said so!"

This time it was Dee Dee who said nothing.

"I'm not going!" Frances marched out of the room, her father at her heels.

"Frances . . ." Lorenzo called after her.

Dee Dee stared after her husband and daughter, long after they both had stomped upstairs and down the hall. Long after Frances had slammed the door to her bedroom. Long after Lorenzo had returned to the kitchen, looking angry enough to have smoke coming of his ears.

"Babe? You all right?" he asked.

Dee Dee's mind was spinning around and around. *What did Frances say? How dare she say that? How dare she!*

"Dee?"

She's not crazy like my mother.

CHAPTER 21

Carmen

Sleep deprived, Carmen struggled through the next yoga class. Her coordination was shot. Her bow pose crumbled and her crow pose was a disaster. Relief came when Sergeant Jasmine lowered the lights, lit candles, and coached her students to set up for shavasana, the final pose for the evening. Carmen settled herself on her mat, closed her eyes, relaxed her shoulders as Jasmine instructed, and took a long, deep breath. *Lovely.* A few seconds into the pose, she realized that someone was shaking her shoulder and calling her name. She swatted at the nuisance with a wild backhand.

"Cut it out! Quit!" she snapped, opening her eyes.

Elise sat back on her heels. "Finally! Welcome to the land of the living."

"W-what?" Carmen yawned and blinked. "What do you mean?"

Dee Dee's laughter caught her attention. "It is called corpse pose," she said, extending her hand to help Carmen to her feet, "but I don't think the old yogis meant it to be taken literally.

You were snoring!" She was grinning. Her delight was almost infectious.

Carmen was mortified. "I was not," she said in a sharp tone, shrugging her shoulders and following the other women to the alcove where their shoes and bags were. She grabbed Dee Dee's arm. "Was I?"

"Sawing logs," Dee Dee said with glee in her voice. "For the whole seven-minute shavasana."

Carmen felt the color rising to her cheeks. "Oh no . . ."

Elise nudged her in the ribs. "Don't worry, you sounded cute. Like a little buzz saw, feminine version, in hot pink. Anyway, it annoyed the sergeant to no end, and that was a joy for the rest of us."

Great . . . Carmen wanted the floor to just open and swallow her up. Now.

"Come on," Elise said as she handed Carmen her yoga mat carrier. "Let's go eat and catch up." She caught Carmen's eye, then looked away. *And then you can tell us what this is all about.*

* * *

Carmen had heard Elise's ESP message loud and clear, long before class. She'd even brought a copy of the obituary with her. She laid it on the table, where the two women could read it.

For a few moments, no one said a word. Their island of silence was closed off, separate from the activity in the Millbank Street Pub. Then Dee Dee's phone pinged, the server set down a tray of drinks, and the spell was broken.

Dee Dee's cheeks colored. "Sorry about that." She picked up

the phone, fumbled with a switch, then glanced at the glowing screen. Mr. Pettiford reporting that Frances had showed up to her appointment with the counselor; Frances reporting that the meeting was "totally pointless."

"A command from number one daughter," she said with a slight smile.

"How is Frances?" Carmen asked, glad to draw the spotlight away from herself.

Dee Dee sighed. "Oh . . . she's . . . Frances."

Elise smiled. "Teenagers. Can't do without them, can't kill them."

Dee Dee slid her phone into her bag. "Okay. Back to the present. So it looks as if . . . I guess we can assume that your mother didn't attend the funeral." Dee Dee frowned. "That's rotten."

Carmen nodded. She had another word in mind.

"No, it's evil," Elise said forcefully. She tapped the table lightly with her fingertips. She frowned, then looked up at Carmen. "Your mother and Richard. They did actually get married, right?"

Carmen nodded and took a sip of her beer, licking the foam away from her lip.

"Remember . . . in one of the letters Dorothy wrote, Mom mentioned that there was resistance from Richard's mother. His father was okay. And his brother helped put the crib together, but his mother . . ."

Dee Dee nodded. "Right. I remember now. His mother acted as if he had died."

"Nasty bitch," Elise growled.

Carmen laughed. "Elise! I'm surprised at you! What a thing to say about my grandmother! That's the kind of thing I would say! Or Dee Dee . . ."

Dee Dee grinned. "Damn right."

"Yes, it is," Elise said, smiling.

"Okay. This is what we have," Dee Dee interrupted, pulling a notebook out of her purse and opening it on the table in front of them. "Richard's mother—what was her name, Belle? No, Bella. Bella was against the marriage and obviously was against Leah . . ." Dee Dee paused and glanced at Carmen. "You. So let's assume she arranged for the obit, organized the services, and cut your mother off." She shook her head. "He was Jewish, so the services were held practically the next day. She . . . your mom . . . probably didn't even get to say goodbye."

The image of her young mother, grieving, cut off, and alone, was one that Carmen had tried to suppress over the past few days. She had tried and she failed.

"I can't imagine it. Except that I can." Elise cleared her throat. "It's beyond cruel."

"What have you learned about the rest of the family? Are any of them still alive? Even Bella? You know, evil never dies."

Carmen shrugged.

"His father?" Elise asked.

Carmen shook her head. "Only that he was a lawyer. He died in 1975. Bella died five years earlier so at least he had a few years of peace without that—"

"Be careful. It's your grandmother you're talking about."

"—woman." Carmen rolled her eyes.

Dee Dee looked down at a page in her notebook covered with writing highlighted in yellow.

"And there was the brother . . ."

Carmen nodded.

"Yes, David. He was the one I looked for first, because, well, he would have been younger and Cousin Dorothy's letters indicated that he kept in touch with Mom and with . . . Richard after they got married." She wasn't ready to call him her father, not yet. Carmen sighed. "He got married. No children, though. Died in 1984. Dorothy's gone now. I don't have anything. Just assumptions based on what I know, and the records from Vital Statistics." She permitted herself to sigh. "If they ever get here."

This time it was Dee Dee who shrugged her shoulders. "Well, I could get one of the services we use at work to do an enhanced web search."

Elise looked at Carmen. "I know that you don't want to hear this. But I think all of your roads are leading to Rome," she said.

"Rome?" Carmen echoed.

"Rome. Your father."

"Oh no." Carmen shook her head. "I can't. Not yet. I don't want to hurt him."

"Carmen, think about it. He married a woman who already had a child. He has to know something. It might not be everything that *you* want to know, but—"

"But it might be . . . enough. You're right," Carmen said,

feeling defeated. She sank back against the cushions, remembering the expression on her father's face when she'd picked up the old worn boxes from the basement. He had been afraid. Then, she hadn't known what was bothering him. Now, well, she was pretty sure she did.

"Are you going to go see him?" Elise asked.

Carmen tapped an icon on her phone and chuckled. "Yes. End of next week, as a matter of fact, Thursday. I'm having dinner with him and The Mrs. Reverend Doctor Oakes."

"Again. So soon? You've barely recovered from the last dinner," Elise quipped.

A disturbing thought popped into Carmen's head. "I hope they aren't planning to make some kind of announcement." She groaned.

Dee Dee giggled. "Is that 'The' with a capital *T*?"

"And do you have to curtsey when you greet her?" Elise piped in.

Before Carmen could answer, the server swooped in with their food. As the plates were arranged, Carmen's mind wandered off. She thought about the recent dinner with her dad, with Elaine Oakes in attendance, about lemon-meringue-colored St. John jackets and long, shiny, fire-engine-red lacquered nails, and her mother's luminous face with its dark, perfect brows and sparkling light brown eyes, a woman she really hadn't known very well at all.

PART 3

CHAPTER 22

Elise

Elise sat at the kitchen island, her elbows on the counter. She looked around at the now empty kitchen cabinets and tried to persuade herself that this was a good sign. The kitchen was finally cleared out, clean, and, except for the Keurig on the counter, ready for the new owner. The sunny outlook did not last long. Elise dropped her head into her arms.

"I'm doomed."

It was early Sunday afternoon, and Dee Dee and Carmen were spending a few hours with her as part of their mutual pact and in response to her call for help. Later in the coming week Carmen would have dinner with her father, when, she hoped, all would be revealed. And the weekend following, the women were meeting Dee Dee at her home to address the four mysterious boxes that had reigned supreme on the family Ping-Pong table for months. But for now, it was Elise's turn in the spotlight. And she was nearly having a panic attack.

"No, you don't understand. I am totally doomed," she murmured from beneath her folded arms.

Dee Dee giggled.

Carmen, emerging from the lavatory as she dried her hands on a towel, made a face of wry amusement. "You sound like Charlie Brown."

"It's exactly how I feel!" Elise whined, exaggerating only a little. She opened her arms and lifted her head. "Look at this place! We packed up twelve sets of china, and it still looks like the first floor of Macy's in here!"

"Fourteen." Carmen's voice was barely audible as she walked into the dining room to finish putting a large packing box together.

"And it does not look like that!" Dee Dee countered, grabbing a handful of grapes as she padded into the kitchen, having relinquished her shoes because of a throbbing bunion. "It looks . . . better than it did."

Elise did not think she sounded convincing.

"You can't give up before you've really started," Dee Dee added.

"Fourteen," Carmen's disembodied voice repeated as she moved into the kitchen from the dining room, where she was now hidden behind the gigantic box she'd assembled.

"Besides, we've got buckets of time. Two months, right? Until the thirtieth of June? That's . . . geez, plenty of time if you count weekends."

"We have twenty-two days. Remember, I met with the attorney last Friday," Elise said in a tone that sounded as if she was announcing the end of the world by killer asteroid. "Cash offer, possession at closing."

Dee Dee's mouth formed an O.

"Okay . . . twenty-two days. No worries. We can do this." Her expression said otherwise.

Elise moaned. "See! That's what I mean! The actual time is getting shorter—it's been cut in half! I'm. Doomed!"

"Okay. You're getting hysterical. You need a drink," Dee Dee concluded, pouring a clear golden pinot blanc into a wineglass and handing it to Elise. "Actually, I need one too." She poured a second glass. "Carmen? Do you want a glass of wine?"

"Fourteen," Carmen barked out again. "Or maybe fifteen," she added under her breath.

This time both Elise and Dee Dee turned to look at her. She was in the living room surrounded by a Gotham City–like landscape of brown packing boxes. Only her eyes, her nose, and the top of her head were visible over the top of a huge box.

"Fourteen what? Glasses of wine?" Elise asked.

"Noooo. Not wine, china," Carmen said. "It was fourteen sets of china, not twelve. You forgot about the second Christmas set we found in the basement next to the furnace filters and the Bavarian silver in the coat closet." She paused and held up a finger as if counting. "Actually, maybe it's fifteen . . ."

Elise took a long sip of her wine and sighed dramatically.

"Like I said: doomed." She looked around at the packing boxes and newspaper, and the legal pad that held her innumerable to-do lists. A lit match would just about take care of all this mess. The idea was very tempting.

The women were silent for a moment. Carmen sipped her wine. Elise scanned the small village of brown boxes in multiple sizes, some full and ready for sealing, others newspaper-lined caverns waiting to be filled with more dishes, glassware, linens, and whatever other treasures of the late Marie Wade's life. Dee Dee sat down on a stool next to the kitchen island and rubbed her aching foot. Now it was Elise's turn to giggle.

"Ah yes, the high cost of glamour."

Dee Dee scowled as her fingers massaged the ball of her foot. "As the man said, it is better to look good than feel good." She glanced at the lighthouses of North America calendar that Elise had tacked up on the wall, the photo picturing a breathtaking structure dominating a rocky and isolated isthmus in Nova Scotia. "Okay. Let's not panic. There's got to be a way to do this," she said. "Your mom got all this stuff into this place. So there's got to be a way to get it out."

Elise chuckled. "True. But remember. Mom got it in here over a span of thirty-some years! We have exactly twenty-two days, but that includes weekdays when we're at work and three weekends."

"Okay," Carmen said, using her best managerial-problem-solver voice. "Don't panic. We have a good plan. We work the plan. We go room to room. Pull everything out, and you set aside the things you want to keep. Everything else goes to either Goodwill, consignment, your kids, or . . . eBay." Carmen was intoxicated by eBay. "Right?" She reached into the box she had just finished filling, pulled out a flower vase molded and decorated to look like an owl, and held it up in the air. "Okay. Elise. Pay attention."

Elise and Carmen grinned.

"Do you want this?"

Elise shook her head. "No."

"Do you think that your sons will want it?"

Elise gave her a look that said, *Get real.*

"Do you want any of these?" Carmen held up a few of the other vases in the box.

"No."

"Perfect." Carmen tucked everything back inside, marked the box, and folded the tabs down.

She opened the next box and repeated the exercise. Again, Elise alternated between sips of wine and saying no.

Once the dining room table was clear, Carmen pointed to the box that held the Bavarian silver dinner service.

"Okay. Dinner service for twelve, Bavarian silver pattern. Yes or no."

Elise saluted her with her wineglass. *"Nein."*

"I don't understand, E," Dee Dee commented. "Don't you want any of the china? Have you thought about this?"

Elise scanned the room, something she'd done so often that the furniture and other items were a blur of colors and shapes. Now they came into focus and registered in her memory as if she were seeing them for the first time.

Maybe that was part of the problem. She'd thought about it too much, just not in the right way.

Do I want the china? Or the art or the furniture or the knickknacks or the books or the jewelry or the baskets or the twenty-five aloe, philodendron, African violet, and jade plants? If I don't take any of this stuff, I'm basically throwing away my mother. These are her treasures, things precious to her, and she was precious to me . . . I don't have her around now, and if I throw away her treasures . . . I won't have anything.

"Elise? Are you all right? You're not stroking out on us, are you?"

Elise hadn't realized that she had zoned out until Dee Dee's face materialized in front of her nose. She swallowed hard, then began sobbing.

"If I throw her away, I won't have anything!"

Dee Dee grabbed a handful of tissues from her handbag and stuffed them into Elise's hand while Carmen topped off her wineglass and patted her gently on the back. The sobs morphed into whimpers, then into hiccups and snorts. Elise blew her nose.

"I-I'm sorry. I guess I was . . . I *am* . . . overwhelmed."

"No worries," Dee Dee said.

"It's understandable," Carmen chimed in. "You've done a lot here. But there's quite a bit left to do and not much time to do it in. The good thing is, the condo's sold. So that burden is off your shoulders."

"Yes," murmured Elise, looking around the room that had been her mother's favorite place to read, entertain friends, and enjoy her fireplace. Memories. All crushed to bits because . . .

The irrationality of her thoughts flooded back again. Her mother's possessions were flush with memories, good ones. And if she gave them away, then those lovely memories, the ones associated with Marie's belongings, would disappear too, or most of them would. The stage would be bare, stripped down. As long as the "stuff" was around, Elise had a shield, a kind of buffer against the loud, painful silence left by one thing: the memory of her last conversation with her mother.

Elise dabbed at her eyes, then blew her nose loudly. She gulped down the wine, then jumped up from the couch and began clicking off the lights. "That's it, I'm done." She glanced at her watch. "It's early. You girls go on home and enjoy the rest of your day. We're finished here."

"Elise, we don't mind staying. I've already blocked off the time," Dee Dee reassured her, exchanging a quick *What the hell is going on?* glance with Carmen, who shrugged her shoulders and said, "I can stay too. Let's finish this room and—"

"No."

The volume and sharpness of Elise's voice startled them.

"I'm not doing *this*." She walked into the kitchen and began gathering up the glasses and stacking them in the dishwasher.

"Okay, well, I understand that you're upset. We can finish this another time—" Elise's voice cut her off.

"No. You don't get it. I'm not finishing this another time. When I say I'm done, I mean I'm done."

"W-well, who's going to clear out all of this stuff?" Dee Dee asked.

"No one. I'll get the junk company to come in, pack it up, and take it to a storage locker."

"Storage locker." The tone in Carmen's voice was flat.

Dee Dee's mouth dropped open, but she didn't say anything.

Carmen stared at Elise for a moment, then continued, "You don't mean to tell us that you're keeping all of this stuff."

Elise nodded. "I do mean that. I'm keeping it. For now."

"Forever," Carmen snapped.

"E, that's ridiculous." Dee Dee frowned.

"That's my business."

"What's really going on here?" Carmen asked in a tone as sharp as Elise's. "I hate to seem dense, but there's something you aren't saying. This whole exercise was your idea. You've walked me through my mother's life, and now I've got a new path to explore, including the conversation with my father, which I'm dreading." She gestured toward Dee Dee. "We have a plan for Dee Dee and we had a plan for you. Why don't you want us to finish? This was all your idea!"

Elise shook her head. "There's nothing up with it. I . . . changed my mind, that's all."

"Bullshit," Dee Dee said.

"You're lying," Carmen added with equal venom.

Elise's light brown eyes seemed to glow for a moment, then she turned away, her purse in her hand. "Get your things so I can lock up."

Dee Dee took a step toward her, but Carmen grabbed her arm. They both gathered up their things and followed Elise out the front door. Elise closed and locked it, and they walked toward the street, where Elise called over her shoulder, "I'll call you." She knew Carmen and Dee Dee had stopped on the sidewalk and were watching her as she moved toward where her car was parked. Once she turned the corner out of their sight, she clicked the key fob and sprinted to her car. She threw her tote onto the seat. Then she put her head against the steering wheel and cried.

Elise jumped when the sound of tapping on her window broke through the flood of tears and sobs. She sniffed, wiped her nose with the back of her arm, and turned the key in the ignition to push the window button. Dee Dee poked her head through the open window and held out a tissue. Carmen stood behind her on the sidewalk.

"Do you want to tell us what this is all about?"

Elise sniffed and leaned against the headrest, her eyes closed. "I . . . don't really know what it's about," she said, her voice cracking. "I just know that I . . . can't let go of Mom's things."

"Why?" Dee Dee asked in a soft voice.

"Because they're all I have of her."

"E, you have your memories." This from Carmen.

"No," Elise answered. "Just one memory."

CHAPTER 23

Elise

Even before Owen Wade died, Elise and her mother were close. Elise was the only daughter wedged in between "two grubby boys," as Marie referred to her sons. The birth of a girl gave her a good deal of joy and an excuse to indulge herself shopping for frilly dresses, in pastel colors, lace-trimmed anklet socks, and patent leather shoes. The baby's nursery was a wonderland of pink gingham and ruffles. If Elise had wanted to be anything but a "girlie girl," she would have been out of luck. Marie decided the moment after she was born that her life would be cushioned and colored in pink. She began life as her mother's "precious darling" and moved into adulthood as her mother's buddy.

Their father's death at age eighty-two was devastating but expected. Once the ordeal of the funeral was over and Elise's brother Warren returned to his home in Seattle, it was up to Elise and her remaining brother, Bill, to keep "an eye" on their mother. A habit takes about twenty-one days to form. By the time twenty-two days had passed, Elise and her mother were as thick as thieves, best friends, inseparable. If you saw one, you saw the other. And because Elise resembled Marie so much, mutual friends began calling them the Black Olsen Twins, the only set of twins in the world who were identical except for a twenty-five-year age difference. They went everywhere together: the grocery store, the movies, club meetings, even yoga class, although Marie preferred Pilates. They sat together in church, they did their part for Walk for the Cure, and they protested the protestors who were picketing the Planned Parenthood center. They sent each other emails and text messages (Marie loved texting); they spoke on the phone every day. If Marie felt smothered by the attention, she didn't mention it. And if Elise was overwhelmed by the energy it took as she tried to fill the void of companionship left by the death of her father, she never let on. Her parents had been close, married over fifty years and soul mates, if such a relationship existed. Elise felt that she was doing her duty as a daughter to help her mother over the "hump" as she coped with being a single woman over seventy-five, maneuvering the world alone. It wasn't a mission Elise spent much time thinking about; she just did it. She wove her mother's life into her own, filling her planner with Marie's appointments in an eye-catching turquoise ink next to her own meetings and obligations. She set timers to call her mother at certain moments every day, included Marie in her social activities. Elise's day was tightly organized around Marie's, and vice versa.

"Sweetie, I don't want to be a third wheel," Marie protested when Elise asked her to attend a charity gala with her and Bobby.

"Mom, don't worry about that. You know that Bobby adores you," Elise said.

"Are you comin' home tonight?" Elise's husband would say when Elise told him she was stopping at Marie's after work or dropping her off after they'd been to Zumba class.

"Maybe not," Elise would say occasionally, staying over at her mother's so much that she stashed a small tote of cosmetics and a nightgown there.

"I don't want Bobby mad at me," Marie told her, her pretty face marred by a frown. "You go on now."

"It's fine, Mom," Elise said, waving off her mother's concern. "He can manage."

"I don't doubt that he can," Marie said. "But you should go home. I don't need a babysitter."

The words stung, but just a little. Elise knew that her mother still had some dark moments, nights when she couldn't sleep because she would have a dream about Owen, days when, even five years after his death, her eyes would well up and she'd reach for tissues.

Mom took care of me, Elise reasoned. *Now it's my turn to take care of her.*

"Best friends forever."

Then came the day when her brother Bill called and Elise realized that her charmed new life with her mother included a ghost.

"Hey, you." Bill's Barry White–like baritone was unmistakable.

"Hey yourself. What's goin' on?"

"Just wanted to hear your voice and . . ." Elise heard her

sister-in-law's voice in the background. "I'm getting to that," Bill shot back. "So pushy, that woman!"

Elise giggled. Her sister-in-law was the least pushy member of her extended family. "So what is it that you have to get to? What's Liz talking about?"

"Buzz and the kids are coming," her brother said, referring to his son and grandchildren. "Liz's having a 'do' here and wants to make sure that you and the Bob come." Elise was available, but maybe now wasn't the time to tell her brother that she and "the Bob" had separated. It would extend their conversation by two hours.

"Do you want me to bring anything?"

"She wants to know if she should bring something!" he yelled into the receiver.

"Oowwww! Billy!"

"Sorry." The bass timbre of his voice couldn't mask the tone of the boy he once was, her bad "little" brother. Elise heard Liz's voice again. "No. She says she's got it covered."

"Okay," Elise said. "I'll let Mom know."

"Mom knows. She's coming," Bill commented. "She and George."

Elise's heart skipped. "George?"

"George, George Bridges, you know. Played in the golf league with Dad. He and Mom have been hanging out a bit."

He and Mom. Hanging out.

The phone felt like lead in her hand.

"Right. Mr. Bridges," Elise said slowly, the only name she knew him by. Okay. Now she remembered. His wife had passed a couple of years ago. What was her name? She and Marie had played cards together on Thursdays at Aunt Edie's.

"Uh-huh," her brother confirmed. "Listen, I gotta go. Lizzie's on me to light the grill." This time Elise did understand her sister-in-law's words: "Don't call me Lizzie!"

"Okay, uh, talk to you later."

She set the phone down quickly, as if it was hot. And it was as if she was having a near-death experience; the scenes of her life over the past few months began to flash before her eyes. She and Mom had been inseparable, except that they hadn't. And suddenly she realized that there had been a subtle and gradual un-pairing.

The Sunday her mother said she didn't feel like going to church. The renewed interest in the fitness facility close to her home, where she was taking a swimming refresher class. The day Elise found her mother cleaning the golf clubs that had been in storage for a couple of years. The evening that Elise called and Marie seemed eager to get off the phone, giving her "the bum's rush," as her dad used to say. Elise had thought it was a little odd, her mother brushing her off like that, but then too much togetherness could be "too much," and anyway, Mom was entitled to private time. Except . . . except Elise had not even considered that the private time her mother had been carving out for herself had anything to do with seeing another man. With . . . dating. She felt her stomach flip.

Because there'd been no odd phone calls, no unfamiliar jacket left behind or socks on the floor or under the bed (an image she quickly suppressed). No one had said to Elise, "I saw your mom the other day at Starbucks with some man." Not some man—he had a name: *Mr. Bridges.* Nothing like that had occurred. But now that she really thought about it, there had been, well, *something.* Something that had triggered a small flashing CAUTION light in Elise's brain. A ghost. She had sensed its presence, felt that the atmosphere had shifted a bit. It was like seeing something out of the corner of your eye. When you turned to look at it, there was nothing there. Little things that she'd had no context for: Marie's expression changing when certain topics were mentioned—Elise could not remember which. A throwaway comment about a film or travel destination that Elise had not seemed interested in, had not mentioned before. Nepal! That was it—Marie had said something about seeing the ancient Buddhist temples and nature sanctuaries in Nepal and Bhutan.

"Why would you want to go there?" Elise had asked her mother, thinking but not saying aloud that it was a stupid idea. "I mean, it's cold. And the altitude. Mom, you'll have to get clearance from your doctor."

"I know that," Marie had snapped back, prompting Elise to look at her. But her mother's gaze had shifted back to the travel brochure in her hand. "I've already emailed her. I have an appointment in a couple of weeks."

There was no more mention of Bhutan, Nepal, or any other place, and Elise had thought nothing more about it. Until Bill and Liz's invitation. Because then the ghost began to reveal itself. *Him*self. And the ghost had a name.

George Bridges.

Her mother had a boyfriend.

CHAPTER 24

Elise

Elise met George officially at the cookout at Liz and Billy's house and remembered, as she took in his lanky build and long legs, where she had "met" him before: a post-concert reception after the symphony when her dad was alive. Her parents and Mr. Bridges and his wife had chatted amiably as they sipped wine; they were playing golf the next week, and Elise, after exchanging hellos, had wandered off toward the bar and gotten a glass of wine too. His wife, she remembered . . . what was her name? Irene? Inez? She had been petite, like Mom, with a reddish-brown complexion and short, startling ebony-colored hair with a silver streak across the top that had made her look like a chic, friendly Cruella de Ville.

"Hello, Elise," George said giving her a friendly toothy grin as he took her hand into his large paw. "We've met, but it's been a long time and you wouldn't remember an old fart like me."

This provoked laughter from Marie and Bill, and for some reason Elise was annoyed. "It was at the symphony . . . afterward, actually."

He paused for half a second. The smile's wattage dimmed a bit. "Two years ago when Ilena, my wife, was living."

She heard her mother's admonition in her head: *Remember your manners.*

"Yes, yes, hello, I do remember," Elise said. "And I was sorry to hear about your wife."

George nodded. "It happens." He glanced down to his left, where Marie was standing. "But . . . life marches on. So they say." He gave Marie's shoulder a squeeze, and she beamed up at him.

Elise thought she was going to throw up.

She murmured her excuses, ignored her mother's pointed look in her direction, and sauntered off toward the grill, where her brother was holding court.

Five slabs of ribs rested in glory across the grates of the grill. They smelled heavenly.

"Whaddya think?" her brother asked, coming up behind her with industrial-size tongs in his hand and wearing his favorite DON'T F—K WITH THE CHEF apron. "Ready for sauce?"

Elise leaned in to get a better look and shook her head. "No. Not yet. A few more minutes . . . maybe ten."

Bill nodded in agreement, then closed the lid and glanced over to the side yard, where Marie, George, and a few other guests had congregated.

"Nice, huh? Mom and George? She's enjoying herself again."

"Uh-huh."

"It's great to see her getting out more. You know they play golf together on Mondays, then go to dinner. Mom says they're thinking of doing a golf vacation to Myrtle Beach."

"Really." Elise had picked up a wooden spoon and was gently stirring the homemade barbecue sauce that Bill had set on the side burner to warm.

"He sent her a dozen roses on her birthday."

Elise felt her head buzzing as if she was about to pass out. "How sweet."

This time her brother said nothing. But he took the wooden spoon from her, picked up the pan of sauce, and began ladling it onto the meat.

"Billy! It hasn't been ten minutes yet."

"No, it hasn't," he said brusquely. "Elise. What the fuck is wrong with you?"

"What do you mean?"

"You know goddamn well what I mean. I'm talking about Mom and Mr. Bridges, and you're giving me these smart-ass, snide answers: 'How sweet.' Give me a break. You sound like a snot-nosed teenager."

"I need to smack you," Elise said, not joking.

"Take your best shot, big sister," her brother fired back. "And take some advice from me while you're at it. Be happy for Mom, okay? She's having fun again, enjoying life, and she deserves that. Don't be stupid about this."

"How am I being stupid? All I did was comment on what you said," Elise answered, knowing for certain that even she didn't believe what she was saying.

Bill gave her a sideways look and turned his attention to the roasting slabs of meat on the grill, brushing them with a layer of the dark reddish sauce. Then he said, "Bobby out of town?"

Elise felt her stomach muscles tighten. "No."

"Then why isn't he here? If there's anything that my favorite brother-in-law enjoys it's a few dozen ribs."

"He, ah, he had something he had to do." Elise grabbed the lid of the grill as Bill busied himself painting the sizzling meat. "Do you want me to close this?"

"I have never known Bob to put anything—work or pleasure related—ahead of food. Especially ribs." Her brother's eyes bored into hers. "So. You guys really are separated."

Mercy. You can't fart sideways in this town without forty people knowing about it.

She avoided his gaze. "We are . . . taking a break." How lame did that sound?

"Taking a . . . what are you, an autoworker at Ford? Do you want to know what I think?"

"Not particularly." She knew that it wouldn't do any good.

"What happened?"

"None of your business. It's a private matter."

"I see."

"No, you don't. You don't see anything about me, about Bobby, or about Mom."

"I see a lot. I see that your marriage might be breaking up. I see that you're mad at Mom for moving on with her life and you think she's cutting you out. She's healing. She's seeing the world in a better light now. Hell, she's almost eighty! Why shouldn't she have some fun? While you . . ."

"While I . . . what?" Elise paused for a moment and noticed that her mother was looking in their direction. She lowered her voice. "What? Spit it out."

It was as if they were eight and ten years old again.

"You need to get your life back. Hell, you need to get a life! Now you can stand down from Mom. She's good now. You've helped her through the darkness, and now she's emerged on the other side."

"This sounds like a sermon from Reverend Pressley," Elise told him, visualizing the televangelist marching from one side of his gargantuan stage to the other while several thousand adoring parishioners waved their open palms and said amen. "How to walk through the shadow of grief and find sunshine on the other side."

Bill shook his head. "Not bitter, are ya?"

"I don't need to 'stand down' from my own mother."

"Yeah, you do."

"Did Mom say that?"

"She doesn't have to," Bill countered, opening the lid of the grill again. The aromas swirled out on light fog-like smoke. He tapped one of the ribs with his fingers and licked off the sauce, smiling.

"Well, you're wrong," Elise snapped, turning her back on her brother, only to see a tableau of Marie and George standing in a huddle with her nephew Buzz and one of his children. George's arm rested around her mother's shoulders. "I just think it's . . . undignified, you know? Mom and George. And disrespectful."

"Uh . . . disrespectful? Of whom?"

"Of Dad, of our father! Don't be an idiot, Billy."

"I'm not," her brother answered, using the deepest register of his already generous bass voice. "And don't call me Billy.

You're the idiot. And *don't* try to make Mom feel bad about this either, Lisee."

She snorted at him. "Please. I'm not a kid. I'm almost sixty years old. I know how to behave."

Her brother's expression was somber this time and opaque. "Yeah? Do you?"

CHAPTER 25

Elise

I think that's sweet," Dee Dee said after Elise finished talking. She absentmindedly moved her water glass around in a circle, leaving little rings of moisture on the table.

After Elise's meltdown, the women had bundled her into Dee Dee's car and driven to a café two blocks over in Oakley.

"I don't think it's sweet at all," snapped Carmen, a frown line creasing her forehead.

Elise looked in her direction with a thoughtful expression of gratitude.

Dee Dee looked over at her and shook her head. "You would begrudge the woman the chance for happiness? For companionship? We're not talkin' hot sex here."

"Or maybe we are," Elise piped in sotto voce. Her tears dried, she held the mug between her palms and stared off into space.

Dee Dee chuckled. "Okay. Maybe we are, but so what? These people are seventy, hell, eighty-plus years old! If they want to have wild sex—"

"Okay, that's enough," Elise interrupted, breaking out of her trance to set down her mug and put together a makeshift cross using a knife and fork, and held it up as if fending off a vampire. "I really don't want to talk about this anymore."

"Really, Dee Dee?" Carmen's expression translated to *I am not amused.*

Dee Dee held up her index finger. "Okay, just listen. Hear me out. If—and that's a big if—they want to have wild sex, travel, just hang out, to have someone to talk to, what's *wrong* with that?"

Elise sighed loudly and picked up a french fry.

Carmen growled. "Sorry, you won't get any votes from me. You forget. My father is seeing that dreadful Mrs. Reverend Doctor Oakes woman, she of the never-ending St. John suit collection in sherbet-hued pastels."

Dee Dee rolled her eyes.

"What was George like?" asked Carmen, blowing across the top of her coffee.

Elise smiled slightly, then said, "He was . . . is a nice man. He has to be over eighty-five now and frail; he fell last year and is still recuperating. I didn't have anything against him. Not really. It's just . . . I felt as if Mom had forgotten my father, that she was disrespecting his memory in some way by seeing someone else."

Carmen nodded and glanced at Dee Dee as if to say, *See? She gets it.*

"Exactly. I know how you feel. It's too soon. Like with my dad. Honestly, that woman." Carmen rolled her eyes.

Dee Dee sat back against the cushions and chuckled. "The two of you need your heads examined. Disrespecting memories, too soon? Just how long do you want your father to mourn?" she asked Carmen. "One year? Two years? Five? How old will he be in five years?"

If looks could kill, Carmen's glare would have been loaded onto an anti-aircraft missile.

"That's beside the point," Carmen snapped, looking over at Elise as if to gather moral support.

"No, that *is* the point. Life is short. And if you're seventy plus or eighty years old, it's even shorter."

"Dee Dee—" Elise warned.

"No, I'm just tellin' you. Think about it. Think about it practically, as if it was a situation at work. I mean, how much sense does it make? How long do you want your dad to sit alone in the dark grieving?" Dee Dee looked at Elise. "How long was your mom sitting around by herself? Huh? 'Cause I can tell you, it isn't pretty and it isn't healthy. My mom died young compared to your mom"—she looked then at Carmen—"and compared to Joan. And my dad didn't date or even look at another woman after her. That's a long time to be alone. And don't forget. My mother was . . . so ill." Dee Dee took a drink of water, swallowed slowly, then cleared her throat. "When Mommy was in and out of the hospital, when my sister and I were still in school, Dad was alone. Her family lived in San Diego. It was too far for them to visit often. He had no one. He had no life. He went to work, he came home, fixed supper, helped Deb and me with homework, then went to bed. The next day, he did the same thing. And this went on, day in, day out. He had to be lonely as hell. I wish . . ." Her voice broke.

Elise bit her lip and wiped a tear from the corner of her eye. Carmen pulled a tissue from her cavernous tote and blew her nose.

"Look. I loved Mommy to pieces. And I know that she loved us, Deb and me, that she tried so hard to fight back against those dark places. And that she was a brilliant artist and an amazing woman. But I'll tell you a secret. Laura O'Neill was one of the most generous people on the planet. She and Daddy were high school sweethearts, but she would not have wanted him to cut himself off like he did, to sit at home night after night, smoking cigarettes by the light of the TV that he wasn't even paying attention to. Mommy loved a party. She loved . . . love. And I know she would not have wanted him to be alone. I think it was his loneliness that made him sick."

For a few moments, the only silence in the café was at table 16, an island of quiet in the middle of the back dining room surrounded by a mélange of smooth jazz and 1990s club music, gabbing teens, fidgety kids, frustrated parents, and hustling servers carrying trays of food and drinks.

Finally, Carmen spoke. "So. Did you?" she asked Elise.

Elise looked up. "Did I what?"

"Follow your brother's advice. Did you behave?"

Elise's eyes filled again. "No."

CHAPTER 26

Elise

For months after *Love Story* left movie theaters, Elise and her friends quoted Ali McGraw's character: "Love means never having to say you're sorry."

What bullshit, Elise thought, remembering with bitterness and several sprinkles of regret the oft-quoted phrase from the film she'd seen with a boyfriend whose name and face she'd long forgotten. Love did not mean you didn't have to apologize— just the opposite. Love meant having to say you were sorry over and over again. And *then* it meant living with the guilt forever if you failed to say you were sorry that one last time, because you couldn't ever know when the last time would be. And the last time was the only time that really counted.

For a few weeks after the cookout, Elise played cat and mouse with her mother, inviting her to lunch (sometimes Marie went and sometimes she said she had "other plans"), offering to drive her to church, calling at odd hours of the morning or at night, to Marie's irritation ("Elise! It's seven in the morning! I haven't even had my first cup of coffee!"), hoping to interfere with Marie's plans, bully her—in a subtle way—to change them, and cut *him* out altogether. Or, in an effort to "catch" her mother with George, to interfere with some of their plans.

Dee Dee's expression was stormy. "Jesus, E. It sounds like a sick version of *Parent Trap.*"

Even Carmen, who had been sympathetic to Elise, piled on. "You were an idiot," she said simply, then sighed. Elise knew that Carmen was thinking about her father and The Mrs. Reverend Doctor.

"Yes, I was," Elise said. "An idiot supreme."

It wasn't as if Elise didn't know it at the time, because she did. But she couldn't stop herself. She couldn't think of anything else. She thought about them at work, when she was at home, and even at night when she should have been asleep. She woke up at three or four a.m. and began spinning her mother's new situation around in her head like a hamster on a wheel, round and round, and she couldn't stop. If she'd had something else to do or someone else to love or some other "useful employment"—a phrase she thought had been penned by Jane Austen—she never would have been so wrapped up in a life that was not her own. But the truth, and the saddest part of all, was that Elise had nothing else to do. Bobby and she had separated—an event fifteen years in the making—he had moved out, and her work, while interesting, was now mundane: she could do it in her sleep, which was a good thing because now she was barely getting any.

You need your head examined.

Dee Dee was right, she should've gotten counseling, grief

counseling—that would have been the intelligent thing to do, the adult thing to do. Instead, she drove over to her mother's place at seven thirty in the morning and let herself in. Something she had done only once: when Marie had called her when she wrenched her ankle and couldn't maneuver the stairs herself, a medical emergency. This was definitely not a medical emergency.

"Mom?" Elise called as she cleared the top step and walked toward the bedroom. She stopped in the open doorway.

"Elise?" Her mother's voice floated toward her. "What the . . . what are you doing here so early? I didn't hear the doorbell! George, did you . . ."

"Oh, sorry. Did I interrupt something?" Even as she said it, Elise heard the one rational voice left in her head say, *I can't believe you did this.*

George hadn't gotten out of bed yet but appeared to be nude, and while her mother had slid on and tied her robe, it was obvious to Elise that underneath it she was nude too, or nearly so.

Marie clicked the lamp on and stared at her daughter, a slight frown on her face. Elise's heart sank. The frown was the one Marie wore when she was concerned about something. But as comprehension flooded her brain, the look in her fawn-colored eyes hardened and her lips pressed together.

"Yes. You did," her mother said in a sharp tone. She looked at George, who was pink with embarrassment, trying to decide whether to make a run for the bathroom or stay put. "George, I'll be right back."

"Sure." George said. "Ah, hello, Elise."

"Hello, George." Elise had not enjoyed her triumphant moment. She suddenly wished that she could click her heels together—and disappear.

Marie closed the bedroom door gently and walked past Elise down the hall and down the stairs, leaving a faint scent trail of Jergens lotion in her wake. Elise followed, feeling very much like a six-year-old who was in trouble instead of a middle-aged woman with a family of her own. She stopped at the bottom of the stairs, where her mother was standing, her hand on the knob of the front door.

"I think I know why you're here. I just don't understand it, or you, for that matter. But it's time for this to stop, Elise, and it's time for you to get some help."

"I don't need any help, you need help. You're not a teenager. What on earth are you doing? You and . . . George . . . are too old for this nonsense! What about Dad? What about his memory? You're disrespecting it!"

Marie's jaw tightened noticeably. "You're right, I'm not a teenager. I am old. I'll be seventy-eight my next birthday. As for your father, as if you have any right to say what you just did, we had a lovely marriage, fifty-five years together, three children. But he's gone now. We talked about this, your dad and I. I told Owen to take a cruise to the Caribbean and cavort naked with Jamaican women on the beach! He told me to hire a trio of gigolos and sail to Rio for Carnival. Because, Elise, both of us realized that life goes on."

"But it's disrespectful . . ."

"Disre—Do you hear yourself? Disrespectful? How? Your father is gone. He is not coming back." Marie paused for a moment and sighed. "Even if I wished on a star, it wouldn't happen. But I can't sit around in the dark, wearing black forever like Queen Victoria. George and I are having a good time—"

"I can see that. But . . . sex, Mother?"

"This is none of your business."

"Of course it's my business! You're my mother!"

"I am not your prisoner! I am not your ward, your slave, or your child. I am a grown woman who wants to enjoy life . . . all of it, for as long as I can."

"Mom, it's not right. People might think—"

"People! I don't care what people think. I never have!"

"And you don't care what I think either."

Marie turned the doorknob and opened the front door. The cool air swirled in and ruffled the hem of her robe, but she didn't seem to notice.

"No. I don't care what you think, Elise. George is a lovely person and a great companion. I'm getting on with my life. You need to get on with yours."

The sound of Marie's heavy mahogany front door closing was hollow. It echoed in Elise's memory, the sound of a stone rolled into place to seal an ancient tomb, a baritone note of finality.

* * *

"That was the last conversation we had. Two weeks later . . ." Elise stopped and swallowed hard. Her voice was so soft that Dee Dee and Carmen could barely hear her. "Two weeks later,

George called me from the hospital. Mom had had a stroke. He was the one who found her." Elise murmured something, then swiped at her eyes with the back of her hand.

"Sorry. What did you say?" Carmen asked, grabbing two handfuls of tissues from Dee Dee's large packet and passing a wad of them to Elise, then to Dee Dee.

Elise sniffed. "I said . . . he never left her side." The memory of George sitting at her mother's bedside, humming tunes, talking to her, holding her hand, well, wasn't that what family did? Wouldn't her dad, Owen, have done that?

The images flashed, then changed with a rhythm familiar only to someone old enough to remember the carousel-style Kodak slide projectors that clicked each time the pictures changed. George changed his position—sometimes sitting, sometimes standing. But he never changed his focus. He had eyes only for the woman lying in the bed and didn't notice Elise standing in the corner of the hospital room when the funeral home staff arrived.

The attendant hovered in the doorway, silent, as if aware that George needed "a moment." Finally, the man cleared his throat and stepped across the threshold. With a reverent nod to Elise and Bill and Warren, he then turned to George, "I'm very sorry for your loss, sir." Before she could stop herself, Elise raised her hand, prepared to correct the man's assumption, to tell him that George was not the grieving widower. But Bill's hand landed on her shoulder, and she said nothing and would be grateful to him forever for preventing her from making another unforgiveable mistake.

The man continued to speak. "You take your time. I'm just letting you know that we're here."

George dabbed at his eyes and stood up slowly, unfolding his limbs gingerly as if they might break.

"You go on," he told the attendant in a gravelly voice that was rough from lack of sleep and from grief. He looked across the room at Elise, who nodded. "It's all right. You can take her."

The man looked over his shoulder at his colleague, who pulled a gurney toward the open doorway. Elise grabbed her purse and followed her brothers as they left the room, pausing to wait for George. Before she could speak, the attendant said, "Perhaps you'd like to step out of the room, sir. If you're ready."

George coughed. "Yes. Of course. I'm ready." He leaned down and kissed Marie on the forehead.

"Good night, my sweetheart," he said. Then he walked past Elise and out of the room, wearing the expression of a broken-hearted man.

* * *

"Talk about a love story," Carmen said, her eyes downcast. She appeared to be studying her hands.

Dee Dee sniffed, then diverted herself by digging through the contents of her seemingly bottomless handbag, extracting more wads of tissues. She offered one to Carmen, who gave her a look that said, *No way*, then shrugged and quietly blew her nose.

"Yes," Elise said sharply. "It was a love story, a beautiful one. And I, like a damn fool, did my best to ruin it for my mother." She felt her throat closing and stopped. She looked across the table at her friends. "I feel as if I'm at a psychological crossroad. I can't keep all of Mom's stuff—I know this. The condo's sold, and I don't have room for her things, either in my house or in my life. Besides . . ." She stopped. "I'm selling my house, too. Bobby and I are divorced. He's moved on. And I . . ."

"You need to get on with your life. Yes, we know. We need to get on with our lives too," Carmen said sharply. "We are just too damn old to continue having these . . . existential crises."

"Exis—what?" Dee Dee asked, grinning.

Carmen chuckled. "Existential crises. We're all having one, or we've had them and we're getting over them. Me . . . with my dad trying to move on with his life and me wrestling with the fact that I, well, that I wasn't exactly who I thought I was." She looked at Dee Dee. "You. Your mother."

Dee Dee looked away.

Carmen glanced over at Elise, who was dabbing at her nose.

"And you. Especially you! You know what you have to do, right? You have to do what you told *us* to do. You're the oldest . . ."

Elise sat up and snorted. "Oh yeah? Well, thanks for that!"

Dee Dee giggled.

"You're welcome! And you know it's true." Carmen sighed. "Elise, we're all trying to face down these . . . fears, terrified as we've been. And you . . . well, you can't keep all that stuff. And you can't keep all the guilt that's preventing you from getting rid of it. From what I see, there's only one way to do that."

Elise's eyebrows rose. "Oh yes? What's that?"

"You have to apologize and ask for forgiveness," Carmen said.

Elise shook her head, tears spilled from her eyes. "Forgiveness? Apologize? To whom? My mother is dead." Her voice cracked. "I-I missed the chance to say I'm sorry to Mom."

"But not to George," Dee Dee said. "You said that he's living over in Madeira somewhere?"

Elise nodded. She couldn't think of what to say.

"When was the last time you saw him?" Carmen asked.

"At . . . at Mom's funeral."

Dee Dee handed over another sad-looking tissue excavated from her tote. Elise took it but held it up as if it was contaminated.

"Well, get on over there. You have a lot of work to do."

"*We* have a lot of work to do," Carmen commented.

Dee Dee nodded. "Yes, we do."

Carmen reached across the table and grabbed Elise's hand. "Go see George. Talk with him."

"I will," Elise said. Her voice was so soft that Carmen barely heard her.

"Yes, go talk with him," Dee Dee echoed. "He isn't getting any younger," she added, her eyes twinkling with laughter. "And neither are you."

CHAPTER 27

Carmen

Carmen received voice messages from only one source: her dad.

"Carmen, I'm just calling to . . . Hello? Are you there?" A pause. Then, "Okay. I'm calling to cancel dinner tonight. I have a cold. Not feeling up to it." There was another pause and Carmen smiled slightly. She knew that her father was still trying to figure out whether to wait—in case she was monitoring her calls—or just hang up. Finally, after a prolonged coughing spell, he made his decision. "All right, Daughter. Bye now. God bless you."

Carmen glanced at the digital clock on her desk. One more meeting and then she could pack up the files in her in-box, call it a day, and take off. A quick stop at Kroger for lemons, soup, and crackers, then she'd drive around to her father's house. She didn't like the sound of that cough.

That wasn't all Carmen didn't like that evening. When she pulled into her dad's cul-de-sac, her usual parking spot was occupied by a smart-looking red Cadillac STS bearing a vanity plate: E-LANE. Carmen parked on the street and gathered up the groceries she'd purchased, smirking as she walked toward the door. Didn't Elaine have an *i* in it? *Geez.* The smirk had barely left her face when the front door opened and Elaine called out to her.

"Hi, Carmie! Come on in! I just got here. I brought your dad some soup. Homemade!" She added that phrase with pride, a huge smile on her face. "Here, let me take those," she added, pointing with a perfectly manicured talon at the Kroger bags.

Carmen, who hated being called Carmie more than she hated liver, repaired her expression in a nanosecond.

"How are you, Mrs. Oakes?" she said, maneuvering deftly away from the woman to avoid a four-layer lipsticked kiss on the cheek. *Homemade, my ass.* "It's nice to see you." *Liar, liar, St. John suit on fire!*

"Oh, please!" the woman gushed, closing the door behind them and leaving a fragrance tailwind of what smelled like Shalimar on steroids. "Call me Elaine!"

Not in this life.

But later, after gulping down a cupful, Carmen had to admit that the soup, homemade or otherwise, was tasty and substantial and just what her father needed. Howard looked pasty and uncomfortable, blowing his nose uncountable times. He coughed continuously until Elaine finally persuaded him to drink a concoction she'd whipped up.

He sat in his leather recliner, palms wrapped around the large white mug, and stared at the contents with a dubious expression on his face. A small spiral of steam rose toward his nostrils. He sniffed, but his sense of smell most likely was gone.

"What's in this?" Howard asked Elaine. He glanced over at Carmen, who shrugged as she took a seat on the couch. She had no idea but had decided that if it was some kind of crazy-ass Geechee woman mess, she was going to take out The Mrs Reverend. Doctor.

Elaine's hundred-watt smile brightened. "Now, Howard, don't be contrary. It's hot and it's good for you." She stood in front of him with her hands on her hips, the gold buttons on her St. John jacket catching the light like little Christmas tree ornaments.

Carmen watched as her father considered this directive for a moment—being used to giving directives, not taking them. Then he sighed—something else that Howard Bradshaw rarely did—and took a tentative sip. He coughed and looked up at Elaine with a poisonous expression on his face. Carmen sat up straight.

"What the . . ." Howard swallowed and coughed again. "There's . . . liquor in this!"

Elaine was nonplussed. "Of course. You didn't think that cup of green tea was going to knock that congestion out of your chest without an infantry behind it, did you?"

Carmen turned away so she could recover her composure.

"Elaine! I don't drink . . . spirits. And you're a Baptist!"

Elaine countered with a look that said, *Oh, grow up!*

Carmen wanted to hug her.

"It's for medicinal purposes, Howard. One tablespoon of

whiskey won't call the devil to your side. He's too busy with that serial killer they're tracking out in Wyoming. He doesn't have time to try to steal your soul over one splash of Wild Turkey. Now, drink up!"

Carmen was surprised to see her father, without another word, drink his toddy. Satisfied that her orders had been obeyed, Elaine turned around and picked up the tray to take it back into the kitchen. She winked at Carmen as she swept by, another trail of fragrance following her. This time it smelled like Shalimar mixed with Lagerfeld.

"Dad . . ."

Howard cleared his throat and looked up. "Yes, Daughter."

"Are you okay?" She couldn't suppress a smile this time.

Her father smiled back. "I'm fine." He glanced toward the hallway that led to the kitchen. "You'll have to excuse Elaine. She can be a bit strong-willed sometimes."

Carmen chuckled. "Dad, I've met five-star generals who are less formidable! But I'm glad she brought you the soup. And the hot toddy."

Howard frowned again. Obviously, the jury was still out as it concerned the toddy.

He coughed a little and then took another sip.

Carmen decided it was time to go. She'd talk with him about her mom another time, when it was just the two of them.

"How's that little . . . project coming along?" her father asked.

Carmen slipped on her coat and paused. She would hardly call the search for her identity "little."

"Fine. Just fine. We're meeting up on Saturday. We're almost finished at Mrs. Wade's home. I don't remember if I told you, Dad: it sold quickly, and the closing is in less than three weeks."

Howard nodded. "Good, good. I'm glad. I didn't think it was such a good idea before, but now I do. You girls are helping each other."

Carmen nodded. "Yes. Yes, we are. It's been good for all of us."

"So . . . have you finished going through those boxes? Joanie's boxes?"

Carmen stopped buttoning her coat and stared at her father. In all her life, she'd rarely heard him refer to her mother as "Joanie." That was a name she heard only from Joan's brothers and their wives. "Joanie" was an Adams family thing. "Joan" was what her father had always called her mother. And then, of course, there was "Jo," the name Richard had used.

"Yes, Dad. I've looked through them." There was no hiding now.

Howard moistened his lips. "All . . . of them?"

"Yes."

He nodded, swallowing slowly. He cleared his throat again and took another sip of Mrs. Reverend Doctor Elaine's solution.

"Then . . . you know." His voice was so low that Carmen barely heard it.

She took a deep breath, glancing again toward the kitchen. "Yes."

The sound of footsteps distracted them. Elaine marched into the room, a gigantic Louis Vuitton satchel draped over her arm.

"Carmie, excuse me, dear." She turned toward Howard. "The dishes are washed, and I put the rest of the soup in the fridge. There's enough for you to have for lunch tomorrow. Don't forget to eat an orange with your breakfast." She reached for her mink-trimmed cape and slid it around her shoulders. "And I've left the pill dispenser on the counter so you have no excuse. One orange pill and one blue one before bedtime. All right?"

She kissed Howard on the forehead, which caused him to blush, and then patted Carmen on the shoulder as she turned toward the door. "Good night, sweetie," she said, her dark eyes flashing with energy, intelligence, and something else that Carmen couldn't quite put her finger on. Elaine leaned close to Carmen and planted a gentle kiss on her cheek. "I knew your mother," she whispered. "We were in Sunday School together." She leaned back and smiled. "She would be so proud of you."

Carmen was surprised into silence. She hadn't known that. The front door closed quietly, and Carmen heard the tweet of car locks. Something else she hadn't known about her mother.

"Dad . . . why don't we talk about this in a few days when you're feeling better? I can imagine that it isn't . . . one of your favorite subjects." She added, lowering her voice, "You know that I'd never want to hurt you."

Howard shook his head slowly. "I'm not that sick. And this isn't painful. It's just that . . . well . . . I can counsel the bereaved, I can referee feuding spouses, but this situation? Well, this is different. Your mother was the light of my life. We grew up together—did you know that? I loved her from the first day

I saw her. She was probably . . . five years old, had dirty skinned knees, braids in her hair going every which way, and a smile that could light up heaven." Her father's eyes were shining with joy. "And I love her still."

At home, Carmen had a file one-inch thick of letters, photos, printouts from and about a man named Richard. But her father knew all this, so why go over it again?

"Even though . . ."

Howard smiled. "That didn't matter. Nothing mattered. What mattered was that she needed me. I knew what she'd been through. I knew . . ." Howard's voice hardened and his tone elevated, as it did when he gave a sermon. "I knew what those people had done to her. They'd cut her out of their lives as if she didn't exist. They were ashamed of her. Of you!" Her father's voice cracked. He shook his head slowly. "I wasn't having that. And then . . ." He started smiling, but a cough took over. "Excuse me. And then, finally, Joanie came home. Back to your grandparents' house. And I met you."

Carmen smiled. "That's not saying much—meeting a baby."

"Oh, I don't know . . ." her father commented.

"You . . . didn't mind?" Carmen asked. "Taking . . . another man's child as your own?" The question sounded archaic, like a sentence from a Victoria Holt novel (one of Carmen's guilty pleasures).

Her father laughed heartily until his laughter transitioned into coughing. Carmen suppressed a smile as he took another sip of Elaine's potion, then set it down on a small table beside the chair. "Are you kidding? Yes, I minded! But not for the reason you'd think. Look, I was an only child. No sisters or brothers. I had cousins, but they were older than I was, some by over fifteen years, and most of them had moved away from Cincinnati by that time. So I didn't have any small children around except for the ones I saw at church. I didn't know what to do with a baby, didn't even know how to hold one! But your mother . . ." Her father's face beamed at the mention of his wife. "Your mother pushed you into my arms." Howard's eyes were shining. "I was done for then!"

"Dad . . . did she tell you . . . what happened? In New York? Did she talk about . . . Richard?"

Howard blew his nose and nodded slowly. "She did. On our honeymoon. She told me. Everything." He paused and smiled sheepishly. "Well. Maybe not everything. Your mother had a thing about secrets."

Now it was Carmen's turn to pause. "Mom? Secrets?" She shook her head. The image of Mrs. Joan Bradshaw sitting in the front pew of Saint Paul AME Church wearing a powder-blue suit, her hands folded primly in her lap, popped into Carmen's head. "I just don't see that."

Her father's eyebrows rose. "No. You wouldn't. But Joanie Ann Adams Bradshaw . . ." Howard stopped and glanced down at his hands, resting in his lap. His gold wedding band was still on his finger. "Joan Adams Topolosky Bradshaw. She had a thing about secrets. She said that every woman needed at least one thing that she kept close to her heart, something that was hers alone." His smile had faded. "And Joanie always meant what she said."

"You didn't ask her?" Carmen inquired.

Howard stared at his daughter for a moment, then grinned. "You didn't know your momma very well, did you?" he asked, though his question was phrased more like a statement. He smiled, a pensive expression on his face, as if he was remembering something. "You just didn't ask Joanie Adams something that she thought was none of your damned business."

"Dad!" Carmen was startled. Her father was not known for cursing.

Howard shrugged. "Hey. Those were her words, not mine. You can't imagine how many times your grandmother Nona got after her for that." Now it was Howard's turn to chuckle.

Carmen laid her coat across the back of the couch and sat down again. "Can you tell me . . . what she said?"

"Yes," he answered with a tone of finality in his voice, corrugated and rough from coughing. "But I want you to know one thing. Joan was always straight with me, about Richard, about her life with him. She never lied, and she didn't hold back. We'd known each other too long for that. I knew . . . I'll always know . . . that she loved me in her own way. But your father, Richard, was the love of her life." He stopped and sniffed, whether from the cold or emotion, Carmen didn't know. "But I want you to know that your mother was the love of my life. And always will be."

CHAPTER 28

Joan and Carmen

"Joanie? Joanie! Cricket's here!" Nona's voice echoed through the house.

Winona must have been a magician. That early spring evening transformed Joan, transformed them all, and made a time traveler of Joan Topolosky. At the sound of those words, in less time than it took to blink an eye, years disappeared and Mrs. Joan Topolosky was no longer a married . . . widowed woman with an eight-month-old baby. That person was gone. Joan was, once again, a ten-year-old girl named Joanie with scraped, knobby knees and a grubby, grass-stained dress.

Even when Joan saw him, standing in the front parlor wearing a suit, shirt, and tie, his wing-tip shoes polished to a glasslike finish, he looked awkward and self-conscious, as if afraid to occupy the space of carpet he stood on. His smile was still crooked, and the tortoiseshell glasses he wore, which should have made him look professorial, made him look goofy. Cricket stared at her for a second, then smiled, and she wondered how she looked to him.

"Hi, Joanie."

"Hi, Cricket."

"I-I am sorry for your loss."

"Thanks," she said with a sigh, something she hadn't done a lot of before Rich died.

"It's good to see you. You look . . ." He'd stopped, realizing that a compliment of her appearance was not the usual offering of condolence. "I'm sorry. What I meant was . . . I'm glad to see you. Your parents are glad you're here too. They've been worried about you."

Joan smiled. "I know. And it's good to see you too, String Bean."

Cricket grinned. "No one calls me that anymore," he said.

"Except me," she said, the old defiance present in her voice.

"Except you."

She smoothed the front of her skirt with her palm.

"Well, it won't hurt you to get pulled back down to earth once in a while, *Reverend* Bradshaw. That's what I'm here for."

He'd opened his mouth to speak but was distracted by the sound of crying.

"Oops! The empress is awake! Excuse me." Joan scurried out of the room.

When she returned several minutes later, she was carrying the baby, in an untidily arranged assortment of pink blankets, and a bottle of milk.

"Here she is!" Joan said proudly, kissing the baby on the tip of her nose. "My little dumpling. That's what Rich called her, his 'little dumpling.'" She smiled, then looked up at Cricket. "What's the matter?"

She knew from his expression.

Cricket stared at the child with a mask of distress coupled with disbelief. He had deluded himself. As long as it had been just Joanie in the room, just Joanie and him, nothing had changed. The world was the same as it was twenty years ago, when they played games in the Adams's vast yard: Joanie Ann Adams and Cricket, a.k.a. Howie, Bradshaw from down the street. But the baby's existence burst that bubble. Leah was the living, breathing evidence that Joanie was not the same anymore. That life, as Cricket remembered it, was different.

"Do you want to hold her?"

Cricket was aghast. "Me? No! I don't know how!" he blurted out, holding up his hands as if he was about to be robbed at gunpoint.

"Really! Cricket! She won't bite you. She doesn't even have teeth yet! She's just a baby. Here!"

When had he ever disobeyed an order from Joanie Adams?

Cricket's arms were trembling, and he looked as if he might drop Leah. He could tell that Joanie was thinking she'd made a mistake. But she didn't take the child away. Instead, she adjusted his arms. "Here. No. *Here*. Like this."

He settled the baby in the crook of his arm and looked down. Reaching up from the profusion of pink blankets was a chubby arm and tiny wiggling fingers. Cricket leaned closer to get a better look only to find his nose captured by a small but tenacious paw.

He giggled. Maybe because of the baritone rumbling from his chest, his laughter deep-seated and athletic, the baby released his nose, and then he blew a raspberry on her forehead.

Leah giggled. Cricket lifted the baby up to his shoulder, where she promptly spit up, then grinned at him with toothless gums. His navy pin-striped suit jacket would have to go to the dry cleaners. But Cricket wasn't dismayed. He giggled again.

Two months later, Joan Adams Topolosky married Reverend Howard Bradshaw at the Saint Paul AME Church.

* * *

"You know we honeymooned at French Lick, over there in Indiana." Howard continued, "It was a gift from my parents."

He hadn't coughed in over half an hour. Carmen suppressed a smile: Elaine's potion was working.

"Grandma and Grandpa?" Carmen commented, realizing too late that she'd sounded incredulous. "That was nice of them." She remembered her father's parents as pleasant but quiet people, old-fashioned and staid. The concept of a "honeymoon" in connection with Eleanor and Gordon Bradshaw just didn't add up to Carmen.

Her father smiled. "I know what you're thinking. You wouldn't have known it to look at her, but my mother was a closet romantic. She loved all of that mushy stuff. Kept a stash of romance novels in an old handbag that she hid in the back of her closet." He grinned. "It was only a weekend getaway, but it was nice. Winona and Hubert had the baby . . ." Howard looked up. "You. And so for the first time since we were kids, almost, we were alone."

Carmen cleared her throat. "But it wasn't quite the same thing."

Howard smiled slightly. His gaze, once fastened on Carmen's face as if trying to read her thoughts, softened and seemed blurry, as if he were far away. And it occurred to Carmen, like a thunderbolt, that he was remembering . . .

Oh Lordy. Carmen hoped she wasn't blushing. Thinking about her parents having . . . an intimate moment . . . Carmen knew her unfiltered thoughts labeled her as a prude. But still. *Mom was married before. She'd had a child. But knowing Daddy, it was probably his first time.* She stole another glance of her father. Howard's face was immobile, but his expression was wistful. This was private stuff and would stay that way. Carmen didn't need a psychic to figure it out: her brother, Howie, had been born that next summer.

Now she had only one question.

"Dad. Did she . . ." Her stomach was jumpy. It almost seemed an intrusion to ask. But she had to. She had to know. "Did she tell you? What happened to Richard?"

Howard looked down for a moment at the soup-bowl-size mug that he again took up in his palms. "Humph. This concoction tastes better than I thought it would." He inhaled and cleared his throat, then looked back at his daughter.

"Yes. Yes, she did."

CHAPTER 29

Joan

R ichard died on an ordinary day. Most days that end in one of the fraternal twins of misery and delight begin with a routine. Rich would always get up first because it took him a while to shave and get ready for work. Joanie had teased him for hogging the closet-size bathroom. Unless the baby was crying, she would stay in bed, savoring a few extra moments of cocooned warmth and quiet. Her day would officially begin with the changing of what was usually a Godzilla-size diaper. She hadn't returned to work yet; her substitute teaching assignment didn't begin until fall. So she had a few weeks left to luxuriate in delicious inactivity, time that was hers to listen to the sounds of morning: the Jeffries's children upstairs thumping around, the door to the stairwell slamming (the super had been promising to repair it since they moved in), the faint sounds of the radio coming from the kitchen, and the smell of coffee. That morning she patted her belly and tried to tighten her stomach muscles, still slack from childbirth. There were few things Joanie disliked more than sit-ups, but if she was ever going to get her favorite slacks zipped again without holding her breath she'd have to start soon. She closed her eyes and sighed with pleasure, wiggling her toes. The sound of water splashing in the bathroom made an odd but soothing lullaby, and since Joanie felt too comfortable to move, and the baby was quiet, she yawned and drifted off again, a dream taking her back to Paris.

Joanie woke with a start. She sat up in the bed, then froze. Had she heard something? No, the apartment was quiet. But something had woken her up, and it wasn't the baby. What was it?

She felt as if she'd slept for hours, but it was only 7:38. Rich wouldn't have left yet; he usually left at a quarter after 8. The sounds of cooing and gurgling reached her ears: the baby was awake. Joanie shook the sleep cobwebs from her brain and scrambled out of bed. She was late. She had so much to do today and . . . She reached for her robe, then paused. Now she realized what was different. The apartment was totally quiet. No radio. Rich always turned on the radio; he enjoyed the jazz station. And she didn't smell coffee. Had he forgotten?

"Rich? Honey? Are you still here? Why didn't you wake me up? Rich!"

Joan shrugged on her robe, then grabbed up the baby, wet diaper and all, and ambled toward the passage that led to the kitchen, then stopped. Richard lay across the doorway to the kitchen, the contents of a Chock full o'Nuts coffee can spread like fine grains of dark chocolate-colored sand across the tile floor.

* * *

"An aneurysm of the brain. He was dead before he hit the floor," the doctor told her, as if that was any comfort. "There was nothing you could have done," he added, his omniscient tone now modified, perhaps by the expression of total devastation he must have seen on Joanie's face. That remark wasn't comforting either. Nothing she could have done would have saved Rich's life. All that statement did was make her feel that her entire existence was for nothing because she wouldn't have been able to save her husband's life, a man named Richard, who now lay on a gurney covered by white sheets. It was over, her life, his life. Gone. Just like that. Baby Top squirmed in her arms, and Joanie's attention returned to the soggy diaper she'd forgotten to change. Again.

"Mrs. Topolosky?"

The doctor's voice pierced her from a second-long daydream of Rich climbing out of bed this morning . . . a moment only two and a half hours ago. She was back in the small waiting room outside the emergency room. The ear-splitting whine of an ambulance was competing with the *swoosh* of a gurney speeding down the hall guided by a circle of medics, its squeaking wheels in need of oil. Joan stared at the doctor with incomprehension. His voice had pulled her abruptly from then to now. Now was not where she wanted to be.

The doctor cleared his throat and smiled slightly. Joan felt sorry for him. Like her, he wanted to be anywhere but here. He—Philip Cohen was his name—looked very young, probably not much older than she was, and Joan imagined that comforting widows whose husbands had dropped dead on the kitchen floor was one of the last duties he had signed on for in medical school. She knew he was trying to be kind.

"Is there anyone we can call for you, Mrs. Topolosky? Your parents? His . . . Richard's parents?"

The baby squirmed and fussed, and Joan adjusted the child, propping her over her shoulder.

She nodded. "Yes. I . . . called my husband's brother. He . . ." Joan closed her mouth. Just the effort of saying those few words aloud had taken all the energy out of her body. Her knees were trembling, and suddenly she felt cold. "He said . . . he'd come. Excuse me." She staggered toward a chair and sank into it.

It had been awful.

"Richard's-dead-I-don't-know-what-to-do," Joanie had blurted out when David answered the telephone, letting the words rush out of her mouth before she could call them back and make them untrue. David had gasped, then roared: a visceral and mournful bellow that did a better job than tears of expressing the way she felt. He and Rich were a year apart and closer than twins.

"Where are you?" he'd asked.

Joan had told him. David had said he would be right there.

He was as good as his word, except he brought his mother with him.

Bella Topolosky swept into the hospital with the grandeur of a Tudor queen. Ira, Richard's father, and David were left in her wake like reluctantly obedient courtiers. She spared a cold smile for a man who held the door for her, nodding slightly to acknowledge the nurses, who stepped aside, but ignoring everyone else: the odd and sundry ordinary folk who sat in the sad-looking chairs that lined the perimeter of the waiting room, including her daughter-in-law and only grandchild. She and Ira continued down the hall, only realizing when they'd reached the double doors that their remaining son was not with them. David had stopped next to Joanie's chair.

"Mom?"

Bella turned around and frowned. "Aren't you coming?" she asked him. "Dr. Bernard said to meet him here."

David turned toward Joan, then looked back at his mother. "Mom. This is Joan and . . . Leah." He put his hand on Joan's shoulder.

Ira stared at his son, then allowed his gaze to rest on Joan and then on Leah, but when he moved slightly as if to walk toward them, Bella put her hand on his arm. Her eyes slid over Joan and Leah like a bath of ice water to look at David.

"David, are you coming?" she said, her words brushed with inflections of the Bronx, where she had been born. Without another word, she turned and went through the double doors, dragging Ira with her.

"I'm sorry about this," David told Joan, his cheeks coloring. "She . . . she doesn't mean it. Doesn't mean to be rude. She's . . . just in shock," he added, glancing in the direction of his parents' exit. "I-I'll be back in a few moments, all right? We need to talk about the arrangements . . . and everything."

David's voice cracked. He leaned down and kissed Leah on the forehead, then walked away. "Wait here."

Joan waited because she was too tired to do anything else. This was the first time she had seen Richard's parents together. Ira was tall, lean, and stooped, with a thick shock of iron-gray hair and the same black-rimmed Buddy Holly glasses that Richard wore. Bella was the polar opposite: short, a little dumpy, but curvy, with a sensuality about her pretty face that reminded Joan of a brunette Lana Turner. She also looked like the ideal *Ladies' Home Journal* housewife—attractive, capable, and friendly, to everyone except her daughter-in-law. And Joan realized, in the half second that they had locked eyes, Richard's looks had come from Bella despite the glasses, while David favored Ira.

David did come back in a few moments, and he spoke to Joan about the funeral arrangements as he rode with her in the cab that took her and the baby home. Bella had already called Epstein's, he explained; they were friends of the family and would coordinate the service and burial.

Dorothy and Washburn met them at the door of the apartment. Washburn took the baby from David, and Dorothy folded Joan into her arms.

"We'll take care of her," Dorothy said to David. "You go on now."

"I'll . . . call you . . . okay?" David's voice faltered. "With the . . . about the funeral."

That was Tuesday afternoon. Wednesday came and went and so did Thursday morning. When Joan called David, either the line was busy or no one answered at all.

When Joan called David on Thursday afternoon, his wife, Greta, answered the phone.

"He isn't in, Joan," she said with cool politeness. "Would you like to leave a message?"

He didn't call back.

Friday morning arrived at about the same time that Dorothy did, bringing a sack of groceries and a newspaper. When Joan answered the door, Dorothy marched in like a general, her expression as grim as Joan had ever seen it.

"Good morning."

"No, it isn't," Dorothy said. She put the grocery bag on the table.

"Hey, I'm the grieving widow, remember? I'm supposed to look like an avenging angel. But you? You look as if you could turn a person into stone."

Dorothy pulled her gloves off and dropped them into her handbag. She picked up the newspaper and waved it at Joan.

"You should read this," she said in a low, angry voice. She pulled out one of the kitchen chairs. "And you'd better sit down."

It was the *New York Times* obituary section. Joanie felt her breath stop in her throat. It was Wednesday's paper.

"Joanie, I am so sorry," Dorothy murmured.

Topolosky, Richard Samuel.

Age 30, died suddenly of a brain aneurysm at his home in Greenwich Village . . . beloved son of Bella and Ira Topolosky, brother of David L. Topolosky. He is survived by his parents and brother, loving aunts, uncles, and cousins, and many

friends. Services will be held Wednesday at Temple Israel,
with burial at The Old Beth Shalom Cemetery, Long Island.
In lieu of flowers, donations may be sent to . . . Arrangements
handled by Epstein's Funeral Service.

Well, they certainly did, Joan said to herself. *They handled*
everything. Without a word to Dorothy, she went to the telephone and dialed her brother-in-law's number. She was not surprised when he answered.

"David."

"Jo, I'm . . . sorry. It . . . My parents . . ."

"You didn't have the decency to tell me—one phone call,
just one!"

"I am so sorry. Mom had everything arranged before I . . .
The way she was acting . . . I didn't think you'd want . . ."

"You were hardly in a position to know what I'd want!"

"I'm sorry! I . . ."

Joanie listened to David's rambling apology. She clutched the
phone with both hands, holding it so tightly that her forearms
ached. She was trembling and yet her voice was not.

"That's real nice of them, I'm sure," Joan said, sarcasm cutting her words with bitterness. "Your parents want to give me
money," she commented. "But they don't acknowledge that I
or their only grandchild exist. I guess the cost of those things
is too high."

"No, JoJo, that's not it . . ."

The anger blew through her like the air coming out of a fail-
ing balloon, and now there was nothing left but pain.

"You don't call me JoJo, do you understand? That was Rich's name for me. You don't call me that. Ever."

"Right. I'm sorry. I-I'm sorry."

"David, you know what? Never mind. I don't care. I just don't. All I know is, you and your parents have robbed me. If you had sneaked into our apartment and taken every stitch of clothing I own and the silver, if I had any, you couldn't have done a better job of it. You took away my last chance to say goodbye to my husband. You've taken that away. And by . . . pretending that I don't exist . . . that Leah doesn't exist, you've insulted me and your niece."

"Jo, wait, please . . ."

"Wait! Wait for what?"

She heard David take a deep breath. She was two seconds away from hanging up when she thought of something.

"Can you do something for me, David?"

This time, her brother-in-law didn't fumble for words.

"Anything."

* * *

It was crowded and old, in use since 1886. When the first grave was dug, the plot of land was out in the middle of nowhere; now it was an island of headstones, many of them carved in the late nineteenth or early twentieth century, surrounded by highways and strip malls. Cars going over sixty miles per hour zoomed past on a two-lane highway, and a black wrought-iron fence separated the grounds from the surrounding housing developments. David carried the baby as they walked carefully through the roughly cut grass along the path between the standing stones, some of them leaning to one side, and Joan silently paid her respects to Mr. and Mrs. Cohen, Ira Myerson, and Moses Hirschfeld, who had lain here since June of 1917 along with his "Wife." The stones were intricately carved, many of them in Hebrew, some with English translations, and so many of them were beautiful, works of art. There were many stories here, Joan thought, so many lives lived, stories of love, struggle, despair, and, sometimes, success. She stepped carefully around a large fallen tree branch following a narrow almost undetectable path through the cemetery, looking over her shoulder at her brother-in-law, who nodded in answer to her unasked question: *Am I going the right way?*

A trio of huge slabs of stone paid homage to three generations of the Gold family, the stones over four feet tall and barely six inches apart. Joanie maneuvered around them and wondered how on earth there was room for anyone else. Then she saw a name she recognized.

It was just the last name, Topolosky, and the first names of grandparents that Joan remembered Richard talking about, a great-uncle who had been a cantor, a grandmother named Leah, a great-grandfather named Reuben. People born in what used to be Imperial Russia and buried in New York. And with them, their great-grandson, his place marked by a mound of dark reddish-brown earth.

For a moment, just one, Joan thought about throwing herself on the dirt—her nutty second cousin Zelma had done this at the grave of her second husband, plopped down on the grave and wallowed around there until she was covered with muddy red clay. Joan thought about dropping to her knees—they were wobbly anyway—and sobbing. She thought about it. She felt like doing it. But she was all cried out. She thought about reciting the Lord's Prayer, then wondered if that was the right prayer to pray in a Jewish cemetery. Or did it matter now? Did anything matter now?

There was a sound behind her, and she turned around. The baby was awake and now being bounced against her uncle's shoulder. Her little round head turned, and she gurgled. David smiled and kissed her on the cheek.

Joan touched the headstone gently, then reached down to pick up a handful of earth. The stone was cold, the earth— mud, really—was cool and mushy, smelling of herbs and wet grass, rocks and ancient bones, stories told and stories left untold. The warm, soft shoulders of her husband were gone, as was his voice, an engaging tenor, his light brown eyes, his laughter after telling her a bad joke. She squeezed her fist closed and felt the squishy mud against her palm. In a nearby tree, a bird called, sharp and annoying. Then silence.

Richard was not here, he was never here, and he would never be here. The stone and the Hebrew carved into it were a memorial, but they were not him. And now she wondered why she had asked David to bring her here. The place wasn't creepy, just . . . empty. The Richard she knew was only in her memory. And in her daughter's smile. She reached into her jacket pocket and pulled out a smooth, cool, light gray stone and kissed it. Then she placed it on the flat top of the Topolosky monument.

"I'm ready to go," she told David as she took the baby into her arms.

"At least you know . . . where he's buried," David said. "So that when you come back . . . for the unveiling . . ." he added hopefully.

"I'm never coming back," Joan said.

CHAPTER 30

Carmen

And she never went back?"

Howard shook his head. "Not as far as I know. And we visited the city many times."

"What happened to David? My . . . uncle."

"I don't know. I wasn't Joan's jailer, you know. I wouldn't have stopped her from speaking with Richard's brother or any of his family. Especially David after all he did."

Carmen frowned. "What did he do?"

Her father studied her for a moment, then smiled. "Of course you don't know. You wouldn't." He paused, his face arranging itself into the same expression he wore when he gathered his thoughts for a sermon. "David paid your college tuition. He said that it was what your . . . what Richard would have wanted."

Carmen shook her head. "No, Dad. No, he didn't. Remember? You and Mom were looking at financial aid packages and then I won that scholarship . . ." She gasped. *Of course.* The name hadn't meant anything to her then. The phone call,

seemingly out of the blue, from the financial aid office, inform-
ing her parents of the scholarship award.

"The Richard S. Topolosky Scholarship," Carmen blurted
out. "I remember telling the financial aid officer that I hadn't
applied for it."

Her father smiled. "You didn't need to. You were the only
person in the world who qualified for it."

"Mom knew. Of course."

"Yes," Howard answered, nodding. "She knew, and I remember that she reached for the telephone, then it seemed as if she
changed her mind. But knowing your mother, her being a stickler
for good manners and all, she probably wrote David a letter."

Carmen's thoughts flew back to the small desk that her
mother had used, the many tiny drawers holding her person-
alized stationery, postcards, and Hallmark cards for every occasion, from baby congratulations to sympathy. In later years,
Joan had set up a laptop on the dark wooden surface, but when
Carmen was in high school, the desk had been topped by a
navy blotter, and her mother had kept a variety of ink pens in
a silver mug. There was no doubt in Carmen's mind that Joan
had written to David to say thank you.

She felt as if the air had been squeezed out of her lungs. What
she'd heard was a love story between two people she had never
known. And a sequel of tenacity and resilience from a woman
she had had the nerve to believe was marshmallow soft. Now
she knew that her mother had been tougher than rawhide. A
woman who had had the courage to start over. Carmen wished
that she had known the real Joan Adams better.

She was still lost in her thoughts when she realized her father had spoken. "Dad? I'm sorry, what did you say? I was daydreaming."

Howard smiled. "I asked if you had requested a copy of the adoption file."

Carmen nodded.

"Okay," her father said. "That's fine. I . . . I knew that you would do that someday. And that it was your right to do that. Don't be too hard on your mom."

"Hard on Mom? What do you mean?"

"I'm talking about your name," Howard said simply. "Carmen."

Carmen grinned. "Dad, no worries. I've gotten used to being named after a Spanish fancy woman."

But her father was shaking his head. "That's not what I meant. The Joanie Adams that you didn't know . . . well, she and your father loved music, and especially, she loved opera. So when you were born, she named you Leah, after your great-grandmother, Ira Topolosky's mother. But Richard gave you your middle name."

She smiled. "I know this, Dad. He named me after his favorite opera. Cousin Dorothy wrote about it in a letter to Mom."

Howard Bradshaw looked down at his hands, wrapped around the mug.

"That is true," her father said in a low voice. "But *Carmen* wasn't his favorite opera, it was hers. Richard named you Tosca. Leah Tosca. But Joanie changed it, because . . . she said it would break her heart again every time she saw it in writing."

* * *

Carmen knew just where they were. A stack of old LPs, tied together with string, buried in the last box she had unpacked. Symphonies, concerti, operas. Several of the covers were water-stained, others were torn, and some were taped, although the adhesive had disintegrated years ago, leaving a faded yellow trail behind. None of them was *Carmen*. But the album on the bottom was a 1953 recording of *Tosca* performed at La Scala with Maria Callas in the title role. Carmen couldn't remember that she had ever heard a recording of Maria Callas. She took the vinyl disc out of its brown cover and held it up. It was warped, and she knew that would affect the sound. One of the song titles on the label was marked with an X in black ink, now fading, an aria from Act 2, "Vissi d'Arte." Carmen pulled it from the internet and listened. And cried.

CHAPTER 31

Elise

It had been ten months since Marie's funeral. Ten months since Elise had seen George Bridges. A lot can happen in ten months. She had heard—through the grapevine—that he was still living with complications from the surgery after the fall he took. She'd also heard that he had given up his condo and moved into an assisted-living apartment north of the city, to be closer to his grandson and other family members.

As Elise maneuvered her way through the café, she was startled to see how thin George was, how frail looking now, even though his smile was bright and his eyes clear with cognition, shining with humor. She noticed a dark mahogany-colored cane resting on a chair nearby.

"Hello, hello, Elise," George said, gesturing for her to take the seat across from him. "I can't tell you what a treat it is to see you!" He looked around the café. "I hope this isn't too noisy. I would've invited you into my apartment, but the painters are there today. It's in disarray, and the smell is bad. I ordered for us. Decaf caramel latte, right?"

"I'm surprised that you remember."

George chuckled. "I'm old, but not that old! In fact, it seems that everything else is going before my memory!" He looked down at his right leg, now stretched out. He bent it gingerly as if practicing an exercise his therapist had recommended.

"How's the leg?" Elise asked.

George shrugged. "Okay. It will never be what it was, but then . . . nothing ever is! I should be off this cane in another month if I keep going with the physical therapy routines." He shook his head slowly. "They're boring, but they work. I guess."

Elise was surprised to catch a tone of sadness in George's voice. It seemed out of character. She fidgeted a bit, working up the courage to change the subject, but was interrupted by the server bringing their coffees. Glancing around the café, she noticed at least three women—over the age of eighty—to every man.

"So what is the female-to-male ratio here, George?" Elise asked.

He chuckled. "Twenty to one among the eighties," he teased. "Much higher than that among the nineties!"

"So you have your pick of the ladies, then," Elise said.

George looked stunned for a moment, then smiled slightly and stretched out his leg again. "No. I'm done with that."

"Come on, George," Elise said, hoping the conversation would continue in a lighthearted way until she worked up more courage to say what was really on her mind.

"Lisee," he said, using Marie's nickname for her, "your mother was the last love of my life."

She stared at George for a few moments. The words she'd

rehearsed over and over, to tell him of her regrets and her apologies, stuck in her throat like pebbles, then disintegrated.

"I know. It sounds ridiculous, doesn't it? An old fart like me talking about the love of his life." He massaged the kneecap on his outstretched leg. "But it's true. Oh, don't misunderstand me—Ilena and I were married for over fifty-five years, she was my childhood sweetheart. But after I'd thought the lights were out for me, forever, here came Marie, with her infectious laughter, her sense of adventure and courage, and her warm heart." George's smile grew into a grin. "And I fell for her like a sixteen-year-old boy. That's how she made me feel. Young, important, and full of life. I'll be grateful to her forever." George sighed and closed his eyes, leaning back against the seat cushion as if he was tired.

It came to Elise just then as she observed him, something she had to remind herself of: George Bridges was old, really old. He was much thinner now, his hair white and fine and lying thinly against his head. His large hands, heavily veined, with long fingers, lying limply in his lap. When her mother was alive and dating him, George was an older man, but not an *old* man.

My mom was his fountain of youth.

George opened his eyes as if he had heard her thoughts.

Elise smiled at him and took a deep breath. "George . . . my timing is bad, I know. I'm late. But I want to apologize to you. For . . . behaving so badly when you and Mom were . . . seeing each other. For acting like a spoiled brat." Elise paused and thought about how embarrassing she'd been. She was mortified. "For ruining the lovely times you and Mom had together.

I am . . . so sorry, sorrier than I can say." *There—I've said it.* She pressed her lips together as if to prevent any more words coming out.

George didn't say anything at first, then leaned over and took her hand. "Lisee, it's okay. Apology accepted, bratty behavior forgotten. You didn't ruin anything. Marie and I had a ball. And we . . . I enjoyed every second we were together. And so did she." He winked at her. "Bratty daughter notwithstanding."

Elise felt the tears coming and blinked. "Thank you. I just . . . wish that I could've said this to Mom." She caught a sob before it could erupt. "I wish that I'd been able to tell her how sorry I was and how much I loved her."

George's grasp tightened on her hand. "Oh, she knew that. She adored you. I hope you aren't beating yourself up or anything." He paused for a moment, then looked at her as if determined to pull her gaze away from the floor and into his eyes. "Elise, your mother took everything in stride. She was the most practical, live-in-the-moment person I ever knew. And she was so grateful to you—you have no idea."

A jolt of electricity ran up Elise's spine. "W-what? Grateful to me? How? Why?"

George grinned. "Because you looked after her when your father died. You didn't allow her to sit at home and feel sorry for herself. You pulled her back into the world, took her places, encouraged her to socialize and stay active. She said that you saved her life."

George chuckled as he released his hold of her hand. She realized then that her mouth had been wide open.

"Saved . . . her life."

He nodded. "Yes. You did for her what my . . . what my kids couldn't do for me because they were afraid of interfering. You pulled your mother back into the world. And she returned the favor by pulling me back into the world after Ilena died. If Marie hadn't been there for me, I would be six feet under today." George's blue eyes bored into Elise. "And if you hadn't been there for her, well, let's say that it's a good thing you were. You are a blessing, Elise Armstrong. Thank you."

She was so stunned that she couldn't think of anything to say. The sound of tapping broke into her mental marathon, George's spoon against his coffee mug.

"Drink your latte. Better yet, let me order you another. That one's probably cold. And let's talk about something different and more interesting." George waved to the server, who was on the other side of the café. "I'm an old guy; I can't sit around here reliving the good old days for too long. I have things to do." He handed her a napkin, which she took from him and dabbed at her eyes. "Can't waste time babysitting a little brat, you know. Time marches on!" He winked at her.

Elise blew her nose into the napkin and winked back.

PART 4

PART 4

CHAPTER 32

Dee Dee

"Mooommm!"

"Frances, I'm done with this. Not going to talk about it any—"

"You don't get it! You never get it!"

"Finished, Frances! Subject closed!"

Lorenzo appeared in the doorway to the front entryway. "Whoa, whoa!" His eyes were wide, his expression distorted with disbelief. "I can hear y'all over ESPN. Now, that's sayin' somethin'! What's this all about?"

Wrong question. The three empresses in his family proceeded to answer the question: at the same time, at the same ear-splitting volume, using similar hand gestures, although Lorenzo wasn't about to point that out. He exhaled, then signaled a time-out. As expected, royalty ignored him. As did the dog, Dallas, who barked and danced around, enjoying the excitement.

The hall echoed with shrieks. The trio of loud voices—Phoebe's plaintive soprano, Frances's evocative mezzo, and Dee Dee's authoritative alto—were not in the same key, but they were singing the same melody, each stanza with different lyrics: of maternal anger, teenage angst, and overall frustration. Lorenzo looked bewildered and put his hands over his ears as he retreated again to the great room.

"Girls, *enough*." This from Dee Dee, who felt as if she were about to do a neutron dance on Frances's head.

"Mom, you're not present," Frances barked out, throwing a garment bag on the floor, then sprinting toward the stairs. "Not. Here."

The *click-click-click* of her footsteps across the tile of the front hall was followed by the *thump-thump* up the stairs, so heavy that it might have been a giant coming home to relax after a long day. *Fee, fie, fo, fum . . . Jesus Christ!*

The cat, Pauly, wasn't taking chances and trotted down the back hall toward his favorite hiding place in the mudroom. Dallas stood riveted in the doorway of the kitchen, looking clueless as usual. Was it treat time? Or doggie park time?

And in the background, as if struggling to be heard, ESPN continued to blare. March madness may be over for the year, Dee Dee thought, but it was still battling on in her *house*.

"You *never* let me wear what I want to wear!" Frances yelled from the top of the stairs. "Everyone's going strapless this year, everyone!"

"France, strapless is one thing, darned near topless is another!"

"Mooommm! You exaggerate!"

"I don't! The lilac—"

"Yes! You! Do!"

"Frances. The dress is too short. You'll need a Brazilian bikini wax to wear it. Which you are not getting, by the way!"

"It *was* short!" A small voice from the peanut gallery—Phoebe trying to be the mediator.

"Shut up, Phoebe!" Frances hissed.

"Make me!"

"If you don't shut your—"

"Frances," Dee Dee growled.

"I'll look like a kid!" Frances's plea had morphed into a whine.

"You *are* a kid" was Dee Dee's retort.

"Jesus Christ!"

"Frances! Cut it out, and stop the whining!"

"I'm not whining! I'm telling the truth. I will look like a kid! I won't wear that stupid dress! And I'm not going to the damn prom!"

"France! You are not . . . You don't talk to me like that . . . *Frances!* Come back here!"

Frances glared down at her mother. "God! Why did you name me that? It's an awful name! Old-timey."

Moments later, somewhere in the back of the house on the second floor, a door closed. Hard.

Then silence.

Lorenzo stuck his head around the doorway. No bullets or arrows whizzed by. Hostilities had ceased for the moment. Dee Dee stood near the bottom of the staircase, feeling as if she were the personification of pestilence, a plague of locusts, and the four horsemen rolled into one.

"Is it safe to come out?" Lorenzo asked, glancing up toward the second floor. "Or is she reloading?" His expression indicated real concern.

Phoebe sighed loudly. She trudged up the stairs, dragging her sister's shopping bags behind her. "Mom's just being a Neanderthal," she said.

Dee Dee's mouth opened, and she took a step toward the stairs but stopped when Lorenzo put his hand on her arm.

"Temporary cease-fire," he said solemnly.

She inhaled loudly. "Traitor."

"No, no, just count to ten."

She looked at him over her shoulder. "Ten won't cut it," she growled, glaring at her younger daughter's back as she reached the top of the stairs and disappeared into the upstairs hall.

"Okay. Count to a hundred. And while you're doing that, I'll get you a drink. What do you want? Wine, scotch, hemlock?"

Dee Dee chuckled in spite of herself. "The hemlock sounds inviting, but no. A cup of hot tea actually. My throat's a little scratchy. Can't imagine why." All of a sudden she felt the energy drain out of her body. She was exhausted. *I am too old for this.* "Lorenzo?"

"Yeah?"

"Is it me? I mean, am I being medieval about this? She wants to wear a dress that even Kim Kardashian wouldn't wear in public!"

Lorenzo's eyebrows rose.

Dee Dee grinned. "Okay. A dress that Kim probably *would*

wear, and that's the problem. Frances tells me that's what everyone's wearing this year and I'm out of touch! And old!"

Lorenzo took her purse and packages and set them on the
steps and guided her toward the kitchen. Dee Dee picked up the
discarded garment bag.

"Well, you are old, but I wouldn't say that you're medieval.
And I don't care if you're out of touch—she is not wearing a
dress that has no sleeves and barely any hem."

"Lo, I'm telling you. That dress comes up to here"—Dee
Dee's hand brushed the upper reaches of her thigh—"and the
neckline is . . ." She glanced down. "Actually, there is no neckline. I can't believe anyone would let their daughter go out like
that. At fifteen?"

Lorenzo shook his head and grabbed the kettle. "Now,
you've seen those emails. The ones Jan sends out."

Dee Dee laughed. "You mean the ones of the ghetto proms?"

"Uh-huh. And you've seen those dresses."

"But, Lorenzo, this isn't that kind of party!"

"I know, I know, babe. But these are the clothes the girls see
on TV and in the movies."

"Well, France can dream about 'em, but she is not wearing
anything like that."

"So did you get her a dress?"

"Oh yeah! But she hates it. And it's lovely."

Lorenzo chuckled. "Ha! So you say. According to the girls,
you have no . . . fashion sense. Let's see it."

Dee Dee picked up the garment bag and unzipped it. A soft
lavender-colored confection emerged with sequins sprinkled

across the front, gleaming like tiny stars as they reflected the light. The dress had spaghetti straps. Lorenzo smiled with approval.

"Lavender, huh? Her favorite color. I like it, but . . ." Lorenzo's expression changed from admiration to mild dismay. Gingerly, he touched a delicate-looking shoulder strap. "Wow. I've been in denial. My little girl is all grown up." He managed to look both proud and disturbed at the same time. "She'll be pretty in this."

"That's what I told her! But nooo . . . She wants to wear something that makes her look like a refugee from slut city! Honestly . . ."

The kettle whistled a welcome distraction. Lorenzo clicked off the burner and retrieved Dee Dee's favorite mug, the one that said SHE WHO MUST BE OBEYED.

"It's puberty. Teenagers."

Dee Dee rolled her eyes. "Yeah. Teenagers. And once I survive Frances, then comes Phoebe. I don't know, Lorenzo. That girl has worn out every nerve I ever had. I keep telling her, one of us is going to survive her teenage years, but it might not be her."

"Uh-oh. You threatened to bury her under the tomato plants again?"

Dee Dee shook her head. "Nope. The collard greens. Tomato plants don't provide enough ground cover."

"She'll be fine. It'll pass. Frances is like a summer thunderstorm. A lot of noise and lightning and then it moves on. It's that artistic temperament," Lorenzo said, a grin brightening his face. "Expression is her thing, and she never half-asses it! Painting, music, dance. She's always been a bundle of emotions, even when she was a baby. Remember, you said she was so much like—" He caught himself before he said it. His smile faded. "Sorry. I meant it in a good way."

"I know you did." Dee Dee dunked the tea bag a few times into the steaming water. "It's all right. Don't worry about it. Actually, Deb's said it too. That France is so much like our mother, it's scary." *Bad choice of word.*

"I'll run up and check on the girls," Lorenzo said quickly and kissed her on the cheek. Dee Dee knew that he was glad to change the subject. "You need anything else? Slow poison maybe?"

"I'm good."

And she was good, or at least she had been. Shopping with the girls always wore her out, and arguing with Frances was a pain, but unfortunately she was used to it. By the time Phoebe graduated from high school, she'd be an expert. And, yes, she and Lo often talked about how much Frances resembled her grandmother. Lorenzo had met Laura only a few times—she had been in the hospital more than out of it—but he'd seen the photos and listened to the stories about her from Dee Dee's father, Dee Dee's aunts and uncles, from Deb and others who had known her. They'd often mentioned the resemblance between Laura and Frances. But it wasn't the physical resemblance now that grabbed at Dee Dee's heart; it was the psychological one.

Frances was an artist, a bright, intelligent girl who painted, sculpted, and sang soprano in the school choir. She vacillated between wanting to be Kathleen Battle when she grew up or Elizabeth Catlett. She played the piano and the cello and wrote poetry of the atmospherically maudlin kind. This year, to her parents' dismay, she was obsessed with Edgar Allan Poe. Frances was spontaneous, volatile, and passionate—about everything, from the water temperature of her shower to environmental issues to her choice of prom dress. Her temper tantrums appeared out of nowhere and were always noisy, full of tears and yelling—had been since she was a toddler—but they never lasted long. Ninety percent of the time, Frances was a gregarious person who got along well with her parents, sister, friends, and teachers. She was happiest when she was playing the piano or curled up on her bed scribbling in her diary or on a sketch pad.

"She's just high-spirited," Lorenzo's aunt would say indulgently, using a term straight out of the Victorian era. She adored the girls, having no grandchildren of her own.

Dee Dee blew on her tea, watching the steam rise, then disappear. She didn't used to worry so much about Frances. If she was honest with herself, Frances probably had no more tantrums than most girls her age. Her outbursts were triggered by all of the usual culprits that plagued every mother of a teenager. And while Frances looked very like Laura physically, Dee Dee consoled herself (the tea helped) by acknowledging that most of the similarities ended there. Frances's loudest meltdowns were nothing compared to the dark lows and speed-of-light highs that had propelled Laura O'Neill into dangerous situations time after time and eventually into a series of mental health facilities. But there was . . . something. Dee Dee could not put her finger on it. Something about Frances fit like a puzzle piece with Laura, and the similarity sent a jolt of dread down Dee Dee's spine.

Laura had been an artist who had used pastels and ink like a master, who had sung jazz with a little trio that Dee Dee's father had played bass in. She had protested against the Vietnam War, studied abroad and smoked Gauloise cigarettes, and graduated cum laude from Ohio University. She had spoken fluent French and Spanish, and had studied Italian and taught a few words of it to her daughters when they were young. Laura had been volatile and engaging. Mercurial in temperament but committed and hardworking. And ill. Seriously ill. Her granddaughter and namesake—Frances's middle name was Laura, and Laura's middle name was Frances—was also engaging and mercurial. How much was Frances like her grandmother? Bipolar disorder had a genetic component. Dee Dee's stomach muscles tightened. There was so much she didn't know about her mother—Laura had spent years of her life in a hospital—and there was no one to ask: Laura had been an only child, and Dee Dee's grandparents had been dead for years. When had Laura begun to . . . get sick? When had the hysterics begun? The dark moods, the voices? Dee Dee was only six years old the first time . . . but even so, she remembered her mother talking to someone who wasn't there, asking her and Debora if they could hear the sounds that she did. The growls that sent her scrambling into the nearest closet, where she would curl up into a ball in the corner, trembling. And when the darkness really descended, she went to bed for days on end or locked herself in the bathroom and hid in the tub. When had Laura O'Neill's nightmare begun? When she was a child? A teenager? Or later? Deb had started having problems at twenty. Would that happen to Frances too?

Dee Dee glanced up at the ceiling, where she heard the *thump-thump* of someone's footsteps in the hall. She thought about Frances's outbursts, becoming more frequent with each passing week. Tears followed by laughter followed by dark moods and the composition of even darker poetry. Some of the poems made Dee Dee shudder: they read like Poe on steroids. Tantrums and screaming matches punctuated with the dull thud of slamming doors. Life with Frances? Or life with teenagers? Dee Dee couldn't tell the difference. Was she making too much of this?

Dee Dee inhaled and closed her eyes. If she was honest, it wasn't really Frances's moods that she needed to worry about; it was her own. Lately, she'd been on edge, jumpy. And it was never anything major that sent Dee Dee into a hissing frenzy. It was just little stuff. Stuff like wet socks, for instance.

CHAPTER 33

Dee Dee

Two weeks ago, Lo was in the kitchen measuring out dog food. Dallas was doing doggy jumping jacks in excitement. He was like a hobbit, always hungry.

"Hold on a minute, buddy, almost there . . ."

"Where is your daughter?" Dee Dee growled, coming through the doorway from the laundry room.

Lo's brows rose.

"*My* daughter? Oh. It's like that, huh? Which of *my* daughters are you referring to? Maybe she isn't mine." His face brightened at the possibility.

"Frances Laura."

Lo shook his head as he poured the kibble into Dallas's bowl.

"Oh, oh. World War Twenty-Four is about to begin." He set the bowl down on the floor, where it was instantly consumed by the chubby but obviously underfed and starving yellow lab. "What did she do now?"

Dee Dee held up one disheveled and gross-looking sock.

Even from the distance of a few feet, it smelled disgusting. Lo's nose twitched. He pointed toward the patio.

She marched through the kitchen and dining room toward the French doors leading to the backyard, a woman on a mission. The mission was to get Frances, once and for all, to be responsible for her own "stuff" and, for God's sake, take the time to empty out her gym bag and hang up the damp items, tee shirts and socks especially, on the line to dry or, better still, pop them into the washer. *Not* leave them in a soggy, balled mess in the bottom of a gym bag that was in the bottom of the laundry hamper that was in the back of the mudroom in the corner and forget about them for a week.

Dee Dee's internal rant came to a screeching halt ten steps from the French doors. Frances was on the patio, walking back and forth, her arms waving in the air, gesticulating wildly as if she was conducting a symphony with the philharmonic. Her face was animated, a mélange of expressions. She grinned, threw her head back and laughed, nodded, shook her head in the negative, and stuck her tongue out. Her steps were light and graceful, reminiscent of the ballet lessons she'd taken but not liked. And all the while, her lips were moving. Dee Dee's eyes scanned the yard. Frances was talking. And talking. Then laughing. And talking some more. To no one.

Dee Dee's blood froze.

Her mother used to do that. Walk around the house, waving her arms in all directions, sometimes hitting her lovely hands against a wall or the side of a counter, which left them bruised and speckled with cuts and scratches at the end of a day. Laura would dance through the house on her toes as if *en pointe*. She'd laugh. And she'd talk. Chitchat. About . . . what? Who the hell knew? Dee Dee and Debora had no idea—they were just kids. Their dad didn't know either, and that pained him. But Laura seemed to know. She would talk and answer questions, carry on conversations as if there was an entire complement of personalities in the room. Talking only to her.

But there would be no one there. She'd float past her daughters as if they were invisible, as if their words were as inaudible as the whispers of dust. Later, timidly, the girls would ask, "Mommy who were you talking to?" And Laura would answer, "Just my friends."

Just what friends?

Dee Dee opened the French doors with the grip of a woman who thought she might be opening the gates to hell.

Frances spun around and stared. "Mom? What's the matter? You look like you've seen a ghost."

"Frances . . . w-what are . . . what are you doing?" Dee Dee glanced around the patio. The sound of the door opening had startled a scavenging squirrel, which sprinted to safety up a tree.

"Doing?"

"Who are you talking to? There's no one here."

Frances's expression of concern morphed into one of disbelief. She lifted the veil of long dark reddish-brown curls from her shoulders to reveal the earpiece and cord attached to her cell phone threaded through the inside of her tee shirt.

"I'm on the phone, Mom. With Austin. Why?" Her features

tightened into a mask of granite. "Is that what's wrong, Mom? You thought I was talking to myself? Talking to invisible people? Like your crazy mother?"

"Frances . . . My mother wasn't . . . She was ill, okay? I'm sorry, I just thought . . ." *What did you think?*

"I'll call you back," Frances said into the microphone at the end of her phone cord. She stuffed the cord into her hoodie pocket as she brushed by her mother. "Yeah, I know, Mom. Grandma Laura was sick. I know that. You say it over and over. She was mentally ill. But I'm not. Okay? Okay? I'm not!" The French doors slammed behind her.

At any other time Dee Dee would have followed her through those doors, right at her heels, reading her the riot act about the laundry, mental illness, and how you don't talk to your mother like that. But this time she could only stand there, in the middle of her beautiful patio, amidst the red and white roses she'd planted in her garden, the lavender now blooming and attracting hummingbirds and slow- and low-flying bumblebees, and the waxy leaves of two magnolias that she was nursing along, hoping they would take off in the now more unpredictable weather of southwestern Ohio. Because in her head, another conversation was playing, a loop that never stopped. Frances had pushed the "Laura button." The button that always made her feel ashamed, that excavated voices and scenes from another day long ago that had spiraled out of control. A day when things had been said that shouldn't have been, that couldn't be taken back or forgiven. Or even atoned for. That day had begun with a seemingly little thing too.

* * *

It was October, a Friday after school. Dee Dee was fourteen.
She and Teena were going to Cydney's slumber party, and home
was on the way. Normally Dee Dee didn't bring friends to her
house, especially to *this* house. They'd moved—again—and the
"new" place wasn't new at all; it was an older home on 14th, a
"fixer-upper," as Dad called it. Debora called it "dilapidated."
After six months, Dad was still fixing it up. He'd told them that
the area was in "transition." And besides that, there was her
mom. But Dee Dee decided to take a chance. It was four thirty.
She and Teena would stop by the house, she'd throw a few
things into a bag, and they'd take off to Fifth to catch the bus.
Deb was at cheerleading practice, Dad wouldn't be home for
hours, and Mom . . . and here was where Dee Dee crossed her
fingers and said a silent prayer. Mom had been sick for a bit and
spent a few days in the hospital. But the doctor had given her
blue pills that made her sleep. With a little luck, Laura would
be under the covers and Dee Dee (with T in tow) could slip in
and out of the house without Laura hearing a peep.

She unlocked the door and tiptoed into the front hall, glancing back at Teena. She whispered, "My mom's sleeping."

Teena nodded.

They slid off their shoes like thieves, then floated up the
stairs and disappeared into the bedroom that Dee Dee and Deb
shared.

Ten minutes later, they floated back down. Quietly, they
wriggled their feet back into their shoes.

"Hi, baby! Whatchu doing?"

The girls froze at the bottom of the stairs and looked over at the person standing next to the couch in the front room. Dee Dee glanced at her friend. Teena looked as if she was staring down a nightmare.

Laura wore the pink nightgown her daughters had given her for Mother's Day, but it looked nothing like it had when it was new. Its vivid pink had faded to soft salmon: the hospital laundry washed everything in hot water and dried the clothes on a high heat setting. The hem was dangling, white thread trailing downward; the wrinkles were deeply set, more like crevasses than wrinkles; and the gown, a size medium to accommodate Laura's height, was now too large. Her appetite had waned, and the gown hung across one shoulder so loosely that Dee Dee thought, her heart in her throat, that it might slip off completely. Worse, Laura had put it on backward, and the label was hanging out. Her feet were bare, the claw-like toenails three months beyond the need for a pedicure. And her long, thick hair had not seen the inside of Elegance Salon in months. The tangled strands were half straight, half not, and some still carried remnants of the Ethel Merman auburn-orange tint that Laura used when she tried to color it herself. She looked like an escapee from *Night of the Living Dead*, part X.

"Is sis one of your friends?" Laura asked. Her voice was deep and raspy as if she'd smoked a warehouse of unfiltered Camel cigarettes. But Laura hadn't smoked for years.

"Yeeessss, Mom. This is Teena Sampson from school. Uh, look, Mom, we gotta go. Cydney's slumber party . . ." Out of the corner of her eye, Dee Dee saw Teena bolt for the door. She heard her friend say, "I'll wait outside," in a terrified whisper before the front door closed with a loud *click*.

"Where'syourfriendgo?"

Dee Dee blinked back tears of embarrassment. "She . . . she left. I . . . I gotta go, Mom. Bye."

"Whatstherush, Dee . . . Deanna? Gimme a hug." Laura grabbed her and folded her into a bear hug with a strength that contradicted her scrawny arms.

"Mommy . . . No. I gotta go. Besides, you . . ." Dee Dee's nose crinkled, and she sniffed back the snot but not the fury. She tried to wriggle out of her mother's arms, and for a moment they were engaged in what looked like a professional wrestling maneuver. "You . . . smell! Mom, when was the last time you . . . took a shower? You look like a . . ." She gasped, the tears and frustration welling up into one big knot in her chest. "Mommy, go back to bed. Please? Go . . . back to wherever you came from!" She finally pushed away from her mother and stepped back.

Laura stared at her, blinking wildly as if she didn't know where to look. Her mouth gaped open slightly lopsided, as if she'd lost control over her muscles. She frowned. "I . . . took a bath . . . Didn't I? Didn't . . . I thought I did." Laura paused as if trying to remember what a bath was. "I don't remember. Maybe . . . yes, maybe I should take one. A bath. Or shower . . ." She glanced toward the back wall of the room as if there were someone there. Then she smiled, sheepishly.

Dee Dee thought, *That's a Mommy smile, a real one.*

"You know," Laura said slowly, forming her words with

care in case she chose the wrong one. "In this new house, I-I forget where the bathroom is." She chuckled at her little joke.

And Dee Dee couldn't help it. "I hate this house. I hate that we had to move. And it's your fault."

Her mother's smile melted away. "What do you mean? Deanna . . ."

"Dad said we had to move. Because of the money . . ." Dee Dee thought, *I shouldn't say this, it'll hurt her feelings. I shouldn't.* But she did. "Because he needs money to pay for your hospital and the doctors and your medicine that doesn't work. So now we have to live in this dump! It's humiliating! I hate to bring my friends here! And then . . ." It was all rushing out, floodwaters of words pouring over a weak and damaged dam. "Why can't you be like everybody else's mom? Why don't you wash? Why are you dressed so . . . weird?"

Laura stared at Dee Dee, then glanced down at her clothing, running her hands across her body as if seeing herself for the first time, totally unaware, as if some other woman was standing in her body wearing a pink nightgown on backward. When she looked up at Dee Dee, her expression reflected fear, sadness, and self-loathing. It was the most heartbreaking thing Dee Dee had ever seen.

Dee Dee turned on her heel and ran. Out of the room, out of the house. She grabbed Teena by the arm and dragged her down the street.

* * *

Dee Dee clasped her mug between her palms. The warmth from the tea should have been comforting, but it wasn't.

Tomorrow. This weekend. Carmen and Elise were stopping by to help her sort through the boxes in the basement and to give her moral support as she finally disposed of—in one way or another—Laura Frances O'Neill Brown's few belongings. Dee Dee saw the boxes in her mind, forlorn looking and deliberately forgotten, sitting on the unused Ping-Pong table, where Lo had put them after the water heater died a few months ago. Four boxes. Luke Brown had packed up his wife's things after her death, and the boxes had remained unopened since then, a sad little quartet usually consigned together to a top shelf in the corner of the basement just above half-full cans of Sherwin-Williams paint the contractor had used on the house. They weren't heavy, and there wasn't any rattling when you shook them, so both Dee Dee and Deb had surmised that there wasn't much in them. Laura hadn't lived long enough to acquire much and had spent over a quarter of her life in hospitals. Eighty percent of the time, Laura hadn't even spoken. She sure hadn't been at Macy's buying things.

"So what am I afraid of? I'm just going to open a few boxes." Dee Dee was startled to hear her own voice. "Okay. Now I'm talking to myself."

Pandora, the first human woman, whose name was Greek for "gift of the gods," —a sick joke, Dee Dee thought—was given a special jar by Zeus. When she opened it—after being warned not to—all the troubles of the world flew out. Dee Dee visualized one of the decrepit water-stained boxes, its flaps wide open while pestilence, plague, famine, and other evils poured out, a dark, howling flood of woe. It made her sad. Nearly every remembrance she had of Laura, even the pleasant ones, had a sepia wash across it, her mother's face tinged with some aspect of her illness that had bubbled up to spoil even the shortest Kodak moment. So how could anything good come out of those boxes?

Dee Dee decided to break the pact and open the boxes herself, before Elise and Carmen arrived, and after Lo left for the gym. That way if there was something awful or embarrassing inside, well, she could deal with it or call Deb. Laura had been haunted by dark things, things that only she could see or hear. Although the memory for Dee Dee was fleeting and fog-bound, Laura had called them "devils"—didn't she? She'd drawn them to show Luke, to show her doctors and anyone else, to "prove" that devils existed. To her, a dark world lived side by side with the light one. If there was something weird in the boxes, Dee Dee would be the first one to see it. And if there was a real devil inside one of them, she'd deal with that too. Besides, she knew of at least one thing that wouldn't be in the boxes.

Her own guilt.

CHAPTER 34

Dee Dee

The next morning, Dee Dee set the four sad-looking boxes side by side on the Ping-Pong table. They'd been on the floor when the water heater broke, and they'd gotten wet—pretty much everything in the utility room had gotten wet. The boxes were water-stained but not damp anymore. They smelled musty and ancient, the odor Dee Dee imagined emanating from excavated Egyptian tombs. Dee Dee's father hadn't looked through them. "There wasn't time," he'd told her. "I had a million other things coming at me." Luke had put them in the cabinet under the bookshelf in the family room, and they stayed there until he died in 2009. There didn't seem to be any order to them, so Dee Dee assigned numbers in her head—*box one, box two, box three, box four*. The lightest box in weight was the noisiest, its contents shifting from side to side when Dee Dee picked it up. The heaviest she assumed was tightly packed with sketchbooks and newspaper-wrapped frames.

"Box number one."

Dee Dee opened the box and picked up the items in it one by

one, wondering why anyone would have taken the time to pack them. It was like cleaning out the junk drawer in the kitchen. One stick of Juicy Fruit gum, mummified to brittle fragility and disintegrating in her fingers; dried-up BIC pens; a Walkman but no earphones, the batteries corroded into white powder; a pencil sharpener; a smiling Buddha paperweight; a fan from Saint Philip's Episcopal Church; a Rubik's Cube; and other miscellaneous and useless whatnots. These were Laura's things, the little personal items she'd kept in her room . . . Had she been in a room? Or had it been a ward with lots of other patients? Or (too sad to think about) a cell? It was so long ago, and Dee Dee had been young and didn't remember. She realized that she had no idea what her mother's living situation had been like at Shawnee Springs Hospital. When Luke had taken her and Deb for visits, they sat in the solarium, the only room with "proper light," Laura the artist had said. She felt ashamed that she didn't know how her mother had spent her days in the last years of her life. Now that Daddy was gone too, there was no one to ask.

She took more time retrieving each of the doodads from box one, examining them and setting them side by side on the Ping-Pong table. She extracted a coffee mug, stained on the inside from the black tea her mother had liked, ironically decorated with the word "coffee" in several languages. An unopened package of incense, and Dee Dee could still smell the fragrance: sandalwood, distant and exotic. An eclectic group of cassettes rubber-banded together, some of the tapes trailing like ribbons; among them was Brahms's Fourth Symphony, Miles Davis's *Bitches Brew*, Nina

Simone, and Alice Coltrane's mystical Eastern riffs. Pulling out a little California Raisin action figure, she hummed "I Heard It Through the Grapevine," fingering his tiny orange shoes. There was a notepad that contained no notes and an address book imprinted with the name of an insurance agency. No addresses; the pages were pristine. *Didn't Mommy have any friends?* Laura had been so fun-loving, smart, and witty.

And then there was a Bible that looked brand-new and a well-thumbed Book of Common Prayer, a ribbon marking the fifty-first psalm. Dee Dee didn't remember her mother being religious. On Sundays, sometimes, they visited Nana and Grandpa Brown's church, Pool of Bethesda Holiness, or attended Saint Philip's with Papa, Laura's stepfather. She glanced at the inside cover of the prayer book: "Property of Saint Philip's Episcopal Church." The pages fell away like a waterfall until they reached the stem of a dried flower.

Have mercy upon me, O God, after thy great goodness . . .

She saw Laura's handwriting in the margin—"Me!"—and an arrow drawn to verse 17:

The sacrifice of God is a troubled spirit: a broken and contrite heart, O God, shalt thou not despise.

Dee Dee closed the little book and set it aside. The meager inventory of the box spun around in her brain. How could her mother's life be reduced to such an obscure and disposable group of objects? Fossilized chewing gum. A packet of incense so old, it had turned to dust. Dried up pens and a prayer book. Was this all there was to Laura? Bits and pieces? Leftovers? All evidence of a troubled spirit?

The second box weighed a ton, full of books, the hardcover variety, so full that it hadn't been closed properly, the peeling masking tape bulging at the top. This time Dee Dee's sorting process broke down: she kept nearly every book. Laura's reading tastes, like her own, were broad and transcendent. The poetry of Nikki Giovanni; *The Prophet* by Kahlil Gibran; *Their Eyes Were Watching God*, Zora Neale Hurston's masterpiece; Toni Morrison's *The Bluest Eye*; P. D. James mysteries alongside those of Agatha Christie and Dorothy L. Sayers; the poems of Sylvia Plath, including the collection *Ariel*; and, interestingly, the four Mary Stewart titles traversing the landscape of King Arthur's tales from the birth of Merlin through his and Arthur's deaths.

This was easy, Dee Dee said to herself, putting the books back into the box so she could carry them upstairs. She placed the Arthurian titles on top.

And now box number three. *What time is it?* Ten fifteen. E and Carmen were coming around lunchtime. Plenty of time to sort through the box, consign some of the items to the fire pit or the recycling bin, the others to a to-be-determined pile, maybe to be sent to her sister in Chicago as mementos, depending . . . Dee Dee opened the box and picked up what looked like a journal. She flipped through the pages, stopping at a sketch that her mother had drawn. She shuddered and closed the book.

Sorting the journals was easy. It only took ten minutes to create a pile of notebooks ready for the recycling bin. The first journal was small and had a "My Little Pony" themed cover. At first Dee Dee thought it had belonged to her or Debora, that the little book had gotten mixed up somehow with Laura's things.

But when she opened the cover, she saw her mother's distinctive handwriting on the title page: "Laura O'Neill Brown," written in fuchsia-colored ink. Inside, many of the pages had been torn out, jerked from the spine of the book, leaving a savage tear. The writing not excised by tearing out the page had been redacted—a tidy word for what it looked like, Dee Dee thought. Laura had blacked over her scribbling with a heavy hand. The Magic Marker ink had seeped through to the pages behind, when there were pages. Dee Dee sniffed. Laura had pressed down so hard with the marker that the ink smell was still sharp and fresh after all these years. She found the same in other journals and diaries. Large swaths of pages were either ripped or scissored out in an ominously neat and precise manner, as if the cutter had measured the pages and drawn lines so that the cuts were razor straight and perfect. Any pages that remained were scribbled over with a black or dark blue marker. Dee Dee closed the diary and sighed. The only legible words inside it were her mother's name and the dates.

The notebooks sentenced to the fire pit held the same story: the scribbling was blacked out or, in some cases (and this was new), graffitied over with black or navy markers. The note-books that held actual writing, some of it legible, were only five in number, and these Dee Dee stacked on the Ping-Pong table. Mentally, she'd noted the time periods each book covered. Even when there wasn't anything else substantive in them, Laura had documented dates. The problem was the dates weren't chrono-logical: her mother had written concurrently in different books but all out of order. There had been bad times: the early and mid 1980s through the mid 1990s, and one book, ascetic-looking moleskin from 1985, had its cover dotted with greasy fingerprints. A shiver went up Dee Dee's spine. She thought about putting the little book in what she'd designated the burn sack. But she didn't. She set it down on the table and ran her fingertips across the cover. She didn't know if she wanted to read it. She was afraid of what she'd find out from Laura's words. Or of what she wouldn't find out.

She turned back to one of the open boxes and extracted another notebook, this one a psychedelic pink with the words "Flower Power" on the cover. She clicked open the lock and flipped through the pages. The diary pages were labeled by date and day of the week. If not for that, there might have been no words at all. The garish cover swaddled an empty landscape of pristine white lined pages. Days, weeks, and sometimes months went by without Laura writing a single word. But when she did, it was only one word:

"Sleeping."

This time no blacked-over words, no torn or cut pages. Just emptiness.

Was Mom sleeping all that time?

"Sleeping."

Dee Dee wasn't sure how long she stared at the word, taking in the ornately looped *l* and the huge *p*, which Laura had drawn rather than written. The period was lovely, a dot made with a flourish. Even on medication, the artist in her would not be subdued. Then the word blurred and Dee Dee started to remember. Shards of memory, really. Bits and pieces. She had been only six, and she had no context in which to place the things she saw. And it was so long ago that she wasn't prepared to acknowledge that each sliver of remembrance was even true, that she actually had seen the images now coming back to her. But deep in the abyss of her memory bank, she realized that, at the very least, she could answer her own questions. The six-year-old she was then didn't know what it meant, but she knew what she had seen.

Was Mom sleeping all that time?

Yes, she was, or so it seemed to Dee Dee. She slept when it was light and she and Debora got home from school. And she slept when it was dark and Daddy came home from work, his brow furrowed with many lines as he smoked cigarette after cigarette after cigarette. Shaking Mommy's shoulder as she lay on her side in the bed. Fully dressed. "Laura? Baby? Are you okay?"

What kind of drugs had her mother been on?

One word came to Dee Dee's mind.

There were so many bottles filled with pills of many colors. There was barely room for the lamp on the nightstand. One day Laura had made a game of it. "The giant white ones and the pixie blue ones," Laura told the girls, laughing as she popped one into her mouth and drank a tall glass of water to get it down. Then she belched, much to the girls' amusement. "There." She picked up another bottle and peered at the label. "Now. Which one shall I take next? Yes. This one. I call it the 'troll.'"

"Which one is that, Mommy?" Dee Dee couldn't remember if it was she or Deb who asked the question.

Laura grinned and stood up, taking their hands. The bottle of trolls fell to the floor.

"It's the teeny-tiny one. Blue and white," she answered, kissing them gently on the forehead. "Those are my favorites."

What kind of drugs had her mother been on?

Dee Dee wiped away a tear from the corner of her eye and closed the book.

Many.

CHAPTER 35

Laura

Barbie diary, 1980-something, illegible:

> *This diary belongs to: Laura Frances O'Neill Brown*
> *Dear Diary,*
> *This is silly. A grown woman writing in a child's diary with*
> *"Ski Barbie" on the cover! It's Luke's fault. That's what happens*
> *when you ask a man to go shopping. The doctor said that I*
> *need a journal, a kind of diary to write in. Luke bought the*
> *first "diary" he saw, Barbie's. You gotta love him. I do. I'm not*
> *sure about actually using it, however. I am not a word person;*
> *I'm a picture person, sketches, paintings, cartoons, that's my*
> *language. But Dr. Christiansen wants me to write things down.*
> *He says to think of it as "The History of Laura." Ever since the*
> *incident. Scratch that, OK? I'm not ready to write about that*
> *yet. I'm not sure that I want to write about anything at all, but*
> *Luke says please try. I will do anything for Luke.*
> *The History of Laura O'Neill (what a title, but I can't think*
> *of anything else)* ☺

Name: Laura Frances O'Neill Brown

Born: April 10, 1955, Ft. Benjamin Harrison, just outside Indianapolis, Indiana

Parents: Agnes Blaine O'Neill, Jack O'Neill

Married to high school sweetheart, Luke Augustus Brown, tall, dark, and handsome (Of course!)

Voted "Girl most likely to paint (over) the Sistine Chapel"

Head cheerleader in high school (OK, I wasn't, but it was a nice dream!)

National Honor Society, aka "egg head"

Alpha Kappa Alpha sorority Squeak! Squeak!

Graduated from OU after two years at Fisk

Same journal, 1984:

I don't want to write anymore

Write. Write write write

Same journal, date illegible:

Big fight with Dr. Christiansen. He says that I'm not living up to our agreement. He agreed to talk with me and make me feel better. I said that I would write so that he would know what was going on with me. I thought I held up my end of the bargain. I just don't use a lot of words. He says I'm cheating. He wants to know who I am and how I feel about things.

Write write write write.

How is that cheatin? He told me to Write!

"*Laura, you write as if you're afraid that you'll run out of words.*"

But now Luke's pissed off, and Mom and Daddy are worried and the girls.

I don't see them as much as I would like, and Deanna's only a baby! Luke says they're being taken care of—his mom has them—but my baby needs her mother. Luke says I was too upset. Dr. Christiansen wants to know why I was upset. I told him that I don't remember being upset.

But of course I do.

It's just that I was so tired. I couldn't even walk straight much less think.

"*Did Luke know how tired you were?*" Dr. Christiansen asked.

Yes yes yes and yes. But Luke was tired too, and he had to go to work. I was off for the summer, one advantage of being a teacher. Luke walked the floor with the baby at night. Sometimes we took turns. Then he took a shower, shaved, grabbed a thermos of black coffee, and left. And it was just me. All day long it was just me.

"*Your mother came to help, didn't she?*" Dr. Christiansen looked down at the tiny notebook he writes in. It intrigues me that it's so small. I could fill the itsy-bitsy pages in a second! He must have the smallest handwriting known to man.

"Yes. No. Mom wasn't able to come until July."

Dr. Christiansen made a mark in his miniature book.

"So you and your husband were on your own with a new baby."

"Yes, but many people are."

This time Dr. Christiansen looked at me with a gaze that cut me in half, examined my insides like an x-ray machine. I felt it! It was searing and sharp like a kid with a stick. Poke poke poke.

"What do you remember, Laura? About the baby? Do you remember that day?"

Which baby? Which day? They'd all melted together like chocolate did when I made fudge. One right after the other, all of them the same: get up stay up change baby feed baby change baby feed baby rock rock rock baby sing sing to baby. She's a sweet baby. Both shes were. Are.

"Yes, I understand," he said. His blue eyes were no longer probing around my intestines. "But do you remember?" He glanced over at the clipboard on the table. "After Debora's birth, do you remember?"

Yes, I remember. After Debora's birth. After Deanna's birth. It was the same.

The baby cried, puked, cried again, then pooped. Pampers didn't make enough diapers to cover this kid. But I cleaned her up, fed her a bottle, and rocked her to sleep and slept a bit myself. Maybe that was it. Maybe if I hadn't slept. But I slept and it felt so good, but when the baby started crying, I woke up. And I felt weird, almost high. And she wouldn't stop crying. She wasn't wet. She didn't even spit up. She didn't want a bottle. She just wanted to cry. And I thought, let's walk a bit. I went back and forth and back and forth and then went to the window and looked out. It was February. This baby *was born in winter. The parking lot was shoveled clean, but the snow was still around. Pretty. But cold. It looked soft and comforting. And I thought of pillows and cotton and sleep. Light and dark. A piece about contrasts. The whiteness. I wondered if I could find a similar white paint, soft like cotton. And what would the baby look like nestled in the white, in the snow? Maybe it wasn't cold at all. But of course it was. I was sleepy. And then I thought that if I breathed the cold air, I'd wake up. My head would clear out. Cold does that, wakes you up. Of course the baby would wake up too, but maybe not. I wasn't thinking straight. I was thinking in curlicues, spirals, and wiry rounds that went "boing, boing" like a Slinky. I know that. Now.*

I unlatched the lock and pulled the window open. Looked down at the snow and thought . . . about the white, white paint on white paper in white snow . . .

I didn't hear Luke come in.

"Laura? Why is it so cold in here? What . . . why is the window open?"

He took the baby from me and closed the window, hard with one hand. Then he grabbed me by the arm and sat me down on the couch.

"Laura, what were you doing? What were you going to do with the baby?"

It was so hard to answer him. I must have talked in circles. I told him. About the snow and the cotton and the whiteness. How precious the baby would look against the soft white snow. A baby painting of snow. And I sounded like a nutcase. Which is what I am. Luke called the doctor, who called another doctor, who called Dr. Christiansen, which is why I'm writing in this silly Ski Barbie diary. Because I'm a nutcase. He asks me to remember over and over. But I felt like this before partum before baby before, didn't I? The only thing I remember is to forget.

Same journal, no date:

Dr. Christiansen doesn't like it when I call myself a "nutcase." He says that what's wrong with me is common in new mothers, it's not unusual. "It's called postpartum depression," he says. "Some people call it the after-baby blues."

Blues? Colors are to me as musical notes are to a violinist. I know about blues. Sky blue, powder blue, azure blue, turquoise, cobalt, navy, teal. What I have? It's not blue. Blue is cool, soothing, fluid like water, and smooth. It comforts and flows. It's soft. It has no form or shape really. This thing I have? It ain't blue. It's black and noisy and hard. It has a head, a big head. And it screams a lot. Through a wide-open mouth that never closes. Never closes. Never.

Closes.

Dr. C asked me if I could draw a picture. I said to him, "Yes, I can, but I won't."

"I don't understand. Why not?" he asked, his tiny pencil positioned between his fingers, poised like a weapon ready to aim, shoot, and fire onto its target, a tiny page. "What is it?"

"It's . . . what it is," I said.

Dr. C's eyebrow rose, and he smiled slightly. And suddenly I was pissed. Really pissed. This is no smiling matter.

"And what's that?" he asked. Then "Who's that?"

That's a place I won't go, so I lied. "It isn't a 'who.'"

"I want to see what it looks like. Don't tell me you can't sketch it out. You are an artist. A good one, from what I've seen."

"I can draw anything," I told him, and it's the truth, I can. But. "It's just that . . . I won't draw this."

"Why?"

I have to explain everything.

"Because drawing it will make . . . it more real," I told him. "And dangerous." I have to be careful what I say. It's listening.

He smiled slightly, the tip of his pencil skating across the elf-size page.

"Laura, if you draw a picture of a spider, it won't leap off the page and bite you."

"No, a spider won't," I said to him. "But this will."

Dr. C kept after me. He said that it's important for me to face it. To know it for what it is: just an image on a sheet of white paper. We argued about this at every appointment until, finally, I did what he asked. I did it as safely as I could. To protect both of us.

He took the notebook and began flipping through the pages. Then he frowned.

"It's in here? I don't see anything. The pages are blank."

I shook my head. "No. It's in there."

Finally he was on the right page. He studied the drawing for what seemed like hours, turned the notebook slowly, clockwise, then set it in his lap.

"What will you put on the rest of the pages? Other sketches?"

"Nothing," I told him. "I don't want my drawings contaminated."

"What do you mean, Laura? What do you mean by 'contaminated'?"

"Just what I said." I reached out to take the book back, and he closed his large hand around it.

"OK. Do you mind if I hold on to it a little while? I'd like to study it more."

"No, I don't mind. But don't leave the book open," I told him. "It's dangerous."

CHAPTER 36

Dee Dee and Laura

D ee Dee knew that drawing. It was in a plain composition notebook with a navy-blue cover, a notebook her mother had left unlabeled and undated. The space indicating "This journal belongs to" was blank. The cover was pristine, as if it never had been used, barely touched by a hand, a fingertip. The pages were all ruled—navy and dark pink on snowy white. No writing anywhere on any page. Laura had not changed her mind. This book contained one thing and one thing only. A single drawing, beautifully executed, the craftsmanship evident in each stroke. A rich, nuanced rendering of a fiend that would be exquisite if it weren't so horrible.

A blob of black, shaded from inky to dark charcoal, no eyes, no nose, just a mouth, open, gaping, stretched out and screaming, full of pointed teeth, vicious looking and huge, like a prehistoric shark's teeth, some with serrated edges. Even without a voice, this thing on the page was . . . real somehow (because it was real to Laura). Real and loud. Its power shattered the eardrum; its plea was desperate, angry, and unforgiving.

Dee Dee closed the book. This was the face of the voice that had tormented her mother. No wonder she . . . *Not going there.*

Dee Dee put the book in the sack destined for the fire pit and picked up the next diary in the box. A My Little Pony diary, its first date unclear.

Not that dates mattered. Half the time Dee Dee couldn't read Laura's handwriting; the other half, Laura left the entries undated or mixed the entries from the 1980s with entries from the late 1970s with entries from the early 1990s, all in the same book. *Crazy.*

Dee Dee sighed. *Okay. Bad choice of word.*

Has it really been a month since I've written in this diary? Yes! I am too busy to write. I feel too good to write about feeling bad. I take one tiny white pill two times a day and one large white pill once a day. And I am me again. I paint. I sing. I dance. I am home with my babies and Luke. I am happy. A little chubby (Dr. Christiansen says it's a side effect) and sometimes I'm constipated. But what's that compared to being home? Every sketch I do is of my girls. And I have made a decision. No black. All blue. All white red gold green. No black. And no yellow either. Hearing Charlie Earland's Hammond B-3 in my head, "Happy 'Cause I'm Goin' Home." Yeah!

Home again. Deb and Dee Dee made me a cake (actually my mom did, but they helped). They are so sweet. Luke says I'm not supposed to drive yet but soon. And then I can take them to school. Like all the other mommies. I adore them.

My Little Pony diary, no date:

Back to normal. Eight hour day. Just like on TV. Routines. Boring. I love it! The yellow pills (they are new) have taken the noise away. I don't even remember now what really happened, and I don't want to remember. Although when I go in next week to see Dr. Christiansen, he'll ask me. And he'll want to see this diary. Won't he be surprised? There is absolutely nothing in it. And that's a good thing.

Same journal, one week later:

Appointment with Dr. Christiansen today.
He wasn't happy that I didn't write much in this diary, but he is happy that I am feeling better. He will give me permission to drive—Hallelujah! He wants me to continue with my writing and with my art. But he wants to look at my sketchbooks.
"Why?" I asked him.
"Well." He looked down at that darned little notebook. It's so small that I don't see how he can even read the writing in it! "You once told me that you'd made another sketch of the dark voice. May I see it?"
I was already shaking my head. "No. It isn't safe," I told him, and I meant it. Why I hadn't destroyed that drawing is still a mystery, but since I drew . . . it, I haven't opened the sketchbook. The longer it stays in the dark, unopened like Pandora's chest, the better.
Dr. Christiansen smiled. "Laura, it's just a drawing."

"I understand what you're saying, but you have to understand what I'm saying. It isn't safe."

"All right. I'll take your word for it."

"Doctor, I don't want to take the horse pills anymore. They make me constipated. And fat." The question is do I want to be skinny, loose as a goose, and crazy or fat, constipated, and sane? To be or not to be . . .

Again, that smile.

"No, Laura, I'd rather you didn't stop. You're progressing so well." He slid out his prescription pad and scribbled something. *"Take this to the pharmacy. It's a laxative. That should help."*

"Okay, thanks," I agreed. *"I'd like to be able to take a healthy dump once in a while."*

We both laughed. I tore up the prescription sheets when I got home. I'll pull back from the white pills for a few days. That should help.

Red spiral-bound college-ruled notebook, date illegible:

Feeling sad. Luke wants me to see Dr. Christiansen. I hate going to the bathroom. There's a shadow in the corner next to the tub.

Same journal, December?:

New pills! Yellow ones with white. Feel much better. Not as tired. No shadows. Teaching art at Provident Middle School. LOVE LOVE LOVE it!

Same journal, date illegible, 19??:

I am teaching full-time! High school! Finally, I can help Luke with the bills (the Bonneville needs work). Hurrah! Mrs. Carson is taking care of the girls after school and on Thursdays when I have practice. Can you imagine? I help Nancy with the cheerleaders! Goooooooooo Tigers! Can't do the splits anymore tho'. Too fat. ☹

Same journal, no date:

The art show. In May, it's all that my students can think about. It's all that I can think about! I've coordinated it from opening the door to closing it. Paintings, prints, collages, sculptures, pottery, creations made of objects found on the street and in the garbage (UGH!), and every darn thing in between. I love it! This is what I can do!

Another sketch of the girls to finish—I've decided to be like Monet—the same subject in different light, clothes, backgrounds, colors. It's the same, but it isn't the same. Just like me. And they are growing so fast, every day is different. Debora is my baby Einstein, numbers, shapes, calculations. Dee Dee is my wordsmith. She has the vocabulary of a college English prof! Love love love my girls.

Same journal, no date:

Barbara has approached me to do a show. Me. Just me! She loves my sketches and the pastels of the girls. She thinks it could make my career as an artist. All I ever wanted. But

I need to work. I need to think about work. But worse than that—they want to take photos of me. And I'm so fat! I have a double chin and my stomach has rolls! I'm actually wearing a maternity top from when I was pregnant with Dee Dee! So OK, no more yellow pills. I have to lose some poundage, have to!! One stone should do it. Two would be better. Three sublime.

CHAPTER 37

Laura

Journal entry, illegible:

"*My candle burns at both ends . . .*" —*Edna St. Vincent Millay, "First Fig"*

And in the middle:

Laura O'Neill

I woke up. My arms ached, felt heavy and broken. I could barely support myself to sit up. I felt so heavy . . . as if I weighed a thousand pounds, my chest thick with breath like concrete. I have to stop taking those damn yellow pills. I feel as if I weigh a ton. No, wait. I did stop taking them. I must have forgotten. But here . . . and here and there . . . a window. Light! How exquisite! Sublime, the brightness! "It gives a lovely light!" Dear Edna, only she could find the words. The sun was out, no clouds, no darkness, and it was so brilliant I wanted to paint it, but I couldn't. My arms were . . . they felt thick and awkward like tree stumps. The window was defaced by stripes . . . stripes? No. Bars. Why are there bars on the windows? I'm not home . . . Where am I? What is this place with bars on the windows and . . . Why am I in a hospital? I'm not sick.

Am I?

"Oh, you awake?" The woman smiled at me. The sound and smell of ripe Georgia peaches filled her voice. "Okay, honey, I'll get the doctor. You just rest a moment. You gotta pee?"

Yes, I did.

She was gentle and very kind. She let me lean on her as I walked to the bathroom. Once I got moving, the heaviness lifted. I was just clumsy. I guess she stayed with me because she thought I was weak. But I couldn't remember why I was there. I wasn't sick. I hadn't even had a cold.

And where were my girls? I looked around the room, but there was nothing, nobody but her—in my head I called her Georgia—and me, the room stark and white and clean. And empty. And it seemed like it was late in the afternoon, not morning. Goodness, I needed to get going. Did I go to work today? Maybe not. Teachers' conference? Hmmm . . . Anyway, school would be let out soon. Dee Dee and Debora would be wondering where I was.

"Listen, I'm feeling fine," I told Georgia. "Could you get my clothes, please? And my purse? I have to pick up my girls from school."

Georgia—her name was Donna, according to the tag pinned on her uniform—smiled at me and patted me on the

shoulder. "Listen, Laura, are you hungry? Do you want
something to eat?"

"No. No, thank you. I just have to get my purse and my
clothes and get out of here." I looked at my wrist, but my
watch was gone. "I had a watch on . . . a little Timex, silver
with a black leather band . . ." I pulled out the drawer in the
stand next to the bed. It was empty except for a penny hiding
in the corner.

"Just sit right there. I'll be back, honey, okay?" She walked
briskly to the door, then turned back, speaking to me over her
shoulder. "You're sure that you don't want anything to eat?"

I shook my head and smiled or tried to. I felt anxious,
worrying how my girls would feel if I wasn't there to pick
them up. Dee Dee would put her thumb in her mouth, and
Deb . . . I smiled thinking about my oldest girl. Deb's lips
would settle into a thin line as she would play her best "big
sister" part, stoic and strong.

"Don't cry, Dee Dee," she'd say. "You don't cry. Be a big
girl. I'll take care of you."

I'll take care of you. Mommy's just sick, that's all.

Mommy's sick?

"Please . . . I've got to pick up my daughters!"

"Don't you worry," Georgia/Donna said as she came back
into the room. "Your daughters are fine."

How did she know?

My heart hadn't been beating, but it was beating then. Hard.
I knew what that was: fear. No. Terror. The feeling I got when
I had to run. To get somewhere, anywhere—it didn't matter

where. I looked out the window, but nothing looked familiar.
I didn't know where I was. It looked like, felt like, a hospital.
I was wearing a white gown with navy stripes, loose and ugly,
fastened in the back. Where were my clothes? My car . . . I
had to get to my car, had to pick up my children, had to get
dressed, had to get dressed, had to . . . and not so much time.
Oh my God, what would the girls think if I wasn't there?
And their father . . . Luke was in Columbus on business. He
couldn't pick them up. It was up to me, it was up to me . . .
I was supposed to be taking care of them. It was up to me.

Debora's voice floated through my thoughts.

Mommy's sick.

Why was Mommy sick?

I tried to breathe, but I couldn't. And then I thought if I
could just stop my heart, then I could breathe. So that's what
I did. I let my heart stop, and then I exhaled, long and hard,
and then I took another breath and let my heart start again,
and then . . .

"Hello, Mrs. O'Neill, I'm Dr. Keller."

"Umm, that's nice. But my doctor is . . ." Geez, what is his
name? Oh, now I remember. "Where's Dr. Christiansen?"
I asked.

The man smiled. "Doug . . . Dr. Christiansen is on
sabbatical. He's in Oslo."

"Oh, it's cold there."

"Yes, it is."

I fumbled with the chair as I tried to get up, but it seemed as
if my legs weren't working properly so I sat down again.

"Well, Dr. . . . Keller. Listen, I'm fine, really. It must have been a touch of the flu or something. I'm okay now. But it's late, and I have to pick up my girls from school. They'll be wondering where I am. If I could just get my clothes and my purse and my car . . ." Where had I parked my car?

"Mrs. O'Neill . . . Do you mind if I call you Laura? Let me begin by reassuring you that your girls are just fine. Their father picked them up from school so you don't have to worry."

"But Luke is in Columbus."

The doctor smiled and put his hand on my arm.

"No. He's here, and Deanna and Debora are with him. Would you like a glass of water? Or something to eat? You must be hungry. You haven't had any food since you've been here."

The caution lights flashed yellow and a deep dissonant honking sound blasted repeatedly in my head HONK HONK HONK HONK. The yellow lights hurt my eyes. I've always had a problem with yellow. That's why I don't use it in my paintings.

"Since I've been here?" I repeated. "Where is here?"

Dr. Keller smiled again. I was beginning to get tired of that smile.

"The Shawnee Springs Hospital."

The caution lights stopped flashing, just froze. Now all I saw was a huge streak of neon yellow. The honking continued HONK HONK HONK . . .

"H-how long have I been here?"

This time the doctor did not smile.

"Two days, Laura," he said somberly. "Today is Thursday."

The honking sound stopped, just froze in place and just blasted in my head to go with the constant yellow light. I blinked my eyes. My head felt as if somebody had slammed it with a baseball bat.

"I . . ." I stopped my heart again so that I could speak. "Why am I here?"

He took a deep breath and tilted his head slightly. "You don't remember? Do you remember anything about . . . the time before you came here?"

"Well, of course I do. I am not an idiot! I took the girls to school, went to work, two classes to teach, went home, did laundry, called my mother, paid the electric bill, sketched out two portraits of Dee Dee and Debora, worked in my sketch pad, ironed the girls' blouses for school tomorrow and their dresses for Sunday school, talked to Luke at work and went to JCPenney's to pick up the new blinds for the kitchen, then stopped at the Sohio station on Long Street, had Bo put air in the back tire. I cleaned the bathroom twice to make sure that the rust stains were completely gone, then I scrubbed out the refrigerator because it was sounding funny and I wanted to make sure that no one could hear it, and then it was time for the school to let out. Debora had a piano lesson with Mrs. Charles. I drove up to the school—they go to North Elm Elementary, and I picked them up and I had to take the back way to get to Mrs. Charles's, so we went down Mill Avenue, then turned left onto Broad and took the Big Mac across, but this truck cut me off and . . ."

Dr. Keller was still not smiling. I was beginning to miss his smile.

"And . . ."

It was like watching a movie with perfectly pitched sound and sharp images full of true-to-life color, not that psychedelic stuff. The traffic on the bridge was heavy, but not gridlocked. The woman in the maroon Pontiac Sunbird . . . me? No. I couldn't have been . . . She pulled over in the outside lane and parked, and I wondered why she did that; there wasn't enough space for a car to park. She got out of the car and ran over to the railing, her face dripping with tears, her mouth spread wide in a smile. Or was it a grimace? Was she in pain? She rocked back and forth against the railing, then swayed from side to side as if she was doing some kind of modern dance. Or maybe she'd been drinking. Or was on drugs. LSD could make you do things like that. And then she raised her hands toward the sky as if willing it or the gods or God or something to come down.

She opened the back door of the car, reached in and pulled out a small child and dropped her over the side. The other child was heavier—she was older, I think—so it took some doing for her to lift the girl, and by that time another driver, a man, had stopped and was trying to prevent the woman from dropping the little girl over. He grabbed the child away from her—the poor thing was screaming in terror. And the woman laughed, climbed up on the railing, and tried to jump off the bridge into the river.

I don't think I've ever seen anyone look so white.

The doctor nodded. He still wasn't smiling.

"Yes. That's . . . exactly what happened. You saw all of that?" Dr. Keller sounded as if he didn't believe me. As if I hadn't seen the movie.

"Yes. Of course, I was on the bridge too, driving to Debora's piano lesson, following right behind a Sears truck, and then . . ."

I rewound the tape in my mind because it seemed to me that I had missed something. The little maroon Sunbird looked so much like my car and the little girl so much like my Dee Dee and the other child resembled Debora and the woman . . .

This time the caution lights did not flash, the horn did not honk. I wouldn't have heard them anyway. The silence was too loud. My heart stopped beating, my lungs stopped inhaling, and I

just

stopped.

"I . . . Did I . . ." My lips felt as if they were as big as pancakes, and my throat felt as if it had filled up with shattered glass, cutting slicing piercing the membranes. I could not bring myself to say the awful words, to ask.

Dr. Keller looked down for a moment at his hands, then lifted his gaze up to meet mine.

"Dee Dee's fine, a broken arm, a few bruises, but she's good. And Debora never even got wet."

"I'll get the death penalty for this," I told him.

He shook his head. "No, Mrs. O'Neill, Laura. You are ill, very ill."

"No, no, I deserve to die . . . really . . . and I can do this,"

*I told him with confidence. "I can die all by myself." I had
already stopped my heart and my lungs. Now all I had to do
was stop my brain and it would be over. The flashing lights,
the horns, the voice that kept growling at me, the pain . . .
I could make it be over. I could die. And then my little girls
would be free to live in safety, and feel secure, and would
never again have to worry about a derangednutcasecrazyass
mother driving too fast and throwing them into . . .*

Oh God! I had thrown them into the Ohio River.

"Mrs. O'Neill? Mrs. O'Neill? Laura!"

*That minute, that very second, the tape started running
again. The woman looked down at the muddy waters, where
flashes of light clothing popped in and out of the water. The
tugboat that had, by providence, been in the area was bobbing
in the waves. The water was choppy, an angry brown in color
and running fast. It had been raining a lot, off and on. The
Ohio River was full of debris, huge tree limbs and litter, and
undercurrents were strong enough to grab a man's toe and
pull him under. But still, a man, a savior, jumped in to rescue
the little girl. And the other annoying man would not let her
cleanse Debora, so what else was she to do? She laughed at
him and tried to jump in too. She wanted to die. To protect
her girls from the growling and the lights. And from her. Most
of all, from her.*

But she didn't die. She'd been rescued.

After trying to kill her children.

CHAPTER 38

Laura

Laura's journal, blue cover, date scratched out:

(I am writing this under duress)

Dr. C is back. He's different. He looks at me different now. His voice sounds odd, strangled, as if there's something cutting off the airflow. Or maybe it's because I'm different. I tried to kill my children. That makes me unique. In a bad way.

"Laura, how are you feeling today?"

I shake my head. I've decided not to speak anymore. The words get stuck in my throat like fish bones. I'm afraid I'll choke.

He doesn't say anything for a few moments, just looks at me, his blue eyes bloodshot and swollen. He feels sorry for me, I know he does. I feel sorry for myself.

"Laura . . ." He holds up my diary, the navy-blue one. "I want to help you. I want to find out what's making you sick."

I shake my head again. I write: BORN SICK.

He smiles slightly. My heart warms. I want to make this

man smile. He's nice. I feel bad that I've made him feel bad.
He flips through the pages of the diary and then stops. I know
what page he's on. He takes a breath, then holds up the book.
 "Laura, will you tell me what this is."
 NO.
 "I'd . . . really like for you to tell me. I have my own theory,
but it's probably wrong." His voice is firm. "I need for you
to tell me. Please. I need to hear your voice, Laura, you
understand. I know that you understand." He taps the page
and turns the notebook around again. "What is this?" And in
a soft voice, its volume so low that it's almost a whisper, he
asks, "Who is this?"
 I shake my head and put the pencil down. I am not saying that.
 Dr. Christiansen bites his lip and sets his notebook and pen
on the table. Then he reaches across and picks up my hands.
His blue eyes—they're almost pink now—they are sad looking,
so weary, like the hymns they sing in church. My soul is weary.
I know what that is, to be weary. A tiredness that seeps into
the bones, travels through the veins, and penetrates the soul. It
breaks my heart to see him like this.
 "Laura, this is serious. And I won't lie to you by saying that
if you speak, this . . . darkness will go away. We just don't
know. But I will tell you that you have to acknowledge . . . it.
And by doing that, maybe we have a chance to help you. But
you have to speak. You have to give . . . the darkness a name."
He sighed. "Can you . . . will you do that?"
 I let go of his hand and pick up the pencil.
 RATHER NOT.

Dr. C sighs again. "Okay." He pushes back from the table, unfolds himself, and stands up. I don't think I've seen anyone look so sad. Except for Luke, of course.

"We'll talk tomorrow, Laura, if that's all right." He walks to the door, his shoulders drooping, his string-bean frame all legs, skin, and bones. I feel so sorry for him.

"It's me," I say.

Dr. Christiansen stops and turns around. His mouth is gaping. He looks hilarious, except there's nothing hilarious about any of this. He isn't laughing, and neither am I. He's looking at me as if I've just landed from the moon, as if he's never seen me before. Maybe he hasn't, not really. But I want him to understand, to be certain that he knows what I am saying to him.

"It. Is. ME."

* * *

Dee Dee's hand was trembling. She closed the notebook and set it gingerly on the Ping-Pong table. Her mother never really came "home" again; she just went from crisis to crisis. Her body went in and out of treatment centers and hospitals. Her mind traveled to a place that only she could explore, secured by a gate to which only she had the key.

It was the first time in Dee Dee's adult life that she had admitted—no, acknowledged—rationally and clear-eyed, through the lens of a grown-up, just what had been wrong with her mother. Even when Laura died—when Dee Dee and Deb were adults—even then she had processed her mother's situation through a glass darkly, because it was, well, easier. It was softer, less embarrassing to say, "She's sick. She's ill," with the grit and serrated edges of mental illness sanded away, or just plain obscured by the nearsighted fog of childhood.

"Mommy's sick." The words she'd heard all of her life. She remembered her dad saying, "Yes, that was before your mother got so ill." But Laura didn't have cancer or ALS. She wasn't "consumptive" like Victorian-era invalids, suffering silently (except for the coughing) and in ethereal beauty as written in historical novels. Laura was bipolar and fought a minute-by-minute battle with her own mind—Laura vs. "It," twelve rounds, for fifty-three years, three months, and six hours. She'd died from a massive coronary, compounded by a stroke, perhaps a side effect of one or more of the psychotropic drugs she'd taken for decades. And when the fight was over, it was hard to know who'd won, Laura or "It."

Dee Dee picked up the notebook again to put it into the I-don't-know-what-the-hell-to-do-with-this pile, then absently flipped through the blue-lined pages once more just in case she'd missed something. She had.

January 13, 1996

I've been drawing for hours. For days! It's b-l-i-s-s! Joy! The wonder of it! All light. YES!

The light's fantastic in here. Brilliant. With all the shades I want and texture! What good is color without texture? Even the ceiling windows, some of them cracked (and grimy—I'd like to give them a good scrubbing), give off amazing light,

*and then the sun filters through, dropping a kaleidoscope of
colors and shapes, drops like rain. A head trip extraordinaire.
Cool. Very cool.*

*My pencil skates across the paper. I love this paper! It
has texture too, it makes sound. As if it lives and breathes,
speaks to me, tells me what it wants. It loves my pencil. I see
the pictures so vividly. My daughters. It's like working from
a live subject, like I did in composition class in school. As
if somehow I've time-traveled back and the girls are small
again. Oh, they were darling. I see the scab where Debora
sucked her thumb, and little Dee Dee didn't want to smile
because her front teeth were gone, taken by the Tooth Fairy
(Haha). I told Luke to leave a dollar for each tooth. He told
me that I was insane, then he stopped and said, "Laura, I
didn't mean it that way. I'm sorry." Oh, Luke, I know what
you mean.*

*I draw on, using the picture in my mind. The girls were so
adorable in the white dresses that Luke's mother bought for
them, their dark hair braided into Pippi Longstocking plaits
that twirled upward. My brushes whish along, they're magic.
They move by themselves, I see them. It's so perfect. Surreal
and all mine. All quiet. No one talking to me. No one getting
in the way. Just my breathing and the singing of the brushes
and chalk and pencils as they sail across the paper, the traces
forming my memories and one, especially, that is now so clear.*

I woke up, left Luke and the girls in the bed.

*Went to pee, looked out the window, porch lights here and
there. It was early or maybe it was late, but it was dark, cool,
October, and quiet. I love the quiet.*

I looked up and there it was, the moon, a crescent with a little halo! A nimbus moon holding its own against the ebony sky, a sky too black for me to paint, and to the left, a star, and I wanted to hold on to that moment, that second, that heaven . . .

And that's when I realized . . .

Heaven isn't a place of clouds like pillows or gold-paved avenues where the souls of pious people stroll. (God, deliver us from pious people, right? They are boring.) Heaven is a moment like this one, one moment of clarity to realize that all you need is a good sleep. The feel of your lover's hand against your cheek. The snoring of a sleeping child. Chocolate! Heaven is one stitch among many in a life, and it's not easy to find, it hides. Because it's only that moment, you only get a few. That moment of joy when you smile, you feel light, and you look at the brilliant moon and mysterious distant star and say thank you.

It's amazing. When the dark thing sleeps, I sneak out and feel grateful and sing and dance and see things that really are

There

And feel gratitude for the slivers and shards and microbes of heaven allowed me, for my exquisite Luke and my fearless Debora. For Dee Dee, she's awake now, and her small, warm body nestles against mine, one of her wild runaway braids tickles my cheek. She picks her nose then uses the grubby little finger to point at the emerging moon.

"Look, Mommy! A toenail!"

And so it is.

Amen.

CHAPTER 39

Dee Dee

Elise picked up her wineglass, then set it down again. "Beautiful."

"She . . . had a way with words, you have to give her that," Carmen commented.

"She never spoke?" Elise asked.

Dee Dee sniffed and shook her head. She blew her nose. "She rarely spoke. Dad said that in her mind, maintaining silence kept the . . ."

"It," offered Carmen.

Dee Dee smiled slightly. "Yes. It. Mommy had rationalized that if she didn't speak, then It couldn't either. So even when she was well—*relatively* well—she was quiet. When we visited her . . ." Dee Dee's voice broke. "She'd hug us and smile. She'd even laugh. But she didn't speak. Not one word. Not to us, not to our dad."

"Do . . . do you remember . . ." Carmen stopped. "I'm sorry. That's totally inappropriate."

Dee Dee closed her eyes. "No. It's okay. Sometimes I think

that I remember. But most of the time I realize that I don't. I've had counseling up the wazoo, but . . ." She sighed. "You know, all I remember is Mom picking me up. After that, it's a blur, then blank. Maybe—"

"Maybe that's a good thing," Carmen interrupted. She took a sip of her cappuccino after blowing away the steam from the soup-bowl-size cup. "I think it's overrated to remember everything. There might be a good reason to forget some things and remember others."

Elise nodded.

"You're right," Dee Dee said.

"Like my ex-husband, I acknowledge and then I forget," said Carmen.

The women laughed and the somber atmosphere faded.

Elise reached out and picked up the small picture frame resting on the counter, within a nest of old Sunday newspapers and disintegrating grocery bags.

"Just so you don't forget this," she said, looking at Dee Dee, holding up the picture. "This is your proof. This . . ." She looked down at the stack of mismatched diaries and journals. "These items should wipe away any notions you might have that your mother was so out of it that she forgot about you and Debora completely." Elise looked at the painting, then passed it over to Dee Dee. "She loved you very much."

"She did," Carmen chimed in.

"Who would've thought . . ." Dee Dee murmured, running her hand across the worn-out flap of one of the cartons. "Talk about a Pandora's box."

"After the woes and the evils and the sad things flew out of Pandora's box to afflict the world, one small presence remained behind, hiding in a corner," Elise commented.

Dee Dee's brows rose.

Elise smiled. "Hope."

Dee Dee studied the little watercolor and smiled. *And sings the tune—without the words* . . . An image came to her—was it a memory or a wish? The scene was as vivid and coherent as this very second: she and Debora posing for their mother as she sketched them, smiling and blowing them kisses from behind her easel, the corners of her eyes crinkling as she worked, the funny faces that she made to hold their attention, flipping the pages off her huge sketch pad, lifting their chins, then kissing them on the tips of their noses and telling them . . .

Dee Dee gasped. Her mother had spoken. Or was this just wishful thinking? But Dee Dee heard Laura's voice in her head, low, alto, soft yet firm, a mother giving instruction to her children, the maternal authority in her tone.

"Look at me, Deb, all right? Look at Mommy."

"Dee Dee, darling, is your nose running? Do you need a tissue? That's a good girl."

Always balanced, a Zen master's attention to design and simplicity, a portrait decades in the making. A background of two shades of blue, turquoise and sage-tinged, two arrangements of flowers, one a tall planter of lean, sparsely foliaged stems, the other delicate and abundant in a squatty vase set on the table: two of everything, and two little girls, dressed in white with blush-colored bows in gently curling black hair, the darkest color on the paper except for their eyes. Two little brown-skinned girls, alike but not identical, one slightly shorter and maybe younger, a little bit chubby, the other taller and leaner, the baby fat gone, and the younger one wearing a red ribbon around her waist. Dee turned the painting over and looked at what her mother had written on the back: "Love, Mother."

* * *

"I'll pick up the girls," Dee Dee said.

Lorenzo was reaching for the car keys. His hand froze in the air.

Dee Dee smiled. "That way you can finish watching *SportsCenter* or *Golf Last Week* or whatever is on."

Her husband's expression was equal parts grin and sneer. "Wrong on both counts. I was watching *Curling Today* on CBC," he said.

Dee Dee's laughter almost choked her. "W-what's CBC?"

"The Canadian Broadcasting Corporation. What?" he exclaimed in response to her reaction of restrained hysteria. "You got something against Canada?"

"No . . ." Dee Dee said, chuckling as she took the keys from his hand. "I . . . just didn't know that you were into curling."

"Oh yeah," Lorenzo said, kissing her on the cheek as he walked back toward the great room. "I'm *big* into curling. Love that sweeping action," he added, demonstrating with comic results. "Hey, when you grab the girls, don't let Phoebe forget her duffel bag. She left it at the gym last week. Those clothes have gotta be ripe by now!"

Frances and Phoebe weren't thrilled to see their mother in the car-pool line. Standing together, looking like near-matching bookends, they quickly exchanged glances when they realized that it was Dee Dee behind the wheel. Dee Dee suppressed a smile since, as far as Frances was concerned, she was supposed to still be in angry-parent mode.

"Hey, Mom," Phoebe said brightly as she clambered into the back seat, duffel bag in tow.

"Mom," Frances echoed cautiously, dumping her gear on the seat next to her sister. She climbed into the front seat.

"Girls," Dee Dee said in as neutral a tone as she could manage. She clicked on her turn signal and maneuvered into traffic. "How was practice?"

The question provoked a detailed play-by-play response from Phoebe, who was beginning to enjoy the soccer that she'd avoided like the bubonic plague last school year. Frances, who'd been in practice on the high school field just opposite the middle school practice area, gave her standard response to parental inquiries: "It was fine."

"Good." As Dee Dee turned onto the freeway, she glanced into the rearview mirror at her younger daughter. "I have something I want to tell you when we get home."

Frances came out of her usual slouch in the passenger seat and then looked over her shoulder at her sister.

Phoebe shook her head slowly, mouthed the words, *You're in trouble.*

"*Me?* Why?" Frances squeaked.

"*Both* of you," Dee Dee said, trying to keep amusement out

of her voice. She knew that Phoebe was planning a fast exit the moment they got home.

"What did I do?" her younger daughter whined.

"No whining, Phoebe, and you didn't do anything," Dee Dee said. "I only want to talk with you. You and Frances."

"Talk . . . with us? What about?" Frances asked.

This time Dee Dee did smile. "Geez! Frances! Talking with your mother is not a foreign concept. What have you miscreants been up to, you sound so suspicious? This is not the Spanish Inquisition. I only want to talk with you. About your grandmother."

Frances frowned. "About Grandma? Why, is she sick?"

Dee Dee shook her head. "No, she's not. And I'm not talking not about Grandma Davis." Lorenzo's mother was the only grandmother her girls had known personally. Dee Dee sighed. "I'm talking about your other grandmother, my mother. Laura." Both of the girls formed an O with their lips.

After they got home, Dee Dee positioned the eight-by-ten painting on a small easel stand and placed it on the kitchen island. The girls padded in together on bare feet, their hair damp from the shower, the smell of coconut and lavender perfuming the air.

Frances picked up the picture. "Who's this? Me and Bean Head?"

Phoebe poked her in the side.

"No, it's me and Aunt Deb."

Frances's teenaged nonchalance cracked. "Oh," she said. "It's good. It's really good. Who painted it?"

"My mother," Dee Dee answered, running a fingertip across the image.

"Let me see." Phoebe nudged her sister aside. She leaned in closer in order to get a clearer view. "It is good." Her light brown eyes caught her mother's. "Grandmother . . . Laura painted this?" Her choice of words amused and saddened Dee Dee. The girls had never known Laura in the flesh and didn't quite know how to refer to her.

Dee Dee inhaled, then leaned back against the countertop.

"Look. Girls . . . I owe you an apology. This is my fault. My mother . . . well, my mother was ill when I was growing up. And she died relatively young—France, you were a toddler when my mother passed away. You girls didn't get to know her. And I . . . well, I admit it. I was ashamed of my mother, of her sickness, even though I knew that she couldn't help it and that she tried very hard to get well. And so . . ."

She stopped for a moment and brushed a tear from the corner of her eye and was surprised that, instead of interrupting her with a snide remark, Frances was pressing a tissue into her palm.

"Mommy was . . . she was what we now call bipolar. One day she would be fine. The next day she wouldn't be. She might stay in bed for days. Then she might stay awake for days. They . . . the doctors didn't have the treatments and medications then that they do now. And even now, well, it's a tricky condition and things . . ." Dee Dee bit her lip, remembering her mother on a new medication regimen that had left her lethargic and disoriented. "Well, things don't always end up well. Mommy wanted to get well. She wanted to be home with us, with me and your aunt. She wanted to paint, to write, she was planning a one-woman art exhibit—did you know that?" Even Dee Dee hadn't known it until she'd read Laura's journals. "She wanted to create a comic book series, you know, like a graphic novel. She wanted . . . so much. But . . ."

"But her sickness wouldn't let her." This from Phoebe.

Dee Dee blew her nose. "No," she said, her voice hoarse. "No, it wouldn't."

She brushed a stray strand of hair away from the lens of Phoebe's glasses. "I tried to pretend that she didn't exist. I never spoke about Mommy, put away most of the photos of her, and never showed you her art, her writing, her . . . the evidence of her life. I didn't tell you stories about her. And so you girls don't know anything about my mother. How lovely she was, how smart and funny she was, and what a talented artist she was! I hid that all away." This time Dee Dee grabbed an unruly curl away from Frances's forehead. "Even though I named both of you after her: Frances Laura and Phoebe O'Neill."

Frances looked up, a small furrow in her forehead, her gold-green eyes shining. *I did the right thing naming her Frances Laura, that's for sure!*

"She was an artist and she wrote too? What kind of things did she write?"

"Was she a reporter?" Phoebe broke in, her dimples now evident in her face. "A foreign correspondent?" Phoebe wanted to be a war correspondent when she grew up even though she declared that she was a pacifist.

"No," Dee Dee said, chuckling, her eyes still on Frances's rapt examination of Laura's painting. "No. Mommy wrote essays and short stories, but she also wrote poetry."

Frances's head jerked up. "Really? Do you have some of it? I mean, can I read it?"

Dee Dee slid the spiral-bound notebook across the slick counter.

"There you go," she said. "And when you've finished, I have some photo albums to show you both, and we'll talk about taking a field trip."

Now it was Phoebe's eyes that lit up. "Where are we going?"

"To Yellow Springs," Dee Dee. "There's a gallery there. The owner was a friend of Mommy's, and she's kept some of her art in storage. I've emailed her. We'll go up and take a look."

"Wow." This from Frances. "I'd really like to see her work. She's good. I mean . . . she was good. Her style is a lot like Elizabeth Catlett's woven into Mary Cassatt's. With a little Vermeer thrown in."

Phoebe rolled her eyes. "Like you're an art critic."

This time it was Frances who poked Phoebe in the side. "Like you would even know who Vermeer is."

"Quit," Phoebe growled.

"Girls," Dee Dee warned.

"Mom." Frances held the picture frame against her chest and for some reason the gesture made Dee Dee feel good, as if her mother was being embraced by her granddaughters. "Izzie's having a sleepover tonight and I thought . . ."

"No, France."

"Mooommm!"

"You're on punishment, remember? The party?"

Phoebe snorted with amusement. Her sister poked her in the side again.

"Quit it!"

The bickering started from there.

"Girls!" Dee Dee bellowed. Hallmark moment over. Real life beginning again.

CHAPTER 40

Elise

Whenever the word "Namaste" popped into her mind, Elise envisioned an artificially serene setting, spare and organized, no wasted space or emptiness, very feng shui, with well-placed bamboo plants, the requisite number of strategically placed mirrors, and a smiling Buddha statuette. She would imagine white walls in a room so silent and so sterile in appearance that a surgeon would feel comfortable using it as an OR. And if you threw in twenty people sitting cross-legged with their eyes closed, you had the perfect Instagram marketing pic for a yoga studio like the one Sergeant Jasmine operated, called . . . Namaste. Of course.

But today the word stretched out syllable by syllable across Elise's mind like a sacred chant of balance, acceptance, and, oh yes, serenity. The real kind. Although silence, order, bamboo plants, and sterility were absent. Elise's "Namaste" found a home amidst towers of brown boxes, street noise, conversation, shouts, and general chaos as she, Dee Dee, Carmen, and a horde of other people came in and out of Marie Wade's condominium like ants moving bread crumbs across a sidewalk.

Instead of transporting precious tidbits of food, however, they carried boxes, lamps, cushions, and other items down the walk to the street, where a large truck was parked, its loading ramp extended. And in lieu of the indefatigable yoga instructor, it was Elise who barked out orders.

"Wade! Stack those cushions neatly in the back of the truck, will you? Push them against the seat—"

"Yes, Mom . . ." her son said, his voice muffled by the tower of cushions he carried.

"Lewis! What do you think? Can we get the washer and dryer in there?"

"Yes, ma'am, no problem," Lewis, the moving crew's leader, answered with an expression that indicated just the opposite.

Dee Dee and Lorenzo emerged from the cavernous darkness of the truck.

"There's tons of room in here," Lorenzo said. "The size of the truck isn't the problem. It's the size and amount of the *stuff*!"

"Yeah," Dee Dee said as she walked down the ramp. She exhaled loudly and drew her hand across her forehead in mock exhaustion. As she passed by Elise, she said, "E, instead of four men and a truck, you need fourteen men and a convoy of trucks. The more stuff we move out, the more there is!"

"Wimps," Elise said, a grin brightening her face.

Carmen staggered toward them carrying a brown-box version of the Leaning Tower of Pisa.

"God, she's heading toward disaster," Dee Dee blurted out as she and Elise moved quickly to intercept her.

Carmen stopped and together the women adjusted the load.

"Thanks. I needed that." As they maneuvered slowly onto the ramp of the truck, Carmen added, "I just want you to know that I'm only doing this because I was told there would be martinis."

"And pulled-pork sandwiches," Dee Dee added.

"And chocolate cake." This remark came from Frances, who grinned as she walked by carrying a lampshade that was as tall as she was.

Elise laughed and turned to go back into the house before she heard a car door slam. Bobby waved at her from the parking lot. She waved back and walked toward him.

"Wow," he said, surveying the activity in the lot and on the walkway. He sidestepped a pair of men who were awkwardly maneuvering a large sofa down the sidewalk toward the truck. "Wade told me that you were finally clearing out the place, but I didn't believe him." He nearly tripped over a pile of furniture covers. "Boy, you weren't kidding. You're not . . . holding on to anything?"

Elise shook her head. "Nope. Everything goes."

Bobby frowned. "Everything?"

"Everything. I have the mementoes from Mom that I want, and so do Bill and Warren." Elise turned toward the moving truck, now half full, and the buzz of activity coming from the regiment of people who surrounded it. "The rest of it goes somewhere. But it isn't going with me!"

"That's wild," Bobby mused. "Honestly, Elise? I didn't think you'd be able to give any of it up."

Elise smiled. "Neither did I. But things change."

"When's the closing?" Bobby asked, his voice muffled by the noise.

"Monday."

Her former husband's eyes widened. "No shit." He turned back to look at the open door of the condo. "And you're almost done? You'll be finished by then?"

"I will," Elise said proudly. "It's all worked out." She gestured toward the moving truck. "That stuff goes to a consignment shop. Dee Dee's buying some of the artwork—her daughter Frances is into art. Carmen's bought some of the jewelry and the brass lamp, the boys have taken what they want, and Mom's books were donated to the library weeks ago. The kitchen appliances stay, the washer and dryer go, the draperies and window coverings stay, and the new owner likes the antique armoire Mom had in her bedroom, so that stays behind too. All of the rest? Gone, gone, and gone. The cleaning crew comes in . . ." She glanced at her phone. "I've scheduled them for six-thirty tomorrow. The house will be empty and clean before the closing."

"I'm impressed," Bobby said, smiling.

"Impressed enough to pitch in?" Elise asked him.

He nodded. "Absolutely."

And, listen, E, I've been thinking . . . Shit."

"What is it?" Elise asked. Bobby pulled her arm.

They turned toward the ramp, where their son was doing a juggling act with a trio of large plastic tubs that were precariously sliding out of formation toward his feet. Bobby broke into a sprint.

"Wade! Son! Stop, hold on . . ."

The disaster was narrowly avoided and the two men managed to restack the tubs and carry them up the ramp and into the truck.

"You are a miracle worker."

Elise smiled at Dee Dee, who was standing next to her. Carmen approached them from the parking lot.

"Naaaaw."

"Oh yes you are," Carmen added, uncapping her water bottle and taking a few loud gulps. "I don't know many women who could persuade their ex-husbands to help them clear out a house."

Elise shrugged. "Well, it wasn't *that* kind of a divorce. It was just a matter of it being over, and we both knew it. No need to get our thongs in a knot."

Dee Dee giggled. "And that's why I love you, Elise. Never at a loss for the right words." She opened the flaps of her jacket to reveal a bright purple tee shirt with an inscription in a Gothic font that read DON'T MIND ME — I'M HAVING AN EXISTENTIAL MOMENT.

"You wore it!" Elise exclaimed, standing back to get a better look. "It looks better than I thought it would!"

Carmen nodded. "Uh-huh. I think it's the color. The purple is just right—royal and riotous at the same time." She glanced over at Dee Dee, who was chuckling. "What? Dee Dee, what is it?"

Carmen and Elise stared at their friend, whose expression had evolved from the satisfied smile of someone who had just completed a challenging task to that of the Grinch who was about to steal Christmas.

"I have an idea," Dee Dee said. "Are you guys coming to yoga class on Monday?"

Carmen and Elise exchanged glances.

"Yeah . . ." Carmen answered. "Why?"

"What are you wearing?" Dee Dee asked.

* * *

Sergeant Jasmine walked slowly across the room, studying each student as they adjusted themselves in their poses pursuant to her barked instructions. She nodded with satisfaction at their progress, especially those devotees who had adapted to her philosophy of yoga etiquette: rapt attention to the instructor, no chitchat, and proper and authorized (as in sold by Jasmine) yoga attire of black, light gray, charcoal gray, or navy only. Solid colors. No logos, no designs.

"Really plant those hands . . . Make suction cups of your fingers. Grab that mat! Tuck in your tailbones. Aaron! Straighten your elbows. Mike, are you okay? Rose? Elise . . ."

The last three students in the second row tucked in their tailbones, puffed out their kidneys, and planted their palms on the mats with regimental precision. Their manicured fingertips splayed in perfect form and clutched their mats like the Jasmine-described suction cups. And so their headstands, although a bit wobbly in the opinion of the instructor, were adequate. As for the rest of their appearance . . . Being upside down, they didn't see the raised eyebrow and pursed lips of their instructor.

Jasmine paused to adjust the foot position of one of the three, then moved on. Any thoughts she had about the message printed across their identical purple tee shirts, she kept to herself.

Just before her headstand dissolved, Elise whispered, "Namaste."

ACKNOWLEDGMENTS

Every writer is encircled by a pantheon of amazing people who go about their business with focus and diligence. I am elevated by them. Thank you to Patrik Bass, editor, who reached out to me; to Amina Iro for her patience; and to my agent Matt Bialer, who lit a lamp to guide my way.

The Secret Women is a story for anyone who has had the thankless task of clearing out the home of a loved one who has died. The "stuff" is overwhelming: boxes, drawers, closets, furniture. But the memories and questions that sometimes emerge from photos, letters, and journals may leave mysteries in their wake. I decided to create a story inspired by this unlikely source.

Gratitude goes to my friends Louise Lawrence and Winona McNeil, whose observations of clearing out their own family members' belongings helped me to see through the clutter. Additional thanks to Winona for graciously allowing me to use her lovely name. My appreciation also goes to Sandra Rivers and Ron Ellis, who answered questions about many subjects, including New York City and the military. Please note that any errors or divergences on these subjects are entirely mine. A special thank you, as always, to my family, especially my husband, Bruce Smith.

This book is dedicated to the memory of my second cousin, Dorothy Turner Johnson, who made up her mind to reach the age of one hundred years—and did. An adventurer, librarian, and Francophile, Dorothy was a WAC during World War II, part of the 6888th Central Postal Battalion, the only unit of African American women to serve overseas. I hope that I've inherited some of *those* genes.

ABOUT THE AUTHOR

Sheila Williams is the author of *Dancing on the Edge of the Roof*, *The Shade of My Own Tree*, *On the Right Side of a Dream*, and *Girls Most Likely*, as well as a contributor to the anthology *A Letter for My Mother*, selected and edited by Nina Foxx. She has been commissioned as the librettist for *Fierce*, an original opera composed by William Menefield for the Cincinnati Opera's 100th season in 2020. She lives in northern Kentucky.